THE BAD BOY & THE TOMBOY

THE BADBOY & THE TOMBOY

NICOLE NWOSU

wattpad books **W**

Copyright © 2020 Nicole Nwosu. All rights reserved.

Published in Canada by Wattpad Books, a division of Wattpad Corp.
36 Wellington Street E., Toronto, ON M5E 1C7

www.wattpad.com

First Wattpad Books edition: October 2020
ISBN 978-1-98936-533-5 (Trade Paper original)
ISBN 978-1-98936-541-0 (eBook edition)

Library and Archives Canada Cataloguing in Publication
information is available upon request.

Printed and bound in Canada

3 5 7 9 10 8 6 4 2

Cover design by Jennifer Yoon
Cover title treatment by Ashley Santoro
Cover image © Nikola Stojadinovic via iStock
Typesetting by Sarah Salomon

To my Wattpad readers. Thank you for everything.

1

ALMOST TOOK OFF HIS HEAD

Competition was the most consistent thing in my life. Whether it was on the soccer field against another team, video games against my fourteen-year-old brother, Justin, or a board game with my group of friends, winning was something everyone around me basked in.

Jasmine, one of my best friends, threw her arms up in the air in victory, her mouth filled with popcorn. "*Yeefffithhh!*"

I captured her victory dance at the end of our popcorn-eating competition with my camera. Andrew, my other best friend, grimaced, "Don't get hotheaded. You won *once*."

The three of us surrounded the kitchen island at my house; empty popcorn bags littered the table. Sun rays streamed into the room through the windows, providing warmth despite the February air outside. The aroma from the multiple bags of buttered popcorn we had heated up in the microwave earlier was strong but not nauseating.

Jasmine flipped her box braids over her shoulder. "Shut up."

Here we go. I flicked through the pictures on my camera as their argument escalated. Andrew's blue eyes settled on Jasmine. "I'm not trying to fight with you today."

"Then let's not try to pick fights," she quipped.

But, oh no. He just had to keep talking. "I know you're having a rough time since the breakup—"

"I don't want to talk to you about it," she said. "I don't want to talk to *anyone* about it." Jasmine got up and left the kitchen, then my bedroom door slammed shut upstairs.

"I told you," I chided. "We should give her space. Sean broke up with her only a few weeks ago."

Andrew ran a hand through his blond hair and looked at the now-empty doorway through which Jasmine had just exited. "I'll try to talk to her."

"You think *you* can get through to her?" The front door opened, and I recognized the person who entered by their footsteps. *Justin.* "She doesn't seem to favor you at the moment."

"She doesn't seem to favor *men* at the moment," Andrew added. "I'll be back."

"Macy!" Justin entered the room, a basketball tucked under his arm, as Andrew exited. My brother unzipped his thick sweater, ears red from the cold weather as he rubbed at his rosy cheeks. "You guys ate my popcorn?"

"*I* didn't."

"*Liar.*"

"I said I didn't." As I nudged him in the ribs with my elbow he hissed, pushing my arm away.

"Anyway," he grumbled, sticking his head in the fridge. "What's Andrew doing?"

"Get me a ginger ale, would you?"

"No."

I gave him a look and he handed me a can as he got water for himself.

"He's talking to Jasmine upstairs."

"Is that a good idea?" Even Justin knew about the strain between Andrew and Jasmine at the moment. "To have those two in a room alone together? The other day she almost took off his head." *Good point.* I took a sip of my drink, put it on the counter, and left the room to head off the potential war.

The two of them jumped when I opened my door, Andrew springing up from my bed to stand. I wasn't sure who to question first—Andrew had a strained smile on his face and Jasmine had a sudden interest in my bedsheets. "Everything all right here?"

"I should get going," Andrew mumbled.

"Are you going to practice tomorrow?" I asked.

"Of course. I'll see you guys then." And without another word he bolted from the room.

"So . . . Andrew?" I teased.

She cringed, a predictable response. We'd all been friends for years. I couldn't even imagine what would happen if one of us got involved in a romantic relationship with another.

"No, definitely no."

Her phone beeped and her eyes scanned the message before she tossed her phone at the foot of my bed. "What's up?"

"Amy's gushing over Sam." Jasmine's friend, Amy, had a crush on *everyone.* I wasn't surprised.

The name Sam didn't ring any bells. "Who?"

"You know Sam."

"I have no idea who Sam is, dude." I raised my arms up to stretch. "Does he even go to our school?"

"Yes."

"Any teams? What grade?"

"He's in our grade."

"What does he look like?"

"He's white," she said, and shot me a look that I should've expected.

"That's literally almost everyone at school except for you."

As I searched for my cleats for tomorrow's soccer practice, she said, "You must've seen him around. He transferred from England this year."

"I know faces, not names. *Finally.*" I put my found cleats in my duffel bag.

I was just reaching to grab my soccer ball near my desk when Jasmine snapped her fingers, sitting up. "Ooh! He was in my history class in the first semester."

"You remember that I *wasn't* in your history class, right? How would I even—you know what? Never mind. Want to go to the rec center?"

"He's kind of low key." I really wasn't going to get out of this conversation. "I think he only talked to, like, three people in that class."

"Not everyone's as outgoing as you," I pointed out.

Jasmine was involved in many clubs in our school. She also played volleyball and softball, which meant she talked to *everyone*. It wasn't solely her interests—her extroverted personality also drew people to her. "I think he plays soccer too."

That got my attention. "Did he try out for the team?"

"You would have noticed if he tried out for the team, Mace."

"You sure? If he did, he could've been one of the guys who were wondering what I was doing at tryouts. I don't think any of *those* guys made the cut."

I'd played soccer since I was a kid and every year, whenever I tried out for my school's team, I'd get the same expression from the rest of the competition. That subtle surprised look over a girl trying out for the boys' team (our school didn't have one for girls). And when I was named captain not too long ago? That surprised look was a little less subtle when people around school heard. After three years on the team, I'd become used to the guys looking at me strangely, but I didn't care—all I wanted to do was play.

Justin popped his head into my room. "Where are you headed?"

"Soccer fields are open right now at the rec center. Might attempt to get Jasmine to pass me the ball."

"No way, I've got to go," she declared. "I have a ton of things to do."

"Want to come?" My question was directed at my brother, even though I knew he had come from playing basketball there.

"Anything to get out of homework."

"Justin." Jasmine shrugged on her jacket. "You know Sam, right? In our grade?"

"How would *he* know?" I asked. "He's in grade nine."

"Curly hair?" Justin said. "Green eyes?"

"*Exactly,*" Jasmine agreed.

"Am I the only one who hasn't seen this guy?" I asked.

"You've seen him," she assured me. "You just don't know his name. See you tomorrow!"

She grabbed her things, swinging her backpack onto her

shoulders as she left the house, her gesture hinting that she wasn't going to give another thought to Sam or anything school related.

~

"When does Dad get home?" Justin asked as we left the house.

"Around five." As I spoke, white air puffed in front of me. The snowfall usually stuck around until March in Port Meadow. Currently, the snow lingered in small traces on the ground, but I wanted it all gone. Canadian spring needed to come faster. I wanted to play soccer outside instead of on the indoor field. Because of the cold weather, the school's outdoor soccer season wouldn't begin until early May, and our current indoor practices focused on upcoming tournaments and exhibition games.

"Maybe he can get me popcorn since you all ate it all," Justin huffed, the tip of his nose already red from the cold. He peered over at my camera as he twisted my soccer ball in his hands, making a face at what he spotted on the screen.

"You made it a competition? And Andrew lost?" His eyes widened at the picture of Jasmine's victorious moment. He flicked through a couple more pictures. "If I was as old as you are, I'd do dumb stuff with my friends all the time to relive my youth too. I don't even blame you." As my brother continued his joking, I placed my camera in my shoulder bag. "When you leave for university, I'm turning your room into a man cave with games, a new TV, and a minifridge."

"I haven't even left yet and you're already thinking of life post-me."

I hadn't decided which school I'd be going to. Acceptance letters from potential universities' science programs were starting to come in and I didn't have to choose until the beginning of June, however, I wanted to be part of a soccer team and get a good scholarship to help with tuition fees. The potential to get scouted for a university team was slim. Scouts came to at least one off-season tournament or exhibition game before the season started, but if I didn't get the opportunity it wouldn't be the end of the world. Academically I was doing well, but soccer was my life. Securing a spot on a team and continuing my journey within the sport would be huge. Justin didn't notice that the weight of the conversation was starting to overwhelm me. *Not now.*

Justin yammered on about what he would add to his man cave during our fifteen-minute walk. We passed by a variety of houses in the quiet, residential neighborhood we'd lived in since we were kids.

This was the usual pattern. Justin would talk about anything and everything, holding the soccer ball, basketball, or both, and I would take pictures. Of the same houses I'd seen for almost the past eighteen years and the faces of people who'd recently moved in. Of two people with a child who held a tablet in their hands who passed us on the sidewalk, similarly bundled up in jackets. Of anything, really, that could capture the moment. When we grew closer to the rec center, I knocked the soccer ball out of my brother's hands, and it rolled onto the grass in front of us.

"Hey!" Justin yelled as I ran with it. I was at my best when the ball was between my feet, no matter how cold it was, the frozen grass crunching underneath my shoes, or any obstacle in my way. I handled the ball with my feet as my brother sprinted after me. "This isn't fair, I *just* played two hours of basketball!"

I slowed down so he could try to get the ball off me. He stuck his foot out to kick it away, but I rolled it back out of his reach. Dodging him, I ran with the ball, loving the feeling of it moving with me while I passed the frosted playground, the trees, and moved closer to the rec center to get away from the cold.

Throwing a look over my shoulder, I heard my brother curse as he struggled to keep up with me. For his sake, I slowed down again, and then promptly tripped over the ball and into some- one's arms.

A flash of pain made me wince as the metallic zipper of their clothing collided with the side of my head. For a second, I was stunned at how distracted I had been to not notice the person in the empty park, but if they hadn't been there, my brother would've watched me fall face first into the grass. As quickly as I landed, I was equally fast to jump out of the stranger's arms. "I'm so sor—"

"Do the world a favor and watch where you're going," he muttered rudely, brushing off his leather jacket as if I'd contami- nated it when my head had connected with the cold zipper. "You have working eyes. Use them."

Taking a step back, I fixed my low ponytail, glad that my brown hair hadn't gotten caught in the zipper. "Okay, jerk, relax."

"It's not my fault you don't know how to use—"

Picking up the ball with my hands, I held it under one arm. His accent gave me the impression that he'd spent a lot of time in the UK. "I know how to use this just fine."

"Doesn't look like it," he mumbled.

Justin appeared. "Aren't you Sam?"

He *did* look familiar—one of those people you'd spot in the hallway but never acknowledge. Based on my first interaction with him, it was a good thing I'd never bothered to speak to him before. It wasn't hard to see why Jasmine would think I'd have noticed him if he was at tryouts. He was tall, with curly brown hair and currently annoyed green eyes. *She* might find him attractive, but with a personality like this? *No.*

"She's your sister?" Sam said.

"I can speak for myself."

"You might want to tell her that the ball is meant to be *kicked*, not tripped over," he said to Justin. "I figured that the captain of the football team would have a much better handle on the ball."

"Justin, go long," I said, annoyed. "Soccer. We call it *soccer* over here."

Justin ran halfway across the field and I kicked the ball in his direction. It soared perfectly over Sam's head in an arc and landed in front of my brother.

"Did I offend you somehow in our fifty-four seconds of conversation?" Sam asked.

Fifty-four seconds of what? He had faint freckles on his nose and his hair looked as if he'd run his fingers through it a few times. "See something you like?"

"Not at the moment."

Sam looked amused. "It's not my fault you're having an off day with the ball. Practice helps, you know?"

"Do you mean to sound this condescending or is it just you as a person?"

"Depends. Watch where you're going next time." Sam brushed his shoulder against mine as he walked in the direction we had come from.

Justin let out a low whistle. "Sh-o-o-o-t."

"Jasmine didn't say he was such a—"

"Dick?"

~

Later that Sunday night, my brother and my dad surrounded the dinner table. Dad was out of the suit and tie he wore when he went to work at the law firm, and sported a T-shirt and jeans. He usually didn't work weekends but he had an important case and, even when he was tired from a long day, he liked us all sitting around the table eating dinner together. From the head of the table, he asked, "What did you guys do today?"

I shrugged, pasta in my mouth. "Nothing interesting."

Justin gave me a weird look, possibly noticing that I was still ticked off from earlier. "What happened to you, Mr. Krabs? Get any big bucks recently?"

As kids, my brother and I were obsessed with *SpongeBob SquarePants*. With our dad being a lawyer, he earned the name Mr. Krabs pretty easily. Justin's favorite character as a kid was Patrick, and I was Sandy because I had taken a month of karate lessons. My dad's expression suddenly grew serious.

"Uh-oh, what did you do, Patrick?" I teased.

"I didn't do anything! What did you do, Sandy?" my brother retorted.

"Neither of you has done anything wrong." Dad paused. "That I know of."

"Careful, Justin."

Justin feigned irritation at my words.

"What do you guys think of going to your grandmother's this spring break?" Dad asked. "You haven't seen her in a long time."

"We just saw her and Grandpa this past summer," I said.

"I mean your mom's mother."

The last time we had seen our maternal grandmother was

years ago, after mom's funeral. I barely remembered the last time we saw her—everything around that time was a blur.

Mom had passed away in the early summer of 2005, when I was nine and Justin was six. She was coming home from the bookstore she owned when a drunk driver collided with her car. Even though she died when we were young, I was lucky enough to have a good memory of who she was and what she looked like outside of the pictures and old videos of us growing up. Justin had her light-brown hair but we both had her brown eyes. However, I was naturally more tanned, like she was, and Justin was more fair, like our dad.

I also shared her love of soccer. She'd played growing up, and was on her varsity college team. She'd instilled in me the foundation of the sport I loved and wanted to carry with me in the future.

As for our maternal grandmother, we hadn't seen her in years. Before Mom died, our maternal grandfather had died as well. After Mom's funeral, she didn't stay in much contact as she traveled to different places over the years, never settling down. Before then, she hadn't lived far from Port Meadow, only two towns over in Redmond. I never pressured Dad to tell us why she had left our mom's childhood home, let alone the country, but I always thought it was linked to losing her husband and her daughter. That was a lot of sadness for one person to handle.

Growing up before Grandpa had died, before Mom had died, we used to go to my grandmother's house all the time. We would meet our grandparents' friends, have nights filled with board games and great food, and hang out as a family. Last I heard, she had been in Italy, where she had lived before moving to Canada with my grandfather after Mom was born.

"I'm in," said Justin.

"Macy?" Dad asked.

He shouldn't have sounded worried. I would jump at any chance to be reconnected with my mom in some form. My brother looked at me curiously and I cleared my throat. "Does she still live—"

"In your mom's childhood home? Yes, she moved back recently. She wants to see you guys. I figured spring break was a good time for you all to know each other."

"I'm in."

A week of the past without any thought of the future was exactly what I needed.

~

On Monday, as I shoved my duffel bag in my locker at school, Andrew approached me. "Jas said you had a little encounter with Sam."

His name was not the first one I wanted to hear this morning. "He's annoying."

"You met him once."

"*And?* I don't like him," I declared. "Besides, how do *you* know him?"

"We had history together."

"Did everyone have the same history class last semester?"

"He transferred this school year," Andrew explained as some classmates greeted us as they passed by. Wellington Secondary School was in the middle of a suburban area, not too far from my house, but a ways away from the downtown core of Port Meadow. With a big population of students, I didn't know or expect to know everyone. "You really didn't know who he was?"

"No clue," I admitted.

"Talk about timing."

Sam—scrolling through his phone—was walking down the hall with someone who was talking animatedly.

"Hey, Sam." Andrew's voice carried down the busy hallway. He and Sam did a subtle fist bump.

"Hey . . ." Sam looked at me as I scowled and closed my locker.

"Nice to see you again too," he said.

I recognized Sam's friend, Caleb. We didn't run in the same circles—he was popular, me, not so much. He had dark-brown hair, tanned skin, and his approachable nature showed in the bright smile on his face. "Caleb, right? We had math together last semester," I said.

"You're Macy. The soccer player?"

"That's her." Andrew slung his arm around me.

"You two are together?" Caleb asked.

Instantly, I gagged. "God, *no*."

Andrew pushed me away. "*Never*."

"*Ever*," I added.

"Forget I said anything." Caleb raised his hands in defense.

"It's not that—" Andrew looked nauseated. "She's like my sister." We'd known each other since preschool. He was my best friend, there was definitely no changing *that*. "The thought of— it's a no."

"A *definite* no." I shivered involuntarily. Sam stared at me. "What?"

The first warning bell cut through the air, and everyone in the hallway rushed to their first-period classes. Caleb followed suit, waving at us. "See you later."

"Bye, Hazel." Sam smirked.

What? "That's not my name."

"Make sure you don't trip on any soccer balls on the way to class." He disappeared into the passing crowd with Caleb.

"He's annoying," I muttered.

"He's playing around," Andrew said as we walked to class. "I'm surprised you didn't know him. Especially with his last name."

"What's his last name?" We got to our desks in time for the national anthem.

When the anthem ended, Andrew still didn't answer. I pinched him and he hissed, "*Fuck.*"

"I'm *waiting.*"

"Wait *longer.*" He smirked. "Maybe I'll keep this information from you; after all, what's in it for me?"

"Would you just—"

"His last name's Cahill."

I gasped dramatically, tapping Andrew's arm frantically. "He's *Cedric's* brother?"

"He's Cedric's *cousin,*" he clarified.

"*What!*"

Cedric Cahill and I met when we were in ninth-grade science class. I wasn't one to be head over heels for anyone—my friends got into relationships, broke up with people, and went through rejection to a point where I didn't want to be involved in any of that. The idea of feeling that way for anyone made me squeamish.

However, meeting Cedric changed my perspective *slightly.* He had moved here from the UK when he was younger. He played rugby, was smart, and had kind brown eyes. Eventually, as I talked to him more often, I began to have feelings for him. Feelings I'd never acted upon.

"Macy Anderson."

The loud voice coming from the front of the room forced the class into silence. My voice had carried throughout the entire classroom, interrupting announcements and violating homeroom's number one rule.

To make things worse, I was given detention, aggravating me further as I stood outside the gym after school with my friends, where practice was going to be held today.

"We'll see you at the next practice," Jon Ming said. "Don't worry about it, the team's not going to fall apart with you missing one practice."

"Cheer up." Jacob patted me on the back before he slipped inside the gym with Jon Ming. Brandon and Austin fist bumped me as they followed the other two inside.

Along with Andrew and Jasmine, Jon Ming, Austin, Brandon, and Jacob were my closest friends. I'd played soccer with them for the past four years, since we'd started high school. They were weird beyond belief, ate as much food as I did, and were the most annoying people I knew. Yet I wouldn't change any of them for the world.

"This is your fault," I snapped at Andrew as we watched our friends start to set up for drills. Where I was supposed to be.

"You're the one who yelled."

Yes, but I shouldn't have gotten detention for it. Not when we had a game next week against our biggest competitors, Crenshaw Hills. Wellington had had a huge rivalry with them for years, and soccer was a sport both schools were known for, making us the biggest competitors in the city.

My phone buzzed as Andrew slipped into the gym and I headed to the classroom to serve out my penance at detention.

Jasmine: sucks that you're in detention

Me: I can feel your sympathy from a mile away.
Please note the heavy sarcasm

Jasmine: ;)

I entered the classroom, gave the teacher who usually held detention, Mr. Malik, my pink slip, and sat down at the desk farthest away from the others who were in the room. I slouched in my chair, putting my earphones in before lifting the hood of my sweater over my head. Suddenly, my earphones were pulled from my ears.

"What are you doing here?"

Sam.

"What are *you* doing here?"

He straddled a chair backward in front of me, his elbows perched on the desk. "Got caught skipping class."

When I proceeded to put my earphones back in my ears, he hooked his fingers on the wires and pulled. "*Dude,*" I protested.

"Why are you here?" he repeated. "You should be at practice, no?"

"It's not your concern." From the look on his face I figured he wasn't going to budge until I gave him a proper response. "I may have sort of accidentally yelled during the announcements this morning."

"Which teacher?"

"Mr. Oliver."

He snorted then glanced over at the now-empty desk where a teacher *should* have been sitting. *Where the heck did he go?*

Sam stood, his chair scraping the floor, and looked at the clock. "Want to get out of here?" I must've made a face of disapproval at his suggestion because he continued. "Mr. Malik usually leaves then comes back toward the end. We're good."

"I don't know you. Why the hell would I trust you?"

"It's not a matter of trust." His green eyes were mischievous. "We're not getting caught." Sam gestured to a few other students who had started leaving the classroom. It was either here, stewing over not being at soccer practice or—"C'mon, Hazel."

"That's not my name." My earphones went back in. "And I'm not skipping detention."

Sam didn't bother me any further, settling in and taking a seat at the desk next to me. We sat in silence for the next hour and a half, him going through his phone and me doing the latest physics homework until the students who had left eventually came back into the classroom. Not long after them, Mr. Malik returned, and detention ended.

I was out the door and headed toward my locker to grab my jacket when Sam caught up to me. "Do you want to hit the diner? You've got to be hungry." He wasn't wrong. My stomach was eating itself from the long day at school. "Practice is probably over. What else do you have to do?"

A few minutes later, Sam and I were sitting at the diner a block away from school. Various people greeted Sam as they passed by, but he didn't pay attention to them. His focus for the next half an hour was annoyingly on the girl over my shoulder, as he gave her flirty eyes. He even had the nerve to send her a little wave that she returned before continuing her conversation with her friends.

"You're related to Cedric?"

Annoyance flashed across Sam's face. "Not exactly who I would like to be associated with. We aren't exactly fond of each other." He took a fry from my plate. I hated sharing. How did someone not like Cedric? Sam said, "Change the topic."

"But—"

"Change. The. Topic."

"Okay!" *Holy.* I moved the plate out of his reach. He held his hands out, stunned. "Wait, the only reason you know me is because of my cousin?"

Outside of my close friends, I didn't pay a lot of attention to anyone else. I recognized faces, but names? There was much more to focus on. Like the soccer team and picking between universities.

"*Hello?* Earth to Hazel." Sam snapped his fingers in my face.

"Not my name," I said. "Unlike you and me, Cedric and I are *actually* friends. I've seen you around but, I don't know, I never knew your name."

Sam didn't reply, his attention drifting back over my shoulder as I shoved a fry in my mouth. He reached for my plate, snagging himself another fry. "Bro, you've got to stop doing that."

"You don't like sharing?"

"Buy your own." I reached into my backpack and pulled my camera out of its bag.

"*Possessive.*" He tilted his chin at the device in my hands. "What's with the camera?"

"I like taking pictures."

"You can do that with your *phone*," he pointed out. "The captain of the football team has a hobby?"

"It's soccer."

"I'm from England. It's football."

"I'm not getting into this argument with you," I said. "I'm going home."

"Hazel, c'mon." He gestured back to my seat as I rose. "Sit, I'll stop being annoying. What kind of pictures do you have in there?"

"You sure you don't want to talk to the girl behind me?"

He reached a hand out for my camera and I gave it to him. He flicked through the pictures and I leaned over the table to get a better look. One was Andrew giving me the middle finger as we walked to his car the other day. "You and Andrew have been friends for a long time?"

"A *very* long time," I said. "What about you and Caleb? You guys seem close."

"We are." Looking at his phone, he cursed under his breath then handed me back my camera. "Shit. I got to go. Maybe I'll see you in detention again, Hazel."

"Don't count on it," I muttered as he shrugged his jacket on. "How often do you get in trouble?"

"Depends on what you consider trouble."

~

I lay on Jasmine's bed later that night, watching her fix the posters along her walls. They covered almost every inch of her room, images of all her favorite movies. I'd watched the collection grow over the years and she'd never taken a single poster down. "Did you know Sam and Cedric were related?"

"Did I know that they're cousins?" she asked. "I think *everyone* knows."

"They're so"—I tried to find the right word—"different."

Jasmine reached up to fix her *Star Wars* poster. "They're cousins, not clones."

I rolled over on her bed, resting my hands under my chin. "I mean Cedric's so *nice* and Sam's so *not*."

"Remember when you had a thing for Cedric?" Jasmine sat down on the bed next to me and grabbed my camera to look through pictures. "I'd never seen you so unlike yourself."

Had a thing for Cedric? Had it gone away? *No.* I didn't admit that out loud to anyone. Although he was a popular guy and we didn't see each other that often, it was strange that he had a cousin I didn't know about.

"Cedric's still cute, no?" Jasmine beamed, eager to hear my response.

If my face is burning up I swear—"I'm not having this conversation with you."

"Who are you going to talk to about boys? Andrew? *Please.*" Jasmine held up my camera. "Mind explaining this?"

I snorted at the sight of Sam making a funny-looking face at my camera. He must've taken it when I wasn't looking. I reached for my camera with no plans of deleting the picture. "He had detention too."

"Look at you, best friends with troublemaker Sam." I grunted out a no yet Jasmine wasn't convinced. "Macy, you never know."

"It's not happening," I protested. Not with someone as irritating as he was.

2
DUMBEGG

The following day, Andrew and I walked into the cafeteria during lunch as he showed me a funny post he had saved on social media. Conversation buzzed throughout the room. Even though Wellington had a huge student body, most people sat with the same group, in the same spot, all five days of the week. Looking around at the familiar faces in their regular spots, I passed by the one face I wasn't fond of: *Beatrice.*

Beatrice and I had known each other since middle school. We were even friends at one point. Close friends. One night at an eighth-grade dance, a boy she liked attempted to kiss me, and that was enough for her to decide that we would never be friends again. And that was just the beginning of her dislike toward me.

Most likely it was a buildup of little incidents. For instance, in grade nine when Austin and I were fooling around with a soccer ball, I accidentally kicked the ball near her face. She called me a freak even though I apologized. Or in grade eleven, when I won an award for female Athlete of the Year. That pissed her off because she wanted it since she was captain of the varsity dance team. She told half of our grade that the only reason I won the award was because I bribed the athletic committee for it, which wasn't remotely true.

As our time in high school progressed, her hate grew as she made comments to piss me off—comments about me having mostly guy friends, or my clothes, or being the only girl on the soccer team.

Her rude remarks only got worse when she involved Jasmine. Sean, Jasmine's ex-boyfriend, had dated Beatrice before he dated Jasmine. When Sean and Jasmine had gotten together months after he and Beatrice broke up, Beatrice wasn't happy, and made it her life mission to make me and Jasmine miserable. Like most mean girls in high school, Beatrice's hate was based on envy, and that didn't help me or Jasmine. It was crazy to me that someone could hate another person for being themselves.

Beatrice was typically pretty, with fair skin, long, light-brown hair, and brown eyes. She was charming, and people gravitated to her. You'd think that because Jasmine was the same way, they'd get along. But in the four years we'd attended school, I don't think I'd ever seen Beatrice without her friends close behind, which worked in her favor when she wanted to say something rude and they egged her on.

A hand came to my shoulder and on impulse, I grabbed it hard, thinking it was one of my soccer friends trying to sneak up on me.

"Relax, it's me."

I spun around and immediately let go of the hand. Sam shoved it into the pocket of his leather jacket, and raked the other through his curly hair. He greeted Andrew, asking him, "Is she always this jumpy?"

"Sorry, I thought you were someone else," I said before they jumped into a conversation. They walked farther into the cafeteria but I didn't follow.

My attention was on the boy sitting in the corner of the room, talking to his friends. *Cedric.* His brown eyes caught mine, and he raised a hand in acknowledgment. I waved back, my heart pounding inside my chest as he gestured for me to come over. *Don't fall, idiot. Don't you dare fall.*

"Hey, Mace," Cedric said.

"Hey," I said. "I haven't seen you around much."

The resemblance between him and Sam was vague, but it was there. They shared the same nose, but Cedric's eyes were brown, and his hair was cropped in a buzz cut. He was more muscular, having played rugby competitively in and out of school, and Cedric's accent was almost unapparent.

"I've been busy. We've got to hang out."

Keep your cool. Relax. "Sure."

"You're probably busy with school and soccer." He leaned back in his chair. "How's it going by the way?"

"We're preparing for the season."

"When does it start?"

"In May. We have indoor exhibition games and tournaments before that."

"Can you squeeze me into your busy schedule?" he teased.

If Jasmine was here, she'd easily slide in something flirty. Banter that proved she was easygoing, fun to talk to. I wasn't her, and so I pretended to play it cool. "We'll see."

"I'll text you then to find out."

"Cool." Saying good-bye to him, I turned on my heel, my grip on my phone harder than it should have been.

Cool? Seriously? When I reached our table, it was filled with my friends—and Sam. "Why are *you* here? That's my spot."

"It's suddenly illegal to sit?"

I slid in next to him and grabbed my lunch from my bag, opening it and putting it on the table. Sam reached out to take a granola bar I had as a snack and I slapped his hand away.

"*Ow.*"

Austin hissed, "Don't mess with Macy and her food, man." He glanced at himself through the camera on his phone as he fixed his hair. Austin was biracial—his father Congolese and his mom Puerto Rican—and he had brown eyes and perfectly straight teeth that had never been touched by braces.

"*Ever,*" Jon Ming added, putting his headphones around his neck. Jon Ming's dyed red hair was as bright as his eccentric personality. He spoke multiple languages, including his native tongue, Korean, and was known for playing the music he created everywhere, at every party he went to.

I pushed Sam's arm off as he tried to put it around my chair. "Hazel here is glad to share food with me, aren't you? She's probably happy to see me."

"Buzz off, dumbegg."

"Buzz off, *dumbegg*?" Sam looked at Andrew. "Who says *dumbegg*?"

"This girl, who doesn't swear," Andrew said. "Be glad you haven't heard her say holy flying lemurs."

"Holy flying what?" Sam chuckled, surprised. "That's weird because you're such a tomboy."

"I'm not—"

"A *tom. Boy.* Do I have to say it slower?"

"Stop being a jerk. I'm not a tomboy."

"You kind of are," Jon Ming agreed. "All your friends are guys except Jasmine." Jon Ming pointed his fork at me, a thoughtful expression crossing his face. "I don't think you've ever owned a dress."

"She has dresses. She just doesn't wear them," Jasmine said.

"And you're like one of the guys." Austin shrugged.

Sam's phone beeped and he got up after he looked at it. His hand reached out to ruffle my hair. "See you later, Hazel."

After he left the busy cafeteria, Jon Ming said, "Sam's interesting."

"And he seems to like talking to you," Austin commented.

"What about *Cedric*?" Jasmine whispered as if someone was going to eavesdrop on our conversation.

"He wants to hang out. It's not like that," I said.

"You're into Cedric?" Andrew said.

"I didn't say that."

"You don't have to." He pointed at me. "You're going red."

I rubbed my cheeks and scowled at my friends. "Can we change the stupid subject?"

Andrew smirked. "I'll put in a good word for you."

"*Andrew.*"

Jasmine got excited. "Can't believe Macy Marie Victoria—"

"It's *Victoria Marie*!" I reminded her for the hundredth time since I'd known her.

"—has a crush," Jon Ming finished. "This is *fucking* weird."

"Who has a crush?" Jacob and Brandon joined us. The fraternal twins shared fair skin and brown eyes but Jacob's brown hair was short while Brandon's longer hair was tied back in a low bun.

"Macy's into Cedric Cahill."

Jacob made a face. "That's a lie."

Was it that hard to believe that I could like someone? Tapping my fingers against the table as everyone kept eating, I asked Brandon and Jacob, "Do you guys think I'm a tomboy?" Jacob laughed. Loudly. Brandon, although politer than his brother, seemed to agree. "I wish you wouldn't turn me into a stereotype."

Jon Ming read off his phone, "A tomboy is 'a girl who likes rough, noisy activities traditionally associated with boys.'"

"I'm not *exactly* that!" I protested.

Andrew held my hands. "You are a tomboy, accept it." He shrugged as if to tell me it was what it was. A disappointed sigh left me as I glanced at Cedric, who was talking to his friends. There was no way he would like a tomboy.

~

That night I lay in my bed with my laptop in front of me, a video playing on the screen: Streamers hung on the walls of the living room. The dining table was loaded with food—potato chips, cheese puffs, pretzels, a veggie tray . . . and my soccer cake. It was my ninth birthday. The last one I had with my mom before she died four months later in a car crash.

The cake was alight and everyone was singing "Happy Birthday to You." My dad was making monkey faces at the camera and my mom stopped him, attempting to flip the focus on me. Five seconds later, they kissed before little me blew out the candles on the cake. Justin's high pitched "ew" tumbled into the shot. Her brown hair was in voluminous waves and her eyes were bright. Even if she'd worn a potato sack she would have stood out. She could light up any room while I blended in with the crowd. Maybe my friends were right, maybe I was a tomboy—but if that meant that I loved soccer like my mom, then I was maybe okay with it.

The back of my head hit my pillow. She would know what to do about me liking a guy. I'd never needed to have that conversation. I could possibly talk to my dad, but this topic would always be a mom thing. The type of thing daughters would go to their moms for, and ask for advice. That's what Jasmine did with her mom whenever the topic of boys came up.

There was a knock on my door. It had to be my dad; Justin normally barged in. He poked his head over the threshold. "Justin made pasta."

"Justin attempted to make food? *Patrick* Justin?" I pushed the covers off. "This I've got to see."

"What were you doing?"

"Watching old videos of Mom."

My dad stepped into the room, eyes now glued to the screen where I had the next video cued up to play.

My family recorded a lot of things. We had tapes saved of the first time Justin and I walked. Of our Halloween costumes every year. And while we had a lot of videos and tapes stored from over the years, we had even more pictures. Most pictures of the family were initiated by Mom. She'd force me and Justin to pose while in line for ice cream during summers growing up. She took pictures of me at every game I had been part of for house league soccer when I was six.

At some point, soon after she died, we stopped taking pictures. This resulted in me asking Dad for a camera one birthday. And since I received it, I haven't stopped taking photos.

"Christmas?"

"Yeah." I pointed at the action figure in my hand on the screen. "Justin hated that I got that. He stole it when I eventually stopped playing with it."

The look in my dad's eyes was distant. "And then you stole it back and he wouldn't stop crying."

I looked back at the screen. "I miss her."

His smile diminished. "I miss her, too, Mace."

~

I ran beyond Jon Ming, passing the ball to Andrew on the right wing. Practice, held at either the gym or rec center after school on given days, was meant to be hard. My body ached from the number of suicides and push-ups Coach Thompson made me do as punishment for getting detention the other day, but I tried to stay focused.

Andrew passed the ball to me and I flipped it back to him before Jon Ming could touch it. Andrew took the shot and in the nick of time, I tipped the ball in, watching it hit the back of the net. The move was great, but it was rare for Coach Thompson to give us praise. We had to earn it.

"Prescott! Anderson! Over here!" Coach yelled. Andrew and I jogged over. "Nice job."

He called our teammates over, ending practice as he said, "Great practice, team, see you tomorrow. Dismissed!"

The rest of the team packed up. Even though practice was over, excited energy bounced inside me. I playfully hit Andrew on his arm. "We are *so* going to win on Monday."

"Someone's happy."

"I'm just saying." My fingers prodded at his stomach in excitement. "We're going to win on Monday. We're going to win the tournament—this team is going to go all the way."

"Mace, we all know how much you love winning."

"Who doesn't?" I straightened my hair in its ponytail as Andrew untied his cleats.

"Staying here?" Andrew asked.

"I'm going to practice a bit more before heading home. You staying?"

"Got too much homework. Although it'll be great to not have your sweaty gear in my car."

"Rude."

"You going to get home safe?" He grabbed his duffel bag and slung it over his shoulder.

"I'll be fine. Don't worry about me. Drive safe!"

"*Danke*," he said exaggeratedly, and walked into the boys' change room.

Growing up over the years, I'd seen different sides of Andrew. We had gone to school together for most of our lives and our parents were close; it was almost inevitable that we would be best friends. I knew how angry he got whenever I took the last slice of pizza or how happy he was when his beloved show got a reboot. I'd seen him cry over movies in which his favorite character died. We'd always been close.

As my feet moved along the ball, adrenaline coursed through my veins and I ran full-out past the set-up pylons, making a quick cut left and shooting the ball. Someone yelled something incoherent that startled me and I looked up to see Sam and Caleb cackling in the bleachers. They left their seats and headed over to me. Caleb was wearing regular clothes but Sam? He was in soccer gear. His cleats were shiny and new, and his clothing top brand. "What are you guys doing here?"

"We could ask you the same thing," Caleb said.

"Training." I pointed to Sam's cleats. "I didn't know you played soccer," I lied.

Caleb patted his friend on the shoulder, excitement all over his face. He was definitely a joy to be around—I could tell. "He's good when he's not being a *pendejo* dick." I must've given him a confused look because Caleb shrugged. "I'm half Latino."

"Why didn't you try out for the team?" I asked.

"Didn't you guys *just* have practice?" Sam asked instead.

"I stayed back for a bit to practice on my own."

"*I'll* practice with you. Unless you can't keep up?" Sam winked and playfully knocked his shoulder against mine as he moved by me, grabbing the ball and luring me out.

Turned out Sam was good.

Sam was *very* good.

He handled the ball as if it were a part of him, eyes darting around the field, always calculating. The only thing that stood between him and the net was me. Caleb sat by the side near my duffel bag, attempting to take pictures. "I hate to break it to you, Hazel," Sam challenged me. "You're a forward."

I am. How did he know that? "I know which position I play."

He hiked the ball up in the air and rolled it off the front of his body. I caged him, focused on his every movement as he attempted to get by me. He was quick but I was too. When Sam realized the lengths that I would go to get the ball off him, we were in the middle of not trying to foul each other. And even though I wasn't fond of the guy, I liked the way he treated me as if I was any soccer player. He didn't go easy on me because I was a girl.

Rolling the ball back and setting up again, Sam surveyed the scene. Obviously knowing he wasn't going to get past me, he took the easy shot, and I whipped around to see the ball enter the net. "Cheater."

"How?" He grinned. "All I had to do was get it in."

"By getting *past* me!" I shoved him lightheartedly and he only seemed amused, running over to get the ball.

"Caleb!" I yelled and he looked up from the bleachers. In his hand was a pen and a notebook; my camera sat next to him. He had alternated between taking pictures and writing in his note-book since we had gotten here. "How do you deal with him?"

"I ask myself that every day." Caleb jogged over to us with my camera. "You take good pictures." He turned to Sam. "Take me home on the bike."

"No," Sam said.

"*Rude.*"

"You're a nice guy," I said to Caleb, who seemed surprised by my compliment. I patted Sam on the shoulder. "You should take notes."

"One, I never said I was a nice person, and two, I can't take him on the bike. My motorcycle's in the shop, but my car's in the parking lot."

"You have a *motorcycle*?" I asked, struggling not to laugh at the new information.

Sam frowned. "How is that funny?"

"Because you're a walking cliché, dude. The leather jacket? Motorcycle? Is this *Grease*?"

Sam shot me a dirty look while Caleb chuckled loudly. Sam was physically attractive, and he knew it. It was obvious in the way he'd flirted easily with that girl at the diner near school, and by his little comments. It added to his entire rude appeal. "Let's go."

Caleb waved good-bye to me as Sam stomped away, picking up his duffel bag from the bleachers and heading into the guys' change room.

There was no way he and Cedric were related.

3
SMALL WORLD

On a cloudy day, I sat at the diner near school with my friends, who were crowded around two tables. It was rare to get all of us together on a Saturday morning, and this was one of the few chances we got. Next to me sat Jasmine's older brother, Drake. He went to university in Willowridge, a town not too far from Port Meadow, and had driven back this morning for reading week. "It's good having you here, man," Andrew said to Drake.

Drake had been on the soccer team before he graduated from our high school two years ago. "Tournament time, right?" Drake asked.

"And we're going to win," Austin promised.

The boys chorused their agreement and I turned to Drake. "Where's your sister?"

"She needs to hurry up." Jacob's knee bounced up and down next to me, his eyes leering at the bright screen listing all the food. "I'm *starving*."

"You're always starving," Brandon said. "Just order."

"I'm here," Jasmine announced, plopping down next to her brother and hugging him. "Sorry, my alarm didn't go off. Was your drive here okay?" Before Drake could answer, Jasmine's eyes caught a figure at the door, and she frowned. All of our eyes turned to see Beatrice, her big group of friends surrounding her.

"*Look away,*" Jacob warned, and our eyes went back to each other before any of them could catch us looking.

"Ignore them and Beatrice." Andrew sighed.

"Are you guys going to postsecondary? Working?" Drake asked.

A few days ago, I'd flicked through pictures of all of us—knowing that I wasn't going to be in the same place as my friends next year at this time had made my stomach twist.

"Mace, did you pick a university yet?"

"I've still got time. I'm waiting to see what happens with soccer later this season."

Beatrice slowed down to greet the boys before shooting Jasmine and me a dirty look. Her face contorted into a conceited smile that I wanted to wipe off her face.

She could put that smile up her—

"I hate her," Jasmine muttered.

"You and me both," I added as my phone buzzed in my pocket. Opening it up as Jacob told the server what he would be ordering, I read:

> Cedric: Next Friday there's a party. I better see you there

Jasmine seized my phone. "He wants you to go to the party?"

"Cahill?" Jon Ming leaned in, intrigued.

Drake looked taken aback by the last name rather than being confused about what was going on. "*Cahill?*"

"Cedric," Andrew informed him, turning back to me. "Answer back."

"*You* answer back," I retorted. Jasmine took charge, typing on the screen of my phone. I read her response as she clicked Send.

> Me: Pick me up then

"*Jasmine.*"

"If he wants you there, he should do it himself." Three floating dots appeared on my phone. He was responding.

> Cedric: Count on it

My phone was snatched out of my hand and Jon Ming and Austin read the text. "*Count on it,*" Austin mocked in a deeper voice. The two proceeded to make kissy faces, which was highly annoying. A lot of things could change regarding our lives, but the way they all acted definitely wouldn't.

~

Later that day, I stood by the side of the indoor soccer field at the rec center, watching the kids on the field doing the drills I'd assigned to them. I volunteered here every Saturday as a house league coach.

Glancing down at my phone, I saw that Cedric had texted me again, which he'd been doing nonstop throughout the day.

I blew the whistle to end the drill and let everyone know they'd done a great job. As the kids were getting ready to head home to their parents, I was in the middle of typing a reply to his message when I spotted Sam with Phillip, one of the kids I coached.

"How did I do?" Phillip asked.

Sam gave him a smile I had never seen before. No arrogance. Sam ruffled his hair. Phillip swatted his hand off but didn't appear vexed. "You did great, buddy."

"Really?" Philip glowed.

"Yes." Sam's eyes zeroed in on me. Phillip turned around, the dimples deepening on his cheeks. I gave him a little wave as Sam stood, handing Phillip a coat to wear. "Change into your shoes, you don't want to stretch out your cleats."

"I didn't know you volunteered here," Sam said to me.

"Every Saturday. What are you doing here?"

Sam gestured at Phillip. The kid had brown hair and brown eyes that resembled the boy I was texting. I couldn't believe I never noticed before.

"You're Phillip's cousin too. He's Cedric's brother," I said.

"Look who's finally using their eyes," Sam mocked. *Jerk.*

Phillip looked at Sam and me in confusion. "You two know each other?"

"We're friends," Sam said.

"We go to school together," I corrected.

But Phillip didn't care for our conversation anymore, his eyes darting over to the water fountain next to the change rooms. "I'll be back," he yelled, running over to fill up his water bottle.

"Small world," Sam said.

"I guess so. Second time I've seen you here."

"I'm here usually the hours others aren't."

THE BAD BOY & THE TOMBOY 37

"I would have noticed if you were here." The rec center was huge—with a gym, indoor soccer field, basketball courts, and different rooms for various activities—but generally you could see everyone coming and going in the lobby or would run into them in the change rooms.

"You would have?" A smirk crept onto his face in a suggestive manner.

"Not in *that* way," I said as Phillip came back.

Sam patted his cousin on the shoulder. "Let's go."

Phillip was making his way to the door when Sam reached toward me. I stilled, his hand holding the top of my whistle as he adjusted the string. My face was heating up. "Hazel, we've got to stop bumping into each other like this."

"Why do you keep calling me that?"

Phillip yelled his name from the exit of the indoor field.

"I'll see you at school," he said. He didn't answer my question.

~

The following Monday I found Jasmine near her locker talking to a girl. "Mace, this is Stevie. She was on the volleyball team with me."

"You're on the soccer team, right?" Stevie asked me.

"Yeah," I said. Beatrice stared at us from down the hall, a distasteful look on her face.

Oh God.

"I haven't seen you around," I said to Stevie, trying to ignore Beatrice.

"I moved here in September." As she was explaining to me where she had lived prior to moving to the city, Jasmine tensed up. "I have to head to class," Stevie said as she waved good-bye.

Jasmine leaned in to me, scowling back at Beatrice. "She's pissing me off and she's not even saying anything."

"She's honestly not even worth it—"

My sentence was left unheard as Jasmine moved down the hallway toward Beatrice and her group of friends.

I followed, ready to back her up in whatever she was going to say. Jasmine stood in front of Beatrice, the two of them nearly the same height, each unwilling to back down. "What do you want?" Jasmine's voice was strong as she glowered at Beatrice.

Beatrice rolled her eyes. "Trust me, I have no reason to waste my time on you."

"Are you sure?" Jasmine's voice was steady. "Because you obviously don't know what you're saying."

"Shut up."

"No." People were listening to the interaction, sensing the obvious tension. This tension didn't involve me. "You look like a complete idiot staring at people like that. I'm doing you a favor."

"Seems to me a favor was done when Sean dumped you."

That wasn't public knowledge—Beatrice put that out there knowing the people listening didn't know, wanting to embarrass Jasmine.

I stepped up to Beatrice, getting in her face, and using my height to my advantage. "Stop talking."

Beatrice wasn't done. "And he moved on *so* fast. I heard he went out with a girl on Saturday."

Jasmine pulled me back. "I don't care who he's with. He can go back to dating you of all people if he wants to."

"What is that supposed to mean, Oreo?"

I froze. While I didn't understand what Beatrice meant, I knew there was a negative weight behind that word. Jasmine lunged at Beatrice, her arm bent to hit the other girl in the face with her fist. I pulled Jasmine back as loud profanities came out of her mouth. Choruses of encouragement for a fight broke out around us. Andrew appeared next to me, and he also held Jasmine tight.

"What is going on here?" An authoritative voice boomed through the crowd, and my physics teacher, Ms. Dawson, walked up to us, eyes on Beatrice, whose friends surrounded her.

Beatrice pointed at Jasmine, whom Andrew was still holding on to. "This psycho attacked me in the middle of the hallway."

"Bullshit." Jasmine broke free from Andrew's grip. "She was being a racist."

"I was *not*," Beatrice spat. Ms. Dawson told Beatrice to head to the principal's office and gestured for Jasmine to come along.

"You okay?" I asked Jasmine.

"I'm fine." As she walked down the hall, she muttered, "I have to be, don't I?"

~

"Get up and go, Mace," Drake reassured me later that day. We were at the rec center and people were filling in the stands as the soccer game was about to start. Jasmine wasn't here—she was currently serving detention for the altercation with Beatrice that morning, which seemed so unfair. Even though Beatrice was serving detention, too, something should have been done for what she had said to Jasmine.

I fist bumped Drake as the ref called for captains. I went over to the center of the field as the captain from Crenshaw Hills approached the middle too.

Michael.

"Anderson!" he smirked. "You're captain this year? Team decided to go with the girl as a joke?"

"Shut up."

Michael scowled. "Watch out."

It took everything in me to focus on the game and not on the words and potential threats from the sexist pig I'd encountered over the years. After deciding who got the first ball with the coin toss, I shook Michael's hand and walked off the field.

Justin was up in the bleachers with my camera in his hand. At the bottom of the bleachers near the bench, sat Sam. He gave me a two-fingered wave as Coach approached me. Once I told Coach that we had the first ball and he blew his whistle to tell my teammates to stop drills and head over to where I stood by the side, Sam said from where he sat, "Caleb says good luck. He had to do some errands so he sent me."

"He *sent* you? You sure you didn't send yourself?"

"Why did it look like the Crenshaw captain was giving you a hard time?"

Michael was frowning at Sam. "Why's he looking at you like you dumped his sister?" I asked.

"I didn't," Sam said. "I had a thing with a girl I thought was his ex-girlfriend, then stopped it when I found out the other guy was still involved."

"Trouble seems to follow you."

"Good luck out there, Hazel." He leaned back and I joined my teammates in the starting huddle.

~

My legs burned as I sprinted for the ball near the end of the game. Michael was right behind me as I ran, getting the ball from the other defender. The score was 2–2, with seven minutes left on the clock. I could feel Sam's eyes on me, like they had been the entire game, and I had a feeling that he was anticipating my every move, and every move the other team made.

Michael's foot connected with my ankle. With a *whomp*, I hit the ground and pain flared. As I turned on my back, Michael was shoved to the side.

"Hazel, can you get up?" I reached for the large hand in front of me and pulled myself up, shaking off the subsiding pain in my foot.

I steadied myself. "I'm fine, go back to the bleachers."

"Are you sure you're okay?"

"I'm *good*, Sam," I assured him. "Go before you get in trouble."

Sam nodded and headed back to the bleachers as Andrew came up to my side. The ref and Michael were in a heated argument, and soon a red card was pulled out. He sent me a dirty look, and walked over to his team as the ref blew the whistle. "Penalty at the box."

Shrugging off all my nervous energy, I waited as the ball was set up. When the whistle blew, I ran, my foot connecting with the ball. The goalie reached for the corner of the post as the ball passed the line and hit the back of the net in a fluid motion. Relief filled my chest as I exhaled. After high-fiving my teammates, we set up again and as if on impulse, my eyes went to Sam, who mouthed *Nice goal*. His praise added to my excitement before my focus went back on the game for the remainder of the half.

Michael stood at a distance. Despite him writing me off as "just a girl," I would challenge him for the rest of this game, and every other game I would play against him.

4
THIS IS NOT A ROM-COM

On Friday night, I sat on the couch in David's living room. David and I had physics together, and he was known for throwing parties I was suddenly thankful for as I sat with Cedric, loud music playing around us.

Cedric had picked me up from my house, and luckily Dad had been out with Justin, which meant he didn't have a chance to talk to Cedric and potentially embarrass me.

The house was hot, possibly from having so many teenagers— and their hormones—crammed into one place. Cedric and I had been talking on the couch for hours, barely moving from our spots. As for my friends, I didn't know where they were, but they were here.

I ran my fingers through my long brown hair, which wasn't encased in a ponytail for once, as Cedric went to get another drink. The chatter around me grew as people took videos of each other. That reminded me of *my* camera, which both Andrew and

Jasmine insisted I leave at home because apparently once I had it in my hands, I "wasn't able to focus on the vibe of a good party." Jasmine's words, not mine.

"Hey." Austin sloppily put his hands on my shoulders. His hat fell off his head, exposing his dark hair.

He was definitely drunk. "You look happy."

"I *am* happy," he gushed. "How are you? How's Cedric?"

"How are *you*?"

Caleb appeared by his side, slinging an arm around Austin to hold him up. "He's good."

"I'm a little *fucked*," Austin whispered as if it was a secret.

"You don't say."

"I kissed someone," he slurred. Caleb's eyes flickered between Austin and me.

"You did? Good for you."

"Miss me?" Sam's voice came from behind me and I twisted around to see him.

His eyes were alert. He wasn't drunk. "Hi, Sam." I turned back to Austin. "Where are the boys?"

"Downstairs—these guys are so cool," Austin said. "Why haven't we hung out before? And Caleb?" Austin jabbed a finger in Caleb's chest. "He's so charming. Like, he walks into a room and people like him because he's so charming. He's so—"

"Charming, like Prince Charming," I added. "I get it."

"Where's your camera?" Sam said. "Rarely ever see you without it."

"I left it at home."

Austin almost fell on Caleb. "All right." Caleb raised him up. "We'll see you after, Macy."

I bid them good-bye, hyperaware of Sam moving from behind

me to follow them. A few moments later, Cedric returned and handed me another drink as he sat down. "I heard about the game. Good job."

Cedric didn't know much about soccer and it showed. "Thanks."

"You must love football."

"Yeah, I'm a volunteer coach on a house league team, and realized the other day your little brother is on it."

"Phillip?"

"Yeah. Sam picked him up. I didn't even make the connection that you and Phillip were brothers."

"Yeah, my family doesn't really come up in conversation," he said. Sam had said that he and his cousin didn't have a good relationship—now, the look on Cedric's face confirmed it. "Aren't you close with Justin?" he asked me.

"Yeah, we're close."

Close enough that even though Cedric had asked me to this party, I'd offered Justin the chance to tag along. He declined, choosing to try to get our dad to buy him new basketball shoes at the mall.

"Did you celebrate your win?"

I shook my head and Cedric's brown eyes lit up. "Good, then let's go out to dinner."

My movements stilled. "To celebrate a game?"

"Macy." *There was no way he was*—"I'm asking you out."

No way. My brain struggled to form words. "*Oh.*"

"'Oh?'"

"Not like that," I was quick to correct, trying to find the proper words. Even this, us at this party together, wasn't enough to be considered a date considering all of my friends were nearby.

This would mean the two of us alone. On a date. "I meant, 'oh' as in a surprised 'oh.'"

"*Oh*," he jested. "I'm kind of hoping you'll say yes, considering . . . I know you like me."

"What?"

"Austin kind of—"

"Austin?!" *I'm never saying* anything *like this to the boys ever again.*

"I kind of got the hint when he was constantly bringing you up, so I thought I'd ask. And now I'm waiting for an answer."

"Uh-hum." I stopped my incoherent response, trying to regain my composure. *I must be in an alternate universe, because this never happens to me.* "Sure."

"Yeah?"

Hands suddenly landed on my shoulders, but recognizing the nail polish, I relaxed my tense shoulders. However, shock and slight confusion lingered from Cedric's question. He asked me out. *Me.*

"I need help in the bathroom." Jasmine dragged me up from my seat, giving Cedric a look of an apology as she pulled me out of the room. She stopped in the middle of a corridor. "How's it going?" She was rocking back and forth on her heels and I had to admit her mood was contagious, making me chuckle. "I mean . . . between you guys?"

"He asked me out to dinner."

"*Shut up.*"

"It's not a big—"

"It's a *huge* deal," she shouted over the loud music. "He asked you on a date, Macy! Please tell me you said yes. You probably did. We're going to figure out what you're going to wear. I have to tell Andrew. Where are the boys?"

"Downstairs, but—" Jasmine pulled me in the direction of the basement. A lot of the guys from the soccer team waved at me and patted me on the back as I moved through, shouting my name as Jasmine ran to Andrew to tell him what I had told her. His eyes went wide as he whipped his head toward me. I never talked about romantic interests. None of the boys talked much about who they were with, either, and, when they did, it was a bunch of jokes, rarely ever deep conversations.

The basement was crowded and was warmer than the rest of the house, filled with half the kids from school. Jon Ming and Brandon were playing a game of pool while loud chatter erupted from where Jacob was talking to a few people in a corner. The scent of alcohol—from the blue cups people held—was strong in the air, and although music was playing loudly through the house, the conversation between everyone here didn't cease, reminding me of the easygoing conversation I had been having with Cedric.

Jasmine and Andrew headed upstairs, dodging people on the steps, as Sam slid up next to me. "What are they talking about?"

"Nothing." I breathed out and he took a sip of his bottled water.

Sam's eyes shifted to a girl who was staring at him and she looked away quickly. Sam's lips quirked up in a smirk. Moving past him, I went upstairs to the kitchen where a never-ending number of people entered and left through the doorway. I wandered over to the hallway that connected to the living room, where two people were chatting at the other end.

"I'm surprised you're here," Sam said and I jumped, startled that I hadn't noticed him follow me.

"I've been to parties," I insisted.

"One party. Just before winter break in December, and you were where the guys were playing video games and stuff. That's the only time I've seen you."

"Is this another attempt to call me a tomboy?" I said.

"It's not a bad thing." He glanced at the clothes Jasmine had put me in, from the top all the way down to the skinny jeans. "You look good. But this outfit isn't you."

"Sam." I flushed. "You don't even know me. How would you know?"

Turning on my heel, I moved to make my way down the hallway and Sam caught my arm.

"Wait, can I start over?"

"All you've done since the first day we met was tease me. You probably think it's funny to get me riled up."

"Have you ever thought that maybe I was interested in getting to know you as a person?"

"No," I admitted. "The only way for you to get to know a person is with flirty banter, a ride on your so-called motorcycle, and it's usually just to find a way into their pants. Your reputation precedes you."

"I like sex, sue me." He shrugged. "No, I'm not trying to do that with you, but if you want to I—"

"I'm *not* like that."

"There's just something about the way you trip over soccer balls that—*I'm kidding, I'm kidding.*"

He had a nice smile and I knew I wasn't the *only* one who noticed—a lot of female eyes went to him as he continued laughing with his hand on my arm.

"You can't let that go, can you?"

"I'm an asshole. You know that," he joked.

"Is that all you want to be known for?"

"I don't really care what people here think about me," Sam confessed. "People can think I'm an asshole, that I'm a jerk—have you heard what people have said about me since I came to Wellington?"

"No." I leaned against the wall. "What have people said?"

Sam scoffed. "Someone once told Caleb that they thought I was involved in an armed robbery. The recent rumor I've heard is that I was a drug lord. It's ridiculous what people make up when they think the new guy needs to be more interesting than just being the new guy."

All of that sounded completely ridiculous. They were making him out to be dangerous. Sam didn't look like he was that much trouble. "What the heck?"

"Tell me about it," he muttered. "With all the rumors, would that stop you from talking to me right now?"

"No. What people think you are isn't you."

"Good to know." He nodded to himself. "About the thing between Jasmine and Bridget. No, wait, Beatrice. That's her name."

"*Bridget?*"

He waved a hand, letting me know that he couldn't care less about her name. "Why does she hate you?"

"It started in eighth grade."

Sam leaned against the wall to properly face me as a group of people passed by him. "Eighth grade?"

"She liked a guy and we had this school dance. He came up to us. She thought he was going to ask her to dance, and he ended up asking me instead. And attempted to kiss me."

Sam's jaw dropped. "You're lying."

I winced at the memory. "I socked him in the eye by accident."

"How do you punch someone by *accident*?"

"I was shocked, okay? It was completely unexpected. Beatrice has never forgiven me."

"You were thirteen," he said. "What the fuck? She hates you for no reason."

"She started hating Jasmine when Jasmine dated Sean. It escalated. Beatrice's dramatic."

Sam pushed himself off the wall. "You can be too."

"Don't compare me to her." My phone buzzed and I pulled it out of my pocket. Cedric's contact name popped up. I'd left him on the couch. "I gotta go." The corners of my lips went up. "I'll bump into you soon."

Was that flirting? What was I doing?

He chuckled over the music. Back in the living room, I spotted Cedric on the couch. Going from one Cahill to another.

~

On Monday, Austin and I entered the cafeteria not long after the bell for lunch rang. "I hate you."

We both sat at our table with the rest of our friends. "I wasn't in the right state of mind!" Austin said. "It all worked out. You got the guy."

"I did not 'get the guy,'" I exclaimed. "This is not a rom-com. This is my life."

"Don't be so dramatic," Brandon added. "I think we should all celebrate this occasion."

"Celebrate what?" Caleb pulled up a chair between Brandon and Jon Ming while Sam took a seat on the other side of me.

"What are we having for lunch today?" Sam teased, looking at my food.

"Mace got asked out on a date," Jasmine said to Caleb. "By *Cedric*!"

Sam tensed, surprise evident on his face. "My cousin asked you out?"

"Right?" Jon Ming agreed.

"Hey, Stevie." Jasmine grabbed a chair and pulled it over for her to sit between us. Stevie looked a little uncomfortable, her eyes flicking over all of the boys at the table.

"They don't bite. Don't worry," I assured her. There were shoelaces wrapped around the strap of her backpack, similar to how my cleat strings were wrapped around my own.

Jasmine groaned when Caleb winked and said, "Unless you want us to."

Austin tilted his chin in the direction of the backpack she put down. "What do you play?"

"Volleyball."

"One question for you to sit with us." Austin leaned forward. "Do you like eating?"

"What kind of question is that?"

Austin's hands hit the table. "Welcome to the group."

"Here we go," Jasmine muttered, eyes on Beatrice as she walked into the loud cafeteria with her group of friends and headed right for us.

"Does she *want* to die?" Jacob asked as Beatrice and her friends approached our table. She wasn't looking at any of us; her eyes were on Sam.

"Hey, Sam."

He raised his head and she took that as an invitation to touch his shoulder, and I coughed. "Can you do that somewhere else? I'm trying to eat."

Beatrice ignored me, focusing on Sam. "What are you doing later?"

The question was casual, as if it wasn't the first time and the realization hit me. *Oh my God.* There would be nothing wrong with that if this was someone else. But this was Beatrice. And Sam. After he called her Bridget at the party. After he said he wanted to know why she was so mean to me, to us.

"Busy," he quipped. "I'll catch you around."

When Beatrice was gone, Jasmine beat me to the question, irritation in her voice. "You hooked up with *Beatrice*?"

Despite everyone's gaze on him, Sam didn't waver, his fingers locked and pressed against his lips. "Kind of."

"When?" Jasmine asked.

"Last term," he mumbled.

"Of *all* people at this school?" I scoffed. "I'm not even surprised."

Sam looked offended. "What's that supposed to mean?"

"You're such a bad boy," Jacob joked, hitting Jon Ming playfully as if he was supposed to find it funny.

Sam didn't bother to comment as he went through his phone and the conversation shifted to a different topic. I was bothered. He wanted to be friends? Hooking up with my mortal enemy wasn't a good start.

~

The cold air partially numbed my face as I ran inside the school after coming from the rec center later that day. A few people still lingered in the hallways as I approached my locker.

"Macy?" Caleb walked over to me. "School ended two hours ago, why are you here?"

"I forgot some of my books. Had practice." I dropped my bag on the ground and sat down on the floor in front of my locker as I caught my breath, rubbing my hands together.

"You look awful," Caleb said.

I raised my head. "How charming of you to say."

He dropped down beside me. "That's me, princess."

"Why are *you* still here?"

"I'm part of the drama club," he answered. "I write plays."

"Did you write the winter play last year?" I hadn't seen it but Jasmine went, and gushed that it had been really good. Caleb nodded. "That's so cool."

I pointed at the notebook he always carried. "You've got a bunch of plays in there?"

"Mostly ideas for stories. I write a bit too."

"My friend Drake used to write a lot. He went to university for journalism," I said, leaning back on my hands.

"Drake?"

"Jasmine's older brother. Graduated about two years ago," I explained, and understanding appeared on his face. "Are you planning on going into screenwriting or something like that?"

"Maybe. I might take a year off, I don't know yet." He shrugged and slouched, his legs extending farther than mine as he moved down. "I got a question. Do you think aliens—" I shot him a strange look. "Hear me out. Do you think aliens exist?"

"Do *you* think aliens exist?" Whenever he had the chance to explain something, his eyes lit up in a wild way. It was funny to see him get passionate about a topic whenever he spoke—especially at lunch, considering he and Sam had joined our table again today.

"Not in space."

"Then where?"

"The ocean." He crossed his legs and my gaze dropped to the ink on his exposed ankle. "We barely know anything about the ocean and the shit we do know is already scary. Imagine what's in the water where we can't see. We're fucked."

"Caleb? I'm going to change the topic," I said, knowing we would have a lot more conversations like this. I pointed at his ankle. "You have tattoos?"

"Yeah, I got a few. Wanna see?" He started pulling off his shirt, and I was quick to protest. "I'm kidding." Caleb lifted his shirt a bit to expose the ink on his abdomen.

"You have a few quotes. For like, motivation or something?" He nodded. "Those are song lyrics, right? Is this a Justin Timberlake song?"

"He's my personal inspiration." He pointed along his body. "I've got a few images here. Small Rubik's Cube on my wrist. My *abuela*'s birthday on my arm."

"I like the lily."

He raised his leg, pulling his sock down slightly. "It's the first one I got."

"How did you and Sam meet? You're so chill while Sam's—"

"Rude?"

"I was going to say *brooding*."

"He has his moments," Caleb said. "Sam moved here last summer but we met years ago. He and his family used to visit over the summer. I met him one year, a few months after I moved to Canada."

"Where did you grow up?"

"El Salvador." His smooth voice changed when he said the

country's name. "I lived in Scotland for a bit, too, before moving here with my *tia* and sister. When I was twelve, I went to a park with my sister, who can't play catch to save her life. Sam caught the tennis ball we were throwing and he said, 'Here you go.' I said, 'We both have weird accents.' And he became my best friend not long after that. We would go to the park every day during the summer and hang out whenever he came back to Port Meadow. Always kept in contact."

It wasn't hard imagining miniature versions of Caleb and Sam interacting with one another for the first time. "You guys are kind of opposites."

"So are you and Jasmine," Caleb pointed out as my phone buzzed in my pocket. Cedric. I was debating how to respond when Caleb suddenly poked me in the side. "Loosen up." He peeked over at my phone. "You look so serious half the time. Maybe Cedric of all people could help you do that."

"Shut up," I mumbled, shutting off my phone.

"Everyone was talking about your date earlier today, you excited?"

"I don't know."

"You don't know?" Caleb looked at me curiously. "Wait, is this your first real date? Ever?" I didn't answer him. "This is why the boys were so riled up about it? Macy, that's fine. It makes sense to be nervous."

"Cedric and I have been friends for a long time and I don't know what exactly to expect," I said.

The date had been on my mind since the party. What would we talk about? Where would we eat? What would I wear? I took a deep breath, avoiding the topic. "Anyway, I heard Cedric and Sam don't like each other."

"There's been a lot of tension in that relationship that I don't think I should get into," Caleb muttered.

"I don't get it. I mean, I can't imagine someone disliking Cedric, and Sam's a jerk but he's my friend. He doesn't seem like a horrible person."

Caleb whipped his head in my direction. "He's your *friend* now?"

"More like an acquaintance who's growing on me," I corrected. "Like a rash."

Caleb laughed so loudly it carried down the hallway. "You're a funny one, princess."

"I wouldn't ever like to be called that, but you're growing on me, Charming." I hit him playfully on the arm while stretching my legs.

"That's my new name? I'll take it." He stood. "Have fun on your date, Macy."

5
ONE OF THE GUYS

I stared at myself in the mirror on Friday night. That long-awaited night that none of my friends had let me forget about throughout the week. Not that I wanted to forget about it. Even Caleb had pestered me about it, and he had more opportunities, too, since he and Sam joined our table at lunch. Jasmine and Drake were over—they came as a pair whenever he was home.

Jasmine noticed my worried expression. "Aren't you excited? Nervous?"

Drake looked up from where he lay on my bed. He was home for the weekend for a job interview.

"I don't think nervous or excited are the right words." If this outing was with one of the boys, it would be different. My guy friends and I were messy, participating in the dumbest things and joking with each other all the time. I wasn't interested in them in a romantic way. With Cedric, I expected to be nervous around him. To focus on not sounding like an idiot around him;

to not blurt out something dumb or stupid. All day my thoughts were filled with multiple questions about what could happen, conjuring up a mixture of nervousness and excitement to fill my stomach. I could puke. *Don't.*

"You look great," Jasmine assured me. "He's going to love you."

She pushed me into my desk chair, holding something in her hand and I stopped her. "No makeup."

"Why not?"

"I don't want to look like a clown." She came at me with one of the brushes and I moved away from her as if she was contagious.

"Makeup doesn't make you look like a clown," she said. "The eyes. *Simple.* I'll give you mascara." Makeup seriously wasn't my thing. However, Jasmine and I being friends for years had taught me that whenever we disagreed, she'd usually win. I sighed when she said, "Look up."

As she prodded at my eyelashes, I said, "Why would he want to go out with me, of all people, when he could go out with someone like—"

Jasmine's movements stopped and her lips pursed. "Beatrice?"

"She's the worst but boys flock to her," I said. "She's pretty. She's not one of the guys."

"You're pretty even if you're 'one of the guys,'" Jasmine said. Drake made a sound of agreement, his eyes on the screen of my laptop. "Cedric's definitely lucky to take you out tonight."

"Are you okay?" I asked her. "Ever since the whole Beatrice thing you've been off."

"What Beatrice thing?" Drake looked up. "What did she say?"

"She called me an Oreo." Jasmine waved a hand in dismissal.

"What did she mean by that?" I asked.

"She's trying to make me mad by saying that I'm not black enough. Because I go to school here, because I live here and not a lot of people look like me." She sighed. "She's basically telling me that I'll never really fit in."

"That's not true," I assured her, but she didn't look convinced.

"Jasmine," Drake said. "She's trying to provoke you."

"Into what?" I asked.

"She's trying to make Jasmine angry," Drake explained to me. "Trying to put her in a box. Jas, don't let her get to you."

"She's done shit like that for a long time," Jasmine mumbled. "It's not only her. A lot of people expect it."

"What do you mean?" I asked.

"I'm, like, one of two black people in our grade. Beatrice calling me that is just another example of her trying to put me in that angry black woman stereotype. *You* may not see it or hear it but it happens."

"That's so dumb," I said. "It's the twenty-first century."

"And racism and prejudice still exist," Jasmine muttered. "I don't want to talk about this anymore. Cedric's going to be here soon." She rummaged through my closet. I didn't want to go out if she was feeling like this. "I've handled almost four years at school. I can deal with it."

"Do you want to talk later?" I offered.

"I'll be fine." Her repetitive response didn't faze me. She'd said the same after her breakup with Sean and now with Beatrice. She never spoke about what was bothering her and I was concerned about how she must be feeling. "I'll watch *Star Wars*."

"Weirdo," Drake muttered.

"And you're going to watch it with me," she said to her brother.

"She still uses the fake lightsabers that you got her that one Christmas," I said to Drake. Jasmine pulled me out of my room once I had grabbed my shoes, bringing me downstairs to where Dad and Justin were watching TV in the living room.

"How does she look?" Jasmine asked.

My dad shot Jasmine a thumbs-up.

"Where are you going?" my brother piped up.

"She is going on a date," Jasmine said, and I took a deep breath, a sudden wave of nervousness flooding me at the word *date*. I bit my lip and Jasmine nudged me with her elbow. "Don't worry. You'll be fine."

Justin's jaw dropped and he got up from his position on the couch. "What the—and Krabs knew before I did? I'm being pranked. Where are the cameras?"

"You're not being pranked." Drake shrugged on his sweater. He pinched my cheek. "Macy's growing up." I swatted his hand away as the doorbell rang.

My dad stood. "What if I scare him a little?"

Drake and my dad were always like this whenever they were together—annoying me with their banter. As Jasmine and I had grown closer growing up, Drake eventually joined her at my house to hang out, playing video games. This resulted in him seeing my dad pretty often even during the summer when he came back from university. Although Drake had his own friends and life outside of this house, he was like my brother, and Dad thought of him and Jasmine as kids of his own.

"Please *don't*." Dad knew all of my guy friends but he'd never met Cedric. "I'm begging you."

"Have fun," Dad said, ignoring Drake and Justin urging him to embarrass me. "Be home before ten."

"Eleven," I bargained.

"Ten thirty."

Drake and Jasmine said good-bye then opened the door and moved past Cedric on their way out. "Hey," Cedric said.

My dad pushed his way through to stare at Cedric. "Hello," he said menacingly.

I immediately pushed him inside. "Dad, *no*."

I hoped there was an alternate universe where Mom was finding delight in this, right along with him. "Have fun, kids."

~

Cedric never left a conversation hanging. That was one of the things I liked about him. We sat at a restaurant that night for hours, catching up with one another. He told me how he was trying to get scholarships to play rugby at college, and talked a bit about his friends. And whenever he spoke, his accent appeared when he articulated certain words.

He held my hand up, looking at the difference between our palm sizes. "For a tall girl, you have very small hands."

"I don't."

"You do." He linked our hands together. He took a sip of his drink and I tried getting comfortable, wanting to lean against the wall and hike my feet up on the chair. "How long exactly have you liked me?"

"I'm seriously debating whether or not I should kick Austin or thank him."

"Why didn't you say anything?" He tilted his head as dessert was placed in front of us and I dug into the piece of the chocolate cake we were sharing.

"Because you're you," I said. "We've always been friends."

"Since science class," he reminisced, taking a piece of the cake for himself. "You'd wear that Messi jersey to class, like, twice a week."

"I think I still have that jersey."

"That jersey's washed out at this point. I don't recall a week where I didn't see you in it."

"Stop." The witty grin I received made me look down for a moment. We dived for the last small bite at the same time. "I want it."

"Try me." He went around my fork, clinging and clashing it with his own.

"You're so weird."

He dominated the piece and held it up in victory before leaning over to put it in my mouth instead.

Even during the car ride home, he was generous and charming. He parked in the driveway, neither of us getting out of the car as our conversation continued, although we were sure that someone had peeked out the window of the house to look at what was happening. "I think your dad did it again," Cedric said.

The curtains closed once again.

"No, that was definitely Justin."

"What grade is he in?"

"Grade nine. What about Phillip?"

"Second. He's turning eight soon. Won't let anyone forget it. If I take him out to eat, he tells the waiter. I take him to his gymnastics class, he tells his instructor."

"He does gymnastics?"

Cedric nodded, his fingers tickling my own lightly. "My brothers all did something growing up."

"You have *another* brother?"

"There's a bit of an age difference. Phillip's still in elementary school and Ivan, my older brother, graduated from university about a year ago. He was more into karate growing up," he explained. "What about you, though?"

There was no way he was getting closer to me. Yet he was definitely getting closer to me; his hand over mine stopped moving and I held in my breath. "You ever do anything outside of soccer?"

"I read a bit. You?"

"I play a bit of drums. What kind of books do you read?"

"Are you any good? I like sci-fi and dystopia."

"I'm decent, I'll play for you one time." His eyes weren't holding my own anymore. "Not a romance person?"

Andrew and I spent a lot of time making fun of rom-coms in my basement. "Not really."

"That sucks because of what I'm about to do."

He kissed me. The surprise made me highly aware of my heartbeat. This was my first kiss and it was with Cedric. *Dude,* I encouraged myself, shutting my eyes as I kissed him back.

When he pulled away, our attention turned to the window where Justin wasn't hiding himself anymore; his face was twisted in disgust.

"Sorry, my brother can be a pain."

"It's okay."

"I should go."

Cedric leaned in and kissed me once again. "I'll call you."

When he had driven away, I stood in the driveway for a split second, still surprised that that happened. That this night happened. As I entered the house, Dad and Justin both stood in the hallway, as if they hadn't been watching us through the window. "How was your date?" Dad asked.

"It was good when you both weren't looking through the window." Pushing past my family, I headed up the stairs as Justin laughed.

~

Andrew's eyes went wide with surprise. He sat on top of my bed on Monday morning as I pulled on a sweater before we headed for school. I had told him about the kiss and his reaction was as expected. "I can't believe we're having this conversation," I muttered.

Part of me had wanted to see both his and Jasmine's reactions right after the date, but we were all busy catching up on homework, and I couldn't tell them over the weekend.

"Then tell Jas."

"I will when I see her," I said.

"How was it?"

"It was good," I said partially in disbelief at how well the night had gone. "The entire night was good—from the date to the kiss, it was good. Do we go out again? What do you do?"

He shot me a look. "Do you want to know?"

"Now that I think about it, *no*." *I'll talk to Jasmine about it at school.*

~

But there was no chance to speak to Jasmine because when I got to my locker, Cedric was leaning against it. "Hi."

"Hi," I said.

"What are you doing after school?" He wanted to see me again.

Raising my duffel bag up as an answer, I put it in my locker. "Practice. What about tomorrow?"

"That's when *I* have practice," he said. "I can meet you after practice tomorrow for a bit?" I agreed just as the warning bell rang and everyone in the hallway scattered to their homeroom classes. "Shit, I got to run. Had to say hi. I'll see you later." Pressing an unexpected kiss to my cheek, he then hurried through the hallway until he disappeared.

My friends appeared behind me, and I knew whatever Jon Ming and Jacob were going to say would be annoying. "Quit it."

They didn't stop their relentless teasing until the end of soccer practice. I was sitting on the bleachers in the rec center after everyone had gone home. "Caleb said something interesting the other day." Sam took a seat next to me.

"What did he say?" I asked.

"He said you called me your friend. Don't deny it now."

"I said you were growing on me. Like a rash."

"Like a rash," he repeated dryly.

He held the ball he'd brought up, gesturing for us to head over to the field. Sam made a quick pass, making a left cut, and I passed it back to him. He shot the ball into the net. Heading over to me once he retrieved the ball, he sat down in front of me, staring up at me with the ball between his stretched-out legs.

"What are you doing?"

"Sit."

"Why?" I took the ball, sitting down.

"Because we're hanging out. It's what friends do."

"Serious question. Why aren't you on the team? You're crazy good."

"I'm not *crazy*—"

"Caleb wasn't joking," I said. "Soccer *is* your sport. You obviously love it. It doesn't make sense."

"Maybe something can happen?" Sam's voice was sharp, making me stop moving the ball under my hand. "Or one day a person could decide that they don't want to play anymore, how about that?"

"Okay, geez." I shouldn't have asked. The same way I didn't push for the story behind the lily on Caleb's ankle. "I shouldn't have asked."

"Fuck, I didn't mean it like that."

"What do you want to talk about?"

"You and my cousin."

"You're trying to see if this thing with Cedric will interfere with our friendship?" I asked.

"You should talk to Jasmine and the boys about that, not me. Our friendship is different. For one thing, you're now dating my cousin. Second, anytime you come over you better not be making out with him where I can see it. My eyes will *burn*. Third, make time for your awesome new friend who has the superior genes of the family. I'm about to make your life more exciting." He snatched the ball from my hand, standing up and dropping it on the ground. "Get ready to experience Sam Cahill."

"How are you going to make my life more exciting?"

"I'm going to show you. Keep up, Hazel."

Despite me calling him my friend, I didn't know much about him, but I wanted to. But I wasn't going to pry into the reasons for his sudden mood swing. And so, for the next few hours, Sam and I played soccer, and I didn't mind it.

6
TAKE A PICTURE, IT'LL LAST LONGER

The following Tuesday, I sat with Cedric in one of the school stairwells, waiting for my soccer practice in the gym to start. Jasmine had pestered me for details about what was happening, constantly mentioning how much time Cedric and I were spending together. Cedric was talking to a classmate in his chemistry class about a new topic they were on when my phone buzzed in my pocket.

Checking the text message, I stared at the device, puzzled by the unknown number.

> Trip over any soccer balls lately?

A little chuckle flew out of my mouth.

> Me: How did you get my number?

Sam: Andrew

I had just changed his contact when Cedric's classmate said good-bye to him, disappearing from the stairwell.

Jerk: Remember that we're friends

Caleb and Andrew were now on the roster with Austin as boys who couldn't keep their mouths shut.

Me: I never said that

Jerk: Caleb says otherwise

"Who's that?" Cedric asked.

"Sam." Turning off my phone, I didn't miss his look of surprise at the mention of his cousin's name.

"My cousin? I didn't know you two talked."

"We're friends. He's okay," I confessed. Annoyance crossed his face at the mention of Sam. "You guys don't have a good relationship?"

"Never have, really." The obvious tension stayed, and I didn't mention Sam any further.

Whatever feud was between Sam and Cedric, it had been something that developed over time because; while Sam could be rude and obnoxious, even I couldn't see myself truly hating the guy.

~

The conversation stayed in my mind when Sam and Caleb approached me the following Wednesday morning before school started. Sam had texted me last night about English, wondering if he and Caleb could borrow my notes from last semester.

"Here." I handed Caleb my old notebook. "I have notes for the play we read in there. Should be the same as last semester."

"Thank you." Caleb and Sam flicked through the book.

"Don't you write?" I asked Caleb. "Why are you so worried about English class?"

"Because I like writing out of my own free will," he clarified. "English class is different."

"He does fine." Sam lightly punched his best friend on the arm. "He just likes knowing every single detail."

"Princess, you're a lifesaver," Caleb joked.

Sam made a face at the nickname and I rolled my eyes. He had no right to criticize the nickname when he was the one calling me Hazel. "We'll see you at lunch?"

Down the hallway, Beatrice was talking excitedly to her group of friends as they passed other people. When she saw me, she looked bothered. *Oh my God.*

Her eyes flicked over to Sam, whom Caleb had handed my notebook to as they walked down the hallway after saying goodbye to me.

Beatrice's annoyed eyes fixated on me, and aggravation overcame me at the sight of her. What she had said to Jasmine the other day crossed a major line. She could have walked past me. She could have. I don't know what suddenly possessed her to stop in front of me because she did with her gaggle of ever-present friends close behind. "Why are you talking to him?"

"You realize that there's more than *one* guy at this school, right? You're going to have to be specific when—"

"Sam," she interjected. "Why are *you* talking to *Sam*?"

Oh. She's into him. "What does it matter to you? Get out of my face."

"Relax." Beatrice flinched dramatically as I slammed my locker shut. "There's no need to be aggressive."

"I'm not being aggressive," I muttered, hiking my backpack up my shoulders.

"Says the girl who slammed her locker shut," Ivy muttered.

"You're not his type," Beatrice said. Her expression was distasteful as she took in the sports headband around my head, my ponytail, and my sweater over leggings. "Then again, you're not really *anyone's* type."

That comment wasn't new. I didn't want to stand here any longer hearing her try to make me feel insecure. "I never said I wanted to be anyone's type." Beatrice stepped in front of me. "Do you think I'm going to talk to you about any guy? Like we're besties? Like you didn't say what you said to Jasmine?"

"This isn't about Jasmine."

"She's my friend, so I'm going to tell you something right now." My plan to get to class on time disappeared. The action grabbed the attention of many others passing through the crowded hallway. "Don't bother her." I got right in Beatrice's face.

"You're not going to do anything to me," Beatrice taunted, crossing her arms.

"Why would you think that?"

"I mean, you're *definitely* capable of channeling that kind of aggressive behavior. After all, they made you captain of the *boys'* team." There was no praise in her words. She wanted me to feel ashamed about it. "But you're not your psycho friend. You're not going to actually attack me like she did."

It was clear that she thought even less of Jasmine than she did of me. And I knew deep down that she was jealous; this need to be the mean girl proved it. But I hated it. My anger was hot, and I wouldn't have cared about any consequences, but thankfully Cedric tapped me on the shoulder.

"Mace."

He didn't notice my tense shoulders or curled fists. Immediately relaxing, I turned my focus to him. "Hey."

"Hey, Beatrice." The smug look on her face changed to a pleasant one at the sight of Cedric. Cedric turned to me. "Ready to walk to class?"

"Yes," I said too eagerly. He didn't notice all the negativity Beatrice brought with her, and for that I was glad.

~

Beatrice didn't bother me for the rest of the week. I didn't mention the incident to Jasmine but I'm sure she heard through Wellington's grapevine. If she did, she didn't bring it up, though. I think we were both sick of thinking, talking, and worrying about Beatrice. We made it through the rest of the week without any further incidents.

On Saturday, I spoke to the youngest Cahill at the end of his game at the rec center.

"At my birthday party, I'm going to have this big Teenage Mutant Ninja Turtles theme cake." He'd brought up his birthday about five times, but it was cute to see the kid excited for his big day.

Sam made his way over to us, and gave Phillip a fist bump. "I didn't know you were picking me up today."

"I'm not," Sam said. "Ivan's waiting for you at the front."

Phillip looked puzzled. "Why are you here then?"

"I left my car when I was at the gym here this morning. Ivan and I had things to do for your mum," he explained. "I'll see you at home later." Sam playfully knocked his hand against the side of his cousin's head, who groaned and pushed it away before waving good-bye.

"What are you doing later today?"

I raised an eyebrow at Sam's question. "That's why you came inside? This is your attempt to make my life more exciting, isn't it?"

"This is my attempt to be an actual *friend* to you." He twirled a set of car keys in his hand. "Any plans? You hungry?"

It hadn't taken Sam long to learn that food was the way to our friendship. "What do you have in mind, Cahill?"

Minutes later, I sat in Sam's car, observing the interior of the vehicle. He and Cedric both had nice, new cars, giving me the impression that their families were better off than most. "Motorcycle still in the shop?"

"Piss off."

I went through the playlists on his phone, my camera in my other hand, as he drove through the bright day, getting farther from the residential areas of the city. He didn't answer my question about where we were going, but we had picked up some food, which was currently stored in front of my feet. "You have an entire playlist dedicated to boy bands and a lot of Spanish music."

"Caleb's always on my phone," he explained.

"You know, if you want to be actual friends you've got to open up a bit. Outside of flirting with half the female population at Wellington, the only person I've ever seen you with when you're not with us at lunch is Caleb."

"I'm not in high school to be *popular*," he said. "The female population thing's a stretch, Hazel. I like to keep to myself. I figured you'd understand since whenever I see you at the rec center, you're practicing on your own."

We were far outside the city at this point and went down a side road I hadn't been to since I was younger. The buildings surrounding us gradually turned into trees. "What's your favorite color?"

"Twenty questions?" he asked as I pointed my camera at him to take a picture.

"I'll go first. Mine's forest green."

"Orange," he answered.

"When's your birthday?"

"January 3."

"Could've been a New Year baby." My gaze focused outside. "No, seriously, where are we going? Because if you're going to do something stupid like push me out of the car and leave me stranded—"

"You're so dramatic," he interjected. "The quarry. Have you ever been?"

When I was younger, kids used to go with their parents to the quarry all the time. It was a great place to take pictures, enjoy nature, go on walks, go to the water and swim, or watch people do so from the cliff tops. Mom and Dad used to take me and Justin during the summer. We would all be near the water, me kicking the soccer ball to Mom. Dad would record every moment while watching toddler Justin try to walk over to us, even though he always ended up getting distracted by butterflies.

"It's been a long time," I said. "Do you go there often?"

"It's kind of my thinking place," he answered.

"With Caleb?" He pulled into a parking spot, turned off the car, then took the key out of the ignition. We got out of the car and my question was forgotten as I climbed up on a rock over-looking the quarry.

There weren't many people—some were walking along the sand in their jackets, others were looking out at the freezing water. "I forgot how pretty this place is."

A few people were coming out of the path down at the bottom of the quarry, yet Sam gestured for me to follow him toward the cliff tops instead. I continued taking pictures and we stopped at a clearing. We were pretty high up—people probably jumped into the deep waters below all the time from here. In February, it was deserted. Sam dropped our bag of food on the ground then started taking off his shoes.

"What are you doing? Are you *crazy*?"

He shot me a look as if I was the crazy one. "I'm introducing adventure into your life. We're going cliff diving."

"No." I pulled him back. "We are *not* doing that."

"We're trying to do *exciting* things."

"Exciting things shouldn't involve getting pneumonia."

"You're probably just scared of jumping," Sam concluded. "It's not even *that* high."

When Sam started taking his pants off I covered my eyes. He laughed. Loudly. *Obnoxiously*. He sounded like he was losing his breath. "Hazel, I'm kidding." He took my hands off my face moments later, his socks and shoes back on, his pants buttoned up.

I took a seat on the ground. "You're a dumbegg."

"Your profanity astounds me." He sat down next to me and took the food out of the bags. "Why are you so into photography?"

"We used to take a lot of videos and pictures as a family before my mom died. After that, I played old videos or pictures that were taken of her. It draws me back to that time, and I wanted to create more memories," I explained.

A wistful expression crossed his face as he chewed. "As if you were there again."

"Exactly." I lifted the hood of my thick sweater over my head, pulling the strings as I faintly overheard people talking below us. Sam used his chopsticks to grab a California roll from my container and put it in his mouth before I could stop him. "You have your own foo—*Sam!*" He indulged in the need to irritate me further by chewing obnoxiously. "You're an actual pig."

"I love it when you flirt with me." He nudged me with the side of a chopstick as he gestured to my camera. "I understand what you mean. Do you mind me asking what happened to your mum?"

"She died when I was nine and Justin was six," I said. "She was coming home from the bookstore she owned. Car accident. Drunk driver."

Suddenly Sam's hand moved to my arm, which somehow gave me comfort. "How did you deal with your mum's death?"

"I couldn't handle not having my mom after she died," I admitted. "It was hard and everyone's constantly pitying you or saying sorry. It came to a point one day where I kind of exploded and couldn't stop crying for a long time because I missed her. Still do. All of us do. I learned to accept she was gone. I visit her grave sometimes and everything, but when I feel like I have to explode, I immerse myself in soccer. That's how I deal with it."

Sam squeezed my arm as I wiped an unexpected tear from the corner of my eye. I gripped my camera. "You want to see what she looks like?"

He nodded, perching his chin on my forearm. My favorite picture: young me in soccer gear and my mom on the other side of me, the two of us smiling wide at our old camera. Sam inspected the picture as we continued to eat. "You look a lot like her."

"I guess so."

Afterward, we stood near the water at the bottom of the quarry. The lack of snow this time of year and the warm streak was a surprise for the city. Farther out, the lake was solid but the ice had thawed closer to where we stood.

Sam took off his shoes and socks, rolling the legs of his jeans up as high as he could and walking into the water. "Hazel, you've been taking pictures for the past forty-two minutes we've been here. C'mon."

"*Pneumonia,*" I warned him, taking a picture.

"*Hurry up.*"

Placing my camera next to his shoes, I took off my own, removed my socks, hiked up the legs of my sweatpants, and then approached the water.

I dipped my foot in, automatically flinching. "Dude, it's freezing."

"*Dude, it's freezing,*" he mocked in a falsetto, coming toward me. "Think fast!"

"*No!*" He sprayed water in my direction. My scream was loud enough to catch the attention of people around the area. Sam pulled me farther into the water and instantly I squirmed at the freezing water nipping at my exposed legs. "I hate you," I muttered, putting my hand in the water to flick it at his face.

He kicked water at me. I kicked water back, the two of us going at it until he put his hands up. He held my arms to stop my movements. I pulled out of his grip and dipped my hand in the water, then wiped the freezing water against his face, to which he hissed. He kicked water at me again, the cold water soaking the front of my sweater, and I gaped at him as he cackled, thinking I wasn't going to do the same to him. "You're irritating."

"I believe the word is irresistible." I kicked water at him again, getting it on his face and his hair. A loud laugh escaped me at the sight. I was making my way closer to the shore to get away from him when my ringtone rang out from where I had put my phone near my camera.

Sam followed close behind, still walking through the water as I answered. "Hello?"

"Are you home?" Jasmine's voice came through strangely.

"I'm out," I said. "You okay?"

"I'm fine." I didn't believe that. "Can I stay over tonight?"

"I have to ask my dad but I'm sure you can." I turned away from Sam. "Are you sure you're okay?"

"Mace, I'm okay," she said. "Let me know?"

"All right."

"Everything all right?" Sam asked me after the call ended.

I put my socks and shoes back on and Sam got the hint, getting out of the water. "I don't think so."

About a half an hour later, Sam's car pulled up to the side of my house. Jasmine was sitting on the front steps, her duffel bag was on her other side.

"Next time we head to the quarry we're having a rematch on the water fight," Sam promised and part of me looked forward to it. "See you at school?"

"See you at school." I got out of the car, grabbing the bag I had brought with me when I was heading to volunteer earlier today.

I pushed the door closed and he drove away as I headed in Jasmine's direction. Jasmine's eyes stayed on Sam's car before it disappeared, and I sat down next to her. "You're hanging out with Sam?"

"We're friends. But are you okay? You sounded really uneasy over the phone."

She didn't speak for a moment, shoving her hands into the pockets of her jacket. "My parents have been fighting a lot more recently and I needed to get out of the house."

She'd never mentioned her parents fighting before. Over the years, Jasmine would mention whenever her parents had gotten into arguments. Their arguments had always been brief, and whenever I went over to Jasmine's home, things seemed fine. Her parents were as extroverted as she was, always inviting Andrew and me to any little gathering their family was having. They'd always *looked* happy, but then again, I didn't live there.

"Are you okay, though?"

She took a deep breath, eyes on the frosted grass of the lawn, and her response was as predicted. "I'm fine. It's just been happening a lot more lately and I'm getting really sick of it. I don't want to talk about it anymore."

Jasmine got up, slinging her duffel bag over her shoulder as I opened the front door to let us inside the house. "If you want to talk about it, I'm here."

She didn't say anything further, just took off her shoes and headed up the stairs to my room.

7
SURPRISE, SURPRISE

Cedric and I were talking by my locker before school started on Monday morning when Sam called my nickname. "Hazel."

"Hey, guys." Sam and Caleb approached us and a frown fell over Cedric's face at the sight of his cousin.

"Still mad at me for Saturday?" Sam asked.

"Almost got pneumonia because of you." I laughed.

"Definitely not. Look at you, perfectly healthy."

Cedric coolly ignored Sam, leaning toward me and pressing a quick kiss to my lips. "I'll see you later."

When he moved past us, Sam's eyes followed his cousin's retreating figure.

"Are you guys together?" Caleb asked me. I shrugged, wondering that for myself. Caleb slung an arm around my shoulder as the three of us walked down the hall. "JM and I played a game yesterday. We had to use these pickup lines from a website and see if they worked on girls at the mall."

"You two are unbelievable. Did it work?"

Caleb showed me a list on his phone of lines that they'd used, check marked if they'd worked and crossed out if they hadn't. "Some of them totally worked. Look."

He proceeded to read the lines off his phone, and Sam and I commented on the stupid lines. "Oh the classic: I lost my number, can I have yours? And: Are you from heaven, 'cause you have the face of an angel."

"But those are such *basic* lines," I pointed out, not impressed. "How did anyone fall for them?"

"It's all about the charm," Caleb said.

Jon Ming had joined us at the doorway, and laughed when he realized what we were talking about. Beatrice sauntered by, giving me one of her infamous dirty looks, which I promptly returned.

Sam tapped my elbow. "How's Jasmine doing?"

"Is Jasmine okay?" Jon Ming asked, puzzled.

"She's got a lot going on. She's been superstressed lately but she's fine."

But she wasn't confiding in me and I didn't think she was talking to Andrew about it either. It was so unlike her, and that had me worried.

~

Sitting in a café with Cedric after school, I was still thinking of Jasmine as I texted Andrew. I used my straw to stir my drink. "Can I ask you a question?" I said to Cedric.

"Am I in trouble?" Cedric looked wary.

"I wanted to know what we . . ." I trailed off, the awkwardness inside me coming out.

Cedric raised his eyebrows. "We're having the *define the relationship* talk, aren't we?"

"Maybe."

"I don't really kiss my friends."

Oh. Judging by the heat rising on my face, this was way more awkward than I wanted it to be. Cedric looked amused. "You can say it." Rolling up the paper that had covered my straw, I tossed it at him. He deflected it. "I'm going to need to hear it."

I pursed my lips, putting my leg up and my foot on my seat as I got comfortable. "Annoying the heck out of me two seconds after this is established doesn't seem like good boyfriend courtesy."

"She said the word!" He raised his arms up in victory. His phone suddenly buzzed and Cedric read the incoming text message. "My mum wants me to pick up Sam from school. He got detention. Again. Surprise, surprise."

"Why does your mom want you to pick up your cousin?"

"Sam lives with us," Cedric explained. "Since summertime. His family always visited during the summers but his parents, my uncle and aunt, back in England, decided he would be better off finishing high school here. He got into too much trouble over there."

How much trouble do you have to get into for your parents to send you to another continent?

"Why did his parents send him here?"

Cedric took a deep breath. "About two years ago, Sam got involved in a car accident."

I straightened, my lips parting in surprise. "What?"

"It was pretty bad." Cedric's voice was quiet. "He and a few friends were coming back from a party one night and a drunk driver hit the side of the car."

"Oh my God." Instantly, tears burned my vision and I blinked rapidly. Cedric didn't notice, his eyes once again focused on the table.

"Obviously, Sam's okay. His friends, too, but there was someone else in the car who got the worst of the accident. Sam's sister. She was in the passenger seat that night. Died on impact."

No words came out of my mouth because I wasn't sure how to respond. Hearing that story hit way too close to home.

"It was a tough time for everyone in the family," continued Cedric. "And her death was unexpected. Sam was definitely the most affected. He's changed since then. We've never been close, but I can tell he's changed. He became really reckless with himself, with other people, and landed himself in a huge incident with a new group of friends he had. His parents decided enough was enough and sent him here."

"That's—" I cleared my throat, taking a deep breath. "That's a lot to go through."

His sister's death was only two years ago.

"When he was sent here, I think my dad thought his behavior would get better, but Sam does things for his own amusement." Cedric put his phone in his pocket. "Even with detention he probably snapped at a teacher, skipped class, got into a fight— wherever he goes, trouble follows, so it could be anything. And he seems to be around you now, so just be careful, okay?"

Cedric looked out the window, a strain on our conversation since it had changed to Sam. Silence fell over the table and I was wrapping my head around the new information when Cedric said, "I didn't mean to make the conversation heavy."

"It's okay," I said, Sam still on my mind. "You don't talk about your family a lot. Like your parents—what do they do?"

"You don't know what my parents do?"

"Oh sorry, I don't know the occupations of my friends' parents . . . what a weird question, Cedric!" He cracked a smile as he typed something into the browser on his phone. "Dude, how would your parents be—" He held up his phone screen to me and my response came out in a sputter. "Your parents are Vincent and Elizabeth Cahill? The business guy?"

"*Business guy?*" Cedric scoffed at my improper word choice yet my mind was reeling at this information. His parents weren't only rich, they were *really* well known. Despite being public figures, their lives were remote and quiet. Almost as quiet as the neighborhood filled with big houses everyone knew they resided in, which wasn't too far from my residential community.

"I don't know anything about business, but I know that guy. Doesn't he own, like, everything?"

"He inherited the family company with my uncle James, Sam's dad, and invests in things like car dealerships and hotels," he explained. "My mum was a model. She designs clothes now."

"You're their son."

"What gave it away? The last name?"

This explained the nice cars he and Sam had. If it wasn't for that, I never would've guessed that their family was wealthy. *Extremely* wealthy. "I didn't put two and two together. You've never mentioned them."

"Because we don't like being associated with them constantly. Don't get me wrong, I love them—yet with their money you keep things under wraps. I avoid most questions about them—people try to take advantage of us. Especially with Dad."

If Sam had said that, I wouldn't be surprised if venom came

out of his mouth, but Cedric? "You must not have a good relationship with your dad."

"I don't hate him. He just expects a lot from everyone. He and Sam, though? Can barely stand to be in the same room with each other since Sam moved in."

"Crap."

Cedric snorted. "That's the closest I've ever heard you come to swearing. He's kind of a workaholic, he's not around as much as he used to be. I'm surprised he remembers Phillip's name with the thoughts brewing through his mind every second."

"If *you* say that about your dad, I wonder what Sam says about him," I blurted out.

"Thank God for a big house—the tension gets awkward. Sam seems to like you." I must've looked disgusted because Cedric was pleased. "It's interesting: Caleb was his only friend here, so it's weird seeing him interact with people and not piss anyone off."

"No, he can still piss me off. I'm just used to him." It was strange to know that besides soccer, a part of me understood what he was going through.

"He's like that," Cedric said, taking a bite of his bagel.

"Tell me about England," I said in an attempt to change the subject.

A distant look fell across his face. "We lived in Bath. All the Cahills have lived in Bath. It's a small town, a lot of nice historical buildings you'd like taking pictures of with that camera of yours. You'd have a great time. Have you ever traveled?"

"The most I've ever traveled is to see Dad's parents every summer and spend Christmas in Scotswood Bay. Or when I was younger, I'd go see my other grandmother. She lives in Redmond."

"Really? My grandmother has lived there for years too. She's one of the reasons why we moved close by."

"What's the main reason you guys moved here?"

"Better opportunity for Dad's business since we're close to Toronto," he explained. "He handles an office there while my uncle James handles the office in England. We visit when we can. We have a lot of family there and around here too."

"There are *more* Cahills?"

Cedric shot me a look, finishing his drink and bagel in record time as he got up. "You don't know the half of it."

Standing on my porch minutes later, Cedric and I were talking as he waited until it was time to pick up Sam from school. The only thing on my mind was what I had learned about Sam.

Cedric was showing me a funny video he had saved on his phone when it hit me: Cedric Cahill was my boyfriend. When he made another joke about me not swearing, I playfully prodded him in the stomach with my hand and he winced. "Shit, you got a hand on you."

He brushed it off, and the two of us had begun kissing when suddenly the front door flew open and I pulled away fast, expecting to see my brother. Jasmine had a hand in my secret box of Pop-Tarts, and was currently chewing the last of the previous one. "Hello, lovebirds. Thought I heard you out here."

"What are you doing here?" She didn't answer my question, heading inside the house. After saying good-bye to Cedric, I followed her inside, closing the door behind me.

She was placing the Pop-Tart box back in the cabinet. "I needed to get out of the house. They're fighting again. I texted you and showed up here. Your dad said I could stay for dinner. Did you do number five in the physics homework? I can't get it."

She headed up to my room as my worry for her only grew. I knew Jasmine. I wasn't going to press it. "Yeah, I got it. I'll show you."

~

"How is she?" Drake asked through the speaker of my phone as I moved around my kitchen the next evening.

Jasmine was in my room doing homework. "I have no idea. She's not talking."

"She's hiding out," he said. "Has she been sleeping over often?"

"Not so much—she comes over after school or after one of her club meetings for a while to do homework or other things, mostly to tell me about things happening at school."

Drake didn't say anything for a moment, coughing uncomfortably, and the sound made me raise my eyebrows. "Speaking of things happening at school, I hear you have a boyfriend."

"Who has a boyfriend?" My dad entered the kitchen.

"Your daughter!" Drake cackled. Even over a distance, Dad and Drake's dynamic never changed.

My dad took off his jacket and set his briefcase on the counter. "The Cedric kid? Drake, do you know anything about him?"

I thought Drake didn't hear him but moments later he answered. "I remember him. He's a decent guy. He'll treat our Macy fine."

"Is it serious or not?" Dad continued with the questions and I sat down at the counter, surveying the pasta on the stove.

"I'm not talking to you both about this," I mumbled.

"Get the pasta, Mace." I did as Dad said, grabbing the strainer from the cabinet as Drake continued talking.

"Mr. Anderson?" Drake asked. "Do you mind if Jasmine is around a lot more often? I can't be there for her with university and stuff."

"She's always welcome here." My dad kept his eyes fixed on my phone and his voice went quieter—the tone he used with me, Justin, and even Andrew whenever we had a problem. "Is everything okay at home?"

"Things are a little rough between our parents right now. It'll get better soon."

"All right." Soon after I had drained the pasta, Drake excused himself to go study, and my dad took over the pot. "I'll set the plates. Go get Jasmine and Justin."

"She won't talk to me," I said. "About what's going on at home or even at school. And when Andrew tries to talk to her about anything, she snaps and they end up fighting with each other."

"She'll talk to you eventually," he promised, unaware of my doubt.

~

We had finished dinner and were sitting around the table talking. My brother had cleared the plates before helping himself to some dessert when my dad asked Jasmine and me about our classes.

"Sam can give me notes," Jasmine said, after stating that she had been having some trouble with biology. "He took biology last semester. He mentioned it today at lunch and Caleb said he did really well."

"Sam?" Justin spoke up. "The rude guy?"

"Who's Sam?" Dad's eyebrows furrowed.

"Sam's our . . . friend," I explained.

"He's kind of a recent addition to the gang," Jasmine added.

"He said rude things to you?" Dad asked me.

"At first. He's not as bad as I thought." With everything Cedric said earlier today, Sam wasn't what I initially thought, or a reckless person.

"Of course you would say that," Jasmine mumbled. "You spend so much time with him."

"Was he the curly haired guy I saw when I picked you up at the rec center that one time?" my dad asked.

"Yes, Sam Cahill."

Realization shone in his eyes. He probably knew him the same way most people knew the Cahill name. By their wealth. "Is he Vince Cahill's son?"

"His nephew. Cedric is his son," I corrected. "Wait, how do you know Vince Cahill?"

"I settled something for his company years ago," Dad explained. "Plus, he and his brother are big names in the media with their company."

"Damn, you might as well insert yourself into their family now," Justin muttered, and I kicked him under the table. "Anyway, onto a more relevant topic: When we see Grandma during spring break, what do we call her?"

"Nonna," Dad answered.

Jasmine looked confused. "Don't you see your grandparents all the time? Those few weeks every summer?"

"We're going to see our other grandmother. Our mom's mom. She lives in Redmond, and we haven't seen her in a long time," I said.

"*Oh.*" Jasmine turned to me, knowing how much it meant to reconnect with my mom by going to the place she had grown up. "Why haven't you guys visited her?"

"She was living abroad for years, and any other time she was back home, the kids were in school," my dad explained. "She's recently moved back for good."

There was excitement every time our visit was brought up, but I was nervous about the actual day to come. Even when I was texting Cedric while walking the halls of the school with Andrew the following day, spring break was the only thing on my mind.

"I got the beta version," Andrew said, talking about a new video game that wasn't out yet. I turned to him with excitement when he asked, "My house after school?"

Suddenly I frowned, recalling the plans I had later today. "Can't. Cedric and I are going out after school."

"You're ditching me for your boyfriend?"

"I don't mean to."

"I'm kidding." He showed me a video game that appeared on his feed. "Aren't you and Justin also waiting for the newest edition of *this* to come out?"

"We've been talking about it for weeks. It comes out next Sunday."

"If only I could play video games with my sister." Andrew chuckled, probably at the thought of his three-year-old sister handling a controller. "Bring Cedric to my place. We can all play there."

Andrew and I were rowdy whenever we played video games— it was worse when the boys and I were together. "I don't think that's a good idea."

THE BAD BOY & THE TOMBOY   91

"What?"

Jasmine ran down the hall toward us then linked her arms with both of ours. "I have news!"

"Is this your way of telling us that you want us to come over and watch *Star Wars* again or something? Not going to happen," Andrew said abruptly.

Jasmine ignored him. "Beatrice was turned down by Sam yesterday and she thinks you have something to do with it."

"We're only friends," I muttered. "Is it my fault he's the only guy who doesn't want her?" I didn't care what Beatrice did, and did *not* need to be involved. "I'm with Cedric."

"But you and Sam are *friends*," Jasmine breathed.

Caleb walked toward us, reading over something in one of his notebooks. He wore a large plaid button-up over a white tank top and held a sweater in his hand. As he approached us, he snapped his book closed, puzzled by our expressions. "Why do we look like someone pissed in our cereal?"

"Beatrice," I answered, no longer surprised by his random analogies. "What's going on with you?"

"I had an awesome idea for a story." He took off his plaid button-up and tied it at his waist.

Spotting Jasmine's puzzled expression, I explained, "He wrote the school play and some short stories."

"I should've known you were involved in the play," Jasmine said to Caleb. "You're so dramatic."

"In other words, the boy version of you," Andrew joked.

Jasmine frowned. "What's your problem?"

"Nothing?" Andrew shrugged.

"Doesn't sound like it."

"Can we not do this here? It's not my fault you're so confusing."

He walked away saying, "By the way, I'm not involved with anyone anymore."

"What is he talking about?"

Jasmine dismissed my question. "Nothing. He's talking about nothing. I'm going to go to class."

She stomped off in the opposite direction. Caleb, like the dramatic person Jasmine claimed he was, pointed in both directions at my best friends. "Which one are you going after?"

"They need a moment to themselves."

"You have no idea what's going on?"

"No idea," I admitted. "I thought it had something to do with her breakup."

"No, it definitely has something to do with *their* breakup, Mace." Caleb put his hands through the sleeves of the sweater he was holding. I stilled, surprised at what he was implying. Something was happening or had happened between Jasmine and Andrew? "I'll see you at lunch. I brought cards to play Crazy Eights—get ready to lose."

As Caleb walked down the hall pulling on his sweater, my eyes caught the exposed ink on his left shoulder blade: *Curiosity can be a risk you sometimes don't want to take. —B. C.*

Cedric approached me, leaning next to my locker. "Phillip wanted me to give you this for his party next Saturday."

The envelope he handed me was covered with Ninja Turtle stickers, and when I opened it up, the card had the blue Ninja Turtle on the cover and Phillip's big writing filled the inside. "Um, gifts 'manatry'?"

My boyfriend chuckled. "He meant *mandatory*, he loves gifts. And girls are required to wear dresses and guys tuxes."

I held in a sigh at having to wear a dress. "It's an eight-year-old's party, not prom."

"My parents are all about making an impression and they thought 'What better idea than to do it at my son's birthday party?' So, how would you like to meet the parents? Beforehand."

What? There was no Jasmine to consult. If Andrew was next to me even *he* would be surprised. It felt too soon and yet the way Cedric was looking at me made me blurt, "Sure!" as if everything inside me was fine.

"Hazel." Sam's voice behind me crackled and his cousin huffed, pressing his lips together in irritation. Sam stood behind me in a white shirt, a noticeable necklace tucked under it.

"Hey." This was the first I had seen him since finding out about his sister. He hadn't been at lunch yesterday. There was no need to bring it up. When my mom had died, I didn't want anyone to mention it.

"Where were you yesterday?" Cedric asked him. "He's back."

Any evidence of Sam previously smiling was wiped away and I got the feeling they were talking about his uncle. "Why do you think I wasn't home?"

"Mum's back too."

"I spent the night at Caleb's. Your mum and Ivan knew." Sam's voice dropped to a whisper. "You don't have to act like you care."

Cedric frowned. The first warning bell rang and Sam turned without another word, heading down the hallway. Cedric pressed a kiss to my cheek, swiftly heading to his class as Sam's retreating figure disappeared.

8
YOU'RE THE RELATIONSHIP EXPERT

Cedric lifted his arms up in victory as the bowling pins fell, turning to me and pointing up at the scoreboard. After school, we had headed to a bowling alley and he was currently winning. "Babe, you need lessons."

"I'm perfectly good at bowling."

"Want me to teach you how it's done?" he teased.

"Don't pull a cliché." I grabbed a bowling ball and slid around in my bowling shoes. I anchored my arm back and let the ball go, watching it roll down the lane and hit the bowling pins. All of them went down.

"I forgot I was dating one of the most competitive girls in the world," he remarked. My phone rang in my pocket.

Andrew's picture flashed on the screen and I was quick to pick it up. He had been ignoring my calls since he'd stormed off earlier today. "Drew?"

"H-e-y, M-a-c-y." Two words in and I knew something was wrong.

"Are you drunk?"

"A lil' bit." It was five thirty. On a Tuesday. Of all the things Andrew could've done, day drinking would never have crossed my mind.

"Where are you? Are you alone?"

"Stop asking so many questions," he drawled. "It's not that serious."

Not that serious? "Are you home alone?"

"Yup."

"Stay put." I hung up then took off my bowling shoes. "I'm sorry, I gotta go. Andrew's drunk."

"What? Why?"

"I have no idea. He doesn't act like this. I'm really sorry."

"It's okay," Cedric assured me. "I'll drop you off at his place."

Cedric drove me to Andrew's. As I walked up front steps, my hand slipped under one of the many potted plants Andrew's mom had in front of their door. Finding the spare key, I used it to open the door. "Anyone home?"

Silence filled the house. Drunk Andrew was usually chatty.

Heading over to the kitchen, I got a glass of water before walking up the stairs to his room. He was lying on his bed looking up at the ceiling, playing with a football. His dog, Freddy, a big golden retriever, was on the ground, and perked his head up at my entrance.

Andrew's eyes slid over to me as he dropped the ball next to his head. Closing the door behind me, I couldn't miss the aroma of alcohol he had been drinking filling the air, and took in the bottle on his nightstand. "Getting drunk in the afternoon wasn't on your bucket list," I said, taking a seat next to him.

He snorted and struggled to sit up, and I took notice of the red splotches on his face. I handed him the water and he chugged it down. "Whoa. Small sips, dude."

He curled his knees up, his face nudging the camera where it hung around my neck. My fingers moved along his blond hair and he sighed contentedly, closing his eyes. "Andrew? What's up? You can tell me anything."

"Yeah," he agreed with a hiccup, looking like the six-year-old I remembered watching *Mighty Morphin Power Rangers* with. "We don't really have secrets."

"No, we usually don't."

"I know everything about you," Andrew said. "When we were ten, you stole Jacob's ruler because he got mud on your new shoes and then you guys fought the day after and you both ended up covered in mud, but he still doesn't know about that ruler."

Jacob will probably never know about the ruler. "What's going on?"

"At the party we all went to, where Cedric asked you out a while ago? I met a girl." He shook his head. "I wasn't feeling it. I could only think about one girl that night." He turned to me with wild eyes, leaning back to lay his head in my lap, lips parted in realization. "I love her, don't I?"

I wasn't sure if he was asking me or convincing himself.

"But I messed up and said it was a mistake," he said. "I knew I was lying but she just confused me so many times because it happened so many times. Imagine being in love with one of your best friends."

Andrew confessing he had feelings for Jasmine made a lot of sense—it explained the constant tension between them since she got out of her last relationship. "I've had a thing for her since, like, seventh grade."

"*Seventh* grade?" I exclaimed.

"Remember when she came to us in grade nine, had her first kiss, and was telling us all about it? I couldn't stand the idea of her being with someone else. But she's Jasmine. She's weird, funny, and people like her, she's going to date other guys. Last summer, you were at your grandparents' and I was over at her place. We were talking, I don't even remember what we were talking about and"—he opened his eyes, holding his tongue between his teeth—"I kissed her."

His boldness made me pause. "Was this before she was dating Sean?"

"Yup." Andrew sighed. "She said we shouldn't have kissed. It got awkward for a couple of weeks until we went to a party. And we were talking and then all of a sudden we were kissing, and the kissing led to . . ." My eyebrows raised. "Yeah, we did. We promised to never bring it up again after that. Then she started dating Sean and I barely hung around with her unless you were with us. Then one day, we were waiting for you and I confessed everything to her. But she was saying how it would affect our friendship. Even when the two of them broke up, a part of me was hopeful, yet she repeated what she said before, that if we ever dated, then broke up, it would ruin everything. How I probably don't even like her and I'm messing around with her. She knows I'm not. And I was a little mad and with everything happening we just keep—"

"Arguing." *Wow.* Andrew wasn't a liar, whether drunk or not. "You really love her, don't you?"

"I think I do."

"*Seventh grade?*"

Andrew let out a tired chuckle and I pushed his head back with my hand. My phone rang in my pocket. "It's Jasmine."

"You aren't here."

"Hi!" I said with too much enthusiasm once I answered the call. "You still at school?"

"No, I'm at home. Listen, can we talk? I need to tell you something about Andrew." I instantly hit Andrew hard on the arm and he made a loud sound. "What just happened?"

"Dang it. Justin fell down the stairs. I have to go. Can I call you back later tonight?"

"No, no, it's okay, I can tell you tomorrow at school. I'll see you then."

After we hung up, Andrew gave me a look, grabbing his pillow to elevate himself. "Justin fell *down the stairs?*"

"I'm a good liar."

"You don't think this is weird, do you?" he asked warily.

"No." Maybe I should've felt weird at the thought of my best friends as a couple. But Andrew was serious about her, and I could not see a downside to them having a chance to be together. "I'm even going to help you plan how to ask her out."

"You get one boyfriend and suddenly you're the relationship expert."

"Listen." I picked up the bottle, planning on disposing of it and the remaining contents on his head. "You're going to ask Jasmine out in the most basic way."

"Basic?" Andrew almost stumbled as he got off his bed. "*How?*"

~

Walking into the library of the school the following day with my brother, I was not expecting to see the person I saw sitting at a table alone. "The library? Not really your scene."

"Believe it or not, leather jacket wearers can excel in school."
Sam moved the papers on the table to make space.

Justin cleared his throat next to me as I took a seat next to
Sam and started looking through the pictures on my camera.
"You remember Justin, right?"

Sam nodded at my little brother, twirling his pen in his hand.
"You look like you're up to something," he said to me. "I'm hoping it doesn't involve my cousin. Speaking of cousin, apparently
you're meeting the 'rents."

He rested his chin on my arm as he looked through my recent
pictures with me.

"Cedric did not tell you that," I said.

"He has very loud conversations with his friends or whenever
he comes back from his runs. Now tell us why you've looked so
deep in thought for the past forty-one seconds."

There was the timing thing again.

"You have a constipated look on your face," Justin said.

"You shouldn't be talking," I snapped.

"Try me," Justin taunted.

"Guys, we're in the library," Sam said. Strange, since he wasn't
one for following the rules.

"You weren't at lunch," I said.

Sam gestured at his homework, eyes still on the screen of my
camera as I went through the pictures.

"Are you nervous about meeting his parents?" He lifted his
head off my arm and slouched back in his chair. "You may or
may not be on your own. I doubt that I can stand to see my
uncle."

"Didn't know I had the chance of having your support."

"We're friends, remember? Why are you guys here?"

"We're waiting for Andrew and Jasmine," I said.

Sam tapped the pen against his mouth. Caleb entered the library, heading toward our table. "So this involves them," Sam said.

"Hey!" The entire library shushed Caleb who exchanged a handshake with Sam. "Sorry. I'm not here often."

"Sit down," I whispered, yanking the earphone out of my brother's ear. "Justin. Caleb."

Jasmine appeared and took the seat next to me. "Why are we here?"

"Hazel was helping me out with a class," Sam lied.

"Oh." Jasmine turned to Justin. "How are you doing?"

Justin looked confused. "Why?"

"Didn't you fall down the stairs last night or something like that?" she asked. "That's what Mace said on the phone."

I lightly kicked Justin to play along. "Yeah, he's fine now. Nothing but a bruise, right, Justin?"

"Yup. I'm all good," he agreed. He was definitely going to use this lie against me in the near future.

Sam nudged me under the table and with his pen wrote "You're a horrible liar" on the corner of one of his papers. I glared at him. Andrew entered the room. He spotted us, greeting everyone until his focus fell on Jasmine.

"We need to talk," he said.

"Now?"

He dropped his backpack next to me, then headed back to the exit of the library.

"What's happening?" Caleb asked as Jasmine left the room too.

"I'll be back." I grabbed my camera and followed my best

friends out the door, standing in the doorway so they wouldn't see me.

"This is how he's asking her out?" A hand landed on my arm and I jumped—Sam. We watched the scene unravel in front of us. I put a finger to my lips to tell him to be quiet.

"You want him to hand her a bouquet of roses or something?" I whispered. "Jasmine's a spontaneous person. Andrew doing it simply seemed appropriate."

"I want us to be together," Andrew said, and Sam commented *ooh* behind me. I hit him with my elbow.

"Drew, we've been over this," Jasmine breathed.

"I know." He sounded determined. "I don't care."

"We can't."

"Yes, you can," I said loudly, walking forward. Sam stayed behind, thankfully not being completely annoying in the moment.

Jasmine's eyes went wide at the sight of me but Andrew continued. "Jasmine, I know you said this would affect our friendship. But I want to be with you."

Her eyes went back and forth between him and me. Her moment of confliction wasn't unnoticed by the people lingering in the hallway waiting for what she would say. Even I grew restless, twiddling my fingers before she asked Andrew, "Why?"

Andrew sighed, reaching forward to grab her in a hug. Her reciprocation was immediate. Andrew's chin rested on top of her head and he whispered, "Because I love you."

The surprise on her face would've been missed if I'd blinked. As if remembering there were others watching, she lowered her voice toward me, "You're okay with it?"

I gave her a thumbs-up. Jasmine didn't waste a second, kissing

Andrew. I immediately turned the other way as Caleb, of all people, cheered loudly for them. He slung an arm around me and gestured at our friends. "That's something we'll have to get used to."

"At least they're happy." I lifted up my camera to take a picture of them. "That's the only thing that matters."

~

"He wants you to meet his parents?" Jon Ming's eyes went wide. The boys were crowded in my basement on Friday night. Andrew paused the game he and Brandon were playing, Jacob stopped eating his slice of pizza, and Jon Ming and Austin stopped their air hockey game, moving over to sit on the couch with me.

"That's quick," Andrew said.

"This still seems so weird," Austin said. "Macy has a *boyfriend*. Andrew and Jasmine are dating."

"We've entered an alternate universe." Jon Ming spoke up. "Prepare to have your mind blown."

"How come you didn't invite Cedric here tonight?" Brandon questioned.

"He had rugby practice earlier and was supertired so he's probably sleeping right now," I said.

"At seven o'clock?" Jacob asked.

"Ced once slept fifteen hours after a conditioning practice. It's normal." The doorbell rang. "Did any of you invite any more people?"

"I may have invited the additional duo," Andrew announced as I went upstairs.

Spotting Justin eating a granola bar on the couch, I was walking in the direction of the door when he grabbed a pillow, whipping it at my head. The pillow dropped to the ground after hitting the side of my face. I headed toward him. "*Dude.*"

The second he put his granola bar on the couch, I jumped him. He tried to push me off, grunting, "God, I swear you've gained weight from the last time you attacked me."

Pushing my elbow into his stomach, I got up. Caleb and Sam were at the front door talking to my father. Sam was wearing his infamous leather jacket and dark jeans, and both his and Caleb's cheeks were a dull red from the cold outside. "Take a picture, Hazel. It'll last longer."

I turned on the flash of my camera and did as he said. "There, you wanted me to take a picture. I'll give it to you tomorrow."

He smirked. "Keep it. Hang it in your room."

Ignoring his comment, I said to my dad, "Sorry, Andrew invited them."

"All is forgiven." My dad pointed at Sam. "I'm not kidding, you're the spitting image of your dad. You look a lot like your uncle too."

Sam nodded in agreement, surprising me that he didn't scowl at a reference about his uncle. "I get that a lot."

"Come in," my dad urged, stepping to the side. Sam and Caleb took their shoes off and I closed the door behind them. My dad pointed them in the direction of the basement and after they left, he said, "He doesn't seem like a jerk. And Caleb, he's a character. He gave me a thorough explanation on how aliens are—"

"—in the ocean instead of space? Caleb's like that." Poking my head into the living room, I said to Justin, "If you want to hang with us, you're welcome to."

"Thanks, Sandy."

"Anytime, Patrick." I picked up the throw pillow from the floor and tossed it at him, knocking the granola bar out of his hand. Running away from his fury, I joined the boys once again. Sam was engaged in a game of air hockey in the corner with Andrew.

As I took a slice of pizza, Jon Ming turned to me while playing a video game with Brandon. "What are you going to do?"

"About what?" I asked through a mouthful of food.

"About meeting the parents."

Caleb took a seat on my other side. "You're meeting the Cahills? Mama Cahill's a sweetheart, she'll love you. Phil says he invited you to his party so you're in with the adorable Cahill. Plus, Cedric's the nice one, and you're best friends with the asshole. You'll be fine."

Sam's hands came down on Caleb's shoulders in an instant and Caleb screamed dramatically. "Piss off, Caleb," he said. I didn't miss the smile on Sam's face.

"What about the dad?" Jacob asked.

"You'll be fine," Sam echoed.

Caleb reached past me to take the last slice of pizza. The *last* slice of pizza. "You guys are animals," I said.

"*You guys are animals,*" Jacob mocked.

"I'm going to make popcorn. Movie?" I made my way upstairs to the kitchen as they discussed suggestions. Despite the fact it was all the guys wanted to talk about, my main focus wasn't on meeting Cedric's parents.

Earlier that day, Coach had pulled me aside after practice and told me news I wasn't expecting. Suddenly, the upcoming tournament after spring break wasn't just about winning anymore for me. Coach said that a scout from a university I had been accepted to was coming to see me because Coach had sent in a couple of tapes from last year. A scholarship might still be in reach, and that had me excited yet nervous.

The shutter of a camera jolted me out of my reverie. Sam looked at the picture. "What were you thinking about?"

"Nothing."

"*Hazel.*" He held up my camera. "You know, you're handy with this. Did you apply for a program in photography?" I shook my head, getting the popcorn out of the microwave and putting in another package. "Why not?"

"It's just a hobby. I like science. I applied to those programs."

"Are you playing football in postsecondary?"

"Why are you asking so many questions today?" I opened one of the cabinets and grabbed a Pop-Tart. "I thought you hated twenty questions."

"I never said that."

"You didn't have to," I joked.

"Answer my question."

With the demanding tone he used, he probably got many answers, because I started talking. "That's the plan. Earlier today, Coach said that a scout is coming to the tournament after spring break."

When I had told my dad after running home from practice he was beyond happy. Someone was coming to watch me. Maybe I would play for their team. *How would my mom have reacted to this news?*

"With the way you play, you should be offered the national team." I struggled to speak as my face flushed. I put the hood of my sweater over my head. "Wait, is Hazel speechless?"

"Shut up."

"Why do you look upset?"

"I'm not a big fan of change."

"When I moved here, I hated it." He shrugged. "Sometimes you gotta accept it. Besides, change is inevitable."

"You know, your accent gets strong when you say *inevitable*." Sam took the strings of my hoodie and pulled on them. "*Dude!*" He took a bite of the Pop-Tart. "*Sam!*"

My dad entered the kitchen. "Glad to see you two are on great terms."

Sam let out a grunt as I elbowed him, taking my Pop-Tart back. "Nick"—*Oh, they're on a first name basis now?*—"your daughter's very weird."

"I know."

"Hey!" I pointed at my dad, who chuckled. "You're supposed to be on my side."

"I'm always on your side, Sandy," my dad said.

"Sandy?" Sam asked.

"We call each other after characters from *SpongeBob*," I explained. "It's a thing from a long time ago."

"What was your mum?"

"Mrs. Puff," my dad answered. "Did Sandy tell you the news?"

Sam grabbed my camera, taking a picture of me. "There's our favorite soon-to-be university football player."

I took the camera from him as my dad snatched the bag of popcorn for himself and said, "Your mom would be proud of you."

When he left the room, Sam was in the process of putting another popcorn bag in the microwave. "Hazel, I'm telling you, if you want me since you keep *staring*, just ask—"

"Shut up!" I pushed the back of his head lightly as I made my way downstairs. And honestly, he was right: change was inevitable. It didn't mean I had to like it.

9
CONTAMINATION ON MY BED

"You're distracting me," I said to Cedric on Wednesday afternoon as I broke the kiss. My eyes darted to the windows looking out on the full parking lot.

Even when he kissed me again, my worry about meeting his parents continued to grow. However, the main topic on my mind was the dynamic between Sam and his uncle. Earlier Sam said he'd probably drop by and I wasn't counting on it. For some reason, that gave me an uneasy feeling.

Cedric's hand was in my hair and he played with the strands. "Congrats again."

His praise was sincere, yet it added to the nerves that always arose whenever the scout and the tournament were mentioned. "It's not like I got it."

"You're going to," he assured me. "What are you doing during the break?"

"Visiting my grandma in Redmond, what about you?"

"Don't know yet. Might go to Bali or visit my other cousins. Family hasn't decided yet. Mace, about my parents—"

"*They're normal people. It's not a big deal, relax.*" I repeated what he had said to me, leaning in to kiss him. His hand gripped my waist as he deepened the kiss but before he could do anything further, a rapid knock broke us apart.

Jasmine was by the side of the car and I rolled down the window. "C'mon, Andrew's waiting in the car." She gave Cedric a two fingered wave. "Hello, lover boy."

"Hi, Jas." Cedric pulled me back toward him, kissing me once more. "I'll see you later. Don't worry, it'll be fine. They'll love you."

~

"How did you feel when Andrew told you?" Jasmine asked an hour later, when we were in my room, changing my clothes.

"Despite not knowing what's been happening with my best friends for a couple of years?"

She winced.

I waved a hand and put my head through the shirt hole. "I'm happy for you both. Don't get mushy around me."

Andrew opened the door, then grabbed Jasmine and kissed her. "Hey!" I yelled, swatting at them with one of my sweaters until they broke apart. "This is a no PDA zone. I don't need your contamination on my bed."

"Maybe you and Cedric have already christened it."

Red in the face, I looked at my outfit in the mirror propped against my wall of pictures. Within my ever-growing collection of photos of my friends, there was one picture I had purposely centered. It was my mom and me after I had won a trophy for playing soccer as a kid. I was hugging her tightly as we grinned for the camera—her other hand was touching the soccer-ball pendant at her neck. She hadn't been wearing that necklace the day she had passed according to my dad. It wasn't in the house, either, or else one of us would have found it.

That picture had been taken at the same park where I had bumped into Sam, near the rec center, under the big maple tree. "What do you think she'd say if she was here?"

"She'd bug you about Cedric more than your dad does," Andrew said. Not too far from that picture was another, showing a younger version of the three of us.

"Remember in third grade when we were painting Justin's room?" I said.

"Your mom told you to call Jasmine," Andrew added. "And when Jasmine came in she tripped on the paintbrush and it went flying and swabbed your mom's pants with paint."

"I apologized so many times that day," Jasmine said. Mom was sympathetic; she hadn't minded.

I looked away from the pictures, turning to my friends. "Let's go?"

In the car, Jasmine, in the passenger seat, gave me pointers as Andrew drove. "Be yourself. Also be a little more polite and eat like a normal person."

"Jas, you told her to be herself," Andrew said as he made a left.

"Right. Mace, be yourself."

"Jasmine, put on your seat belt!" Andrew exclaimed.

She pulled the seat belt across her chest and added, "Also, when we were talking earlier today at school, Stevie was telling me how Beatrice was staring at you."

Even the sound of Beatrice's name left me irritated. "I feel like she's going to do something to me."

"It's not your fault Sam is ignoring her." I'd seen Sam flirt with other girls, not just me. It was so like Beatrice to just focus on me.

"We're here," Andrew announced as he pulled into the driveway.

"Holy shit," said Jasmine. It was a Victorian-looking home, similar to the rest of the houses in the rich neighborhood, but the biggest in the area. It had a long driveway and an elaborately landscaped garden, and a narrow pathway led to the front steps.

"They're *loaded*," Jasmine sang.

"Good luck, Mace," Andrew said.

"Have fun!" Jasmine yelled out the window as Andrew drove out of the long driveway.

Walking up the steps, I was raising my hand to knock on the door when it flew open. The youngest Cahill looked elated to see me. "Macy!"

He closed the door behind me. "Hey, kiddo," I said, my voice trailing off as I took in the interior of the home. A wide staircase led to the second floor. "*Wow*."

I had just managed to take off my shoes when he grabbed my hand and dragged me down the corridor and into another room. We entered the living room, which had couches, an otto-man, and a large flat screen perched on the wall. *Boy Meets World*, playing on the TV, was being watched by a person on the couch.

"Macy's here," Phillip announced, and the person's eyes darted to me.

With blue eyes not as intense as Sam's but nevertheless piercing, he had the same Cahill charm, lean build, and a familiar smirk on his face as he stepped toward me, his hand out. "Ivan."

The brother. "Macy."

"We've heard." The voice came from a woman who entered the room. She was tall with straight, shiny dark hair and had blue eyes shaped similarly to Ivan's, and a mouth like Cedric's. When Mrs. Cahill spoke, her English accent was prominent. "Cedric's told us so much about you."

"It's nice to meet you, Mrs. Cahill." I shook her hand, her motherly presence allowing me to relax.

"Call me Liz," she said as a phone rang.

Ivan took his out of his pocket. "I have to work on a few things, I'll join dinner in a bit, Mum." As he passed by me on the way out, he shot me a wink. "Good luck."

"Sam should have been home by now." She *tsked* as Ivan left the room. "And Cedric too."

"Here, I'm here." Cedric rushed into the room. "Had practice. Was in the shower. Macy, my mum. Mum, this is Macy."

"We've been introduced." Liz patted him on the back. "I'm going to go get your father. Show her to the dining room. Give her a tour of the place afterward, hmm?"

"A tour?" I asked when she left.

"There are a lot of rooms. C'mon." Cedric pulled me by the hand and we followed Phillip into the dining room.

Phillip gestured for me to sit across from him at the table. "You and Cedric are"—he gagged—"*dating*?" He pointed his fork at Cedric, who took a seat next to me. "This isn't illegal?"

"How would it be illegal?" Cedric asked as Liz walked in and put some food on the table. My stomach growled.

"She's my coach," Phillip said.

"You coach Phillip?" Liz took a seat next to her youngest.

"I'm a volunteer coach for house league soccer at the rec center."

Liz's eyes lit up. "Oh yes! I heard you play footy."

"I've played for years," I said.

"What position?"

"Forward," a familiar voice answered. "Hazel here is the captain of the boys' team." Sam took the seat on the other side of Phillip. I hadn't been expecting him to actually show up to this dinner. Cedric cleared his throat, looking discomforted at the sight of Sam.

"Really?" Liz asked. "Also, her name is Macy, Samuel."

Samuel? "I'm her friend," Sam proudly stated. "It irritates her when I don't call her by her name."

"Friend?" Mrs. Cahill's eyes ran me over as if she hadn't seen me properly. "Besides Caleb?"

"Yes, I *do* have friends, Aunt Liz." Liz glared at him. He immediately cringed. "Sorry."

She turned to the rest of us. "Let's get started with dinner, shall we?"

"Not without me, you won't." A deep voice boomed through the dining room. The way Sam's fist clenched on the table made it clear this night wasn't going to run smoothly.

Mr. Cahill stood at the door in a suit, his black shirt topped with a deep-magenta tie. I recognized Cedric and Phillip's brown eyes and Phillip's wavy hair. However, my dad was right: Sam shared similarities with his uncle. Their nose, face shape, and mouth were alike, yet Mr. Cahill's voice was deeper, his accent more pronounced. His eyes turned to me when he sat down at the head of the table. "And who's this?"

"This is my girlfriend, Macy Anderson," Cedric said.

Ivan entered the room, taking a seat next to Sam as Mr. Cahill said, "Vince Cahill."

"Nice to meet you," I responded, shyness suddenly overcoming me. Phillip was quick to turn the conversation to his day at school as everyone ate. I struggled to not inhale everything in front of me; someone tapped their foot against mine under the table. Sam had an amused expression on his face as he put chicken in his mouth. I shook my head in disbelief at how good the meal was and he snorted, getting a weird look from his aunt.

"Macy, I've heard you play football," Mr. Cahill said to me. *The question period of the evening. You got this.* The uneasy feeling that overcame me when I fiddled my thumbs told me otherwise.

"On the school team and usually at a soccer club. It's off-season for both."

"Any plans after high school?" Mr. Cahill asked me.

"I'm deciding on different places. Haven't made a choice yet."

"What kind of student are you?"

That was vague. "Pardon me?"

"Do you take Advanced Placement classes?" Mr. Cahill clarified. I nodded. "Any awards?"

"I got the physics award last year."

"That's wonderful!" Mrs. Cahill praised me.

"Are you coming to my party on Saturday?" Phillip asked me.

"Yup. I have a great present for you." A jersey for a soccer player he couldn't stop talking about whenever I saw him.

"Is it a laptop? Is it a new phone? A trampoline?"

Phillip's enthusiasm put a halt to my fiddling thumbs. "You'll have to wait."

"I don't like surprises."

"What does your father do?" Mr. Cahill interjected.

"Why do you care? Her dad isn't her," Sam said. *Oh crap.*

"What does your father do?" Mr. Cahill repeated, not bothering to acknowledge his nephew.

"He's a lawyer," I answered. "He says he knows you. Nick Anderson."

"Nick! Good man. And your mother?"

"She died in a car accident nine years ago."

They all fell silent—even Mr. Cahill, who wasn't expecting my answer. "I'm sorry."

"Don't act like you know what to say when something like that happens," Sam muttered. His grip on his fork was tight.

"Sam," Ivan started but Sam was glowering at his uncle.

Mr. Cahill ran a hand through his hair as if this happened all the time. "Let's continue with dinner."

Cedric found his phone more interesting than the conversation and everyone else was quiet, but Sam wasn't having it. "'Let's continue with dinner' and just forget things, right? That's not how life works, Uncle Vince."

"You wouldn't know how life works." Mr. Cahill's tone was quiet. "All you do is constantly get into trouble."

"Don't turn this on me," Sam said.

"With all the detentions? I'm surprised you haven't been suspended yet." His uncle's gaze held nothing but failed expectations. "And do we need to remind you of the arson incident? Why do you think you're here?"

Sam stood up. "That's irrelevant. At least ask her proper questions instead of being condescending. She doesn't deserve that. Honestly, I can't fucking do this." He walked out and the door slammed shut behind him. Everyone stared at that door in a heavy silence, but I exhaled slowly. Vince's jaw clenched as he continued eating while I remained stunned by how normalized their argument was by the rest of the family regardless of Sam attempting to defend me.

The rest of the dinner proceeded with no more questions from Vince as Phillip filled the air with conversation about his upcoming birthday party. I was tense, only relaxing a little bit when Mr. Cahill excused himself to take a phone call.

After dinner, I was saying good-bye to Mrs. Cahill at the front door when Cedric walked over to us, twirling his keys in his hands. "Ready to go?"

I nodded. "It was nice meeting you, Liz."

"You too, Macy." Although the evening did not go as planned, she didn't show it, saying good-bye as Phillip waved at me as he ran in the direction of the living room.

Cedric and I headed in the direction of his car parked in the driveway when he sighed, "That could have gone worse."

"It wasn't that bad," I said with some encouragement. Cedric shot me a look. "Okay, yes, it could've gone better. It's always like that?"

"Sometimes," Cedric said when we got into his car.

"Do you think Sam's okay?"

Cedric started the car. "Don't worry. Sam's fine."

~

Sam was not fine.

He hid it pretty well during lunch on Thursday, talking to our friends and me as if the blowout at dinner or his uncle didn't affect him. That afternoon, after my soccer practice was over, I came back from filling up my water bottle to see him juggling a soccer ball.

Today, Cedric offered to pick me up after I spent time here despite me living fifteen minutes away by foot. Usually, I was used to spending time here with Sam after practice, but he didn't seem like good company today; Sam looked mad.

He had three soccer balls lined up a good distance from each other. He stood behind one, hands on his hips as he paused for a moment before running and kicking it straight into the net. I wouldn't have thought something was bothering him by the first shot. But as he proceeded to make the same precise goal with each of them, his movements were rigid.

As the last ball hit the net, he said, "I know you're watching, Hazel."

"How did you know?"

"Your size thirteen feet could be heard all the way from here." He smirked at his lame joke, retrieving a ball from the net. Clearly, he was feeling better. He walked toward me with the ball. "I saw you come in."

"There's nothing wrong with having big feet."

"Can I call you bigfoot instead of Hazel?"

Despite his jokes, I wasn't going to pretend that yesterday's dinner didn't occur. "Are you okay?"

Sam became serious. "I didn't mean to scare you."

"You didn't," I assured him as he played with the chain of his necklace.

"The man bothers me. And the way he was treating you didn't help at all." He leaned his head back, as if in pain. "I don't care if he's my uncle or not—you need to act like you're with the guys when you're talking to him. You don't let them push you around, so don't let him push you around either."

Sam turned, dropping the ball he had been holding. He dribbled forward a bit before taking the shot, and the ball curved into the air before hitting the back of the net. Sam was about to move to get the ball when I stopped him.

"When I mentioned my mom at dinner, I know why you reacted in the way that you did."

His eyes went down to the turf of the indoor field. "Who told you? Cedric?" When I didn't answer he nodded to himself. "You would've found out eventually."

Sam's hand went to his necklace. He shifted the chain and brought out the pendant that had been underneath his shirt: a small golden *B*. "Bethany. She was my twin sister."

I took a step toward him. "It's pretty. Was this hers?"

"Originally." He wasn't looking at me.

"Your uncle mentioned an incident," I said. "Involving arson. I mean, you don't have to tell me—"

"I got caught up with the wrong people last year." He placed the pendant back under his shirt. "Luckily, I didn't face any serious charges. Only a warning."

"What did you guys do?"

"We did a bunch of shit. We weren't friends or anything. One incident—the arson one—was a little too serious. My parents found out who I was hanging around with when everyone got into trouble. They decided it was the last straw and I got sent here."

Without thinking I asked, "If you weren't friends with them—with anyone besides Caleb—then why did you become friends with me? And the group."

"I became friends with you because I wanted to."

That was too vague. "What's the real reason?"

He didn't answer. This conversation pertaining to his sister or even his time in England was over. His eyes went to my duffel bag slung over my shoulder. "This heart-to-heart conversation has been fun. Football?"

~

Half an hour later, Sam stood in the net, gloves on his hands. I took a few steps back and kicked the ball in the direction of the top right corner. He dived, coming forward as the ball threatened to soar over his head, and caught it in his hands, hissing slightly at the force. He rolled the ball back to me. "Stop being predictable. You only got, like, two goals in."

"Shut up."

"Don't look at where you're going to shoot," he said. "You can but don't linger on that spot too long. Okay?"

He took his position, hands on his bended knees, eyes on me. Once I found my target area, I ran forward and fake kicked the ground before kicking the ball. It swerved into the net, barely missing Sam's fingertips and he fell to the ground. "Good."

"Macy!" Phillip's voice cut through the air. He ran over to us, Cedric not far behind him.

"Hey." Cedric's cheerful expression faltered when he saw his cousin.

Phillip ran to the ball I had previously set up, kicking it in Sam's direction. Sam moved out of the way, letting the ball go in the net. "Nice one, buddy. What are you doing here?"

Surprisingly, Cedric answered as Phillip ran over to the bleachers to grab Sam's duffel bag and jacket. "He wanted you to take him to gymnastics today."

Sam nodded. The tension of their exchange made me shift uncomfortably when Phillip came back. "You ready to go?" Cedric asked me as Sam changed out of his cleats and into regular shoes.

"Give me a second, I have to go to the change room."

"Bye, Macy!" Phillip said, running off the field. "C'mon, Sam, we have to go!"

Sam didn't say anything further, hiking his duffel bag over his shoulder as he followed his cousin out of the building.

10

BENJAMIN IAN THE GREAT

My best friends being a couple was completely fine with me. However, where Jasmine and I usually chatted during the four minutes before we had to get to class, she now spent it making out with Andrew in front of her locker. When Stevie and I were going to get a ride in Andrew's car a few days ago, the couple delayed us once again. And again during lunch the following day.

"Guys." The pair turned to me. "I love the fact that you both are happy with one another. But this is something *everyone* has to get used to."

"Tone it down," Austin said. "It's school, not your bedroom."

"Sorry." Jasmine linked her arm with mine, all of us walking into the cafeteria.

Cedric sat across the room with his friends. Despite the two of us dating, I liked that we didn't have to sit at the same table with each other. Sometimes we'd hang out together at lunch, but for the most part lunch was spent with our separate friends.

Cedric walked over to me. He told me a few days ago that he had a rugby game about an hour away from the city. "Are you leaving right after school?"

"Yeah, I'll text you after the game," he said.

"What game?" Austin asked.

"I have a rugby match," Cedric explained, saying his greetings to the boys and Jasmine before turning back to me. He pressed a kiss to my cheek then headed back to his friends.

"Sometimes it's hard to believe that Sam and he are related," Austin commented.

"Tell me about it," I mumbled as Stevie joined us.

"Sam has his surprising moments," Caleb said. "He's a freaky genius. You guys should see his marks in math."

"His rep around school is definitely different than he appears," Jon Ming mumbled.

My friends listed off their plans for tonight, most of them heading to a party. I turned to my best friends, awaiting their answer. "Movies," Andrew said. "You want to come with?"

I didn't want to intrude on a date. "It's all good."

Sam sat down next to me and pointed to my sandwich. He hummed in appreciation when I allowed him to take a bite out of it. Beatrice was staring at him. When she realized I was looking at her she scowled, turning away. "You don't have plans tonight?" Sam asked. "Then I'm coming over."

"You don't want to go to the party? Hook up with someone? Beatrice maybe?"

Sam didn't bother commenting on the jab. "I'll come over to yours, Hazel."

~

"It's Friday night." Sam walked into my house later in his usual wear. His car was parked in the driveway and he kicked off his shoes.

"I'm glad you know your days of the week." Just then my dad came out of his office; he and Sam greeted each other pleasantly. Then Dad reached for his jacket. "Where are you going?" I asked.

"I have plans with Andrew's dad," he said.

"Wait, where's Patrick?"

"He's sleeping over at a friend's house."

So it would be just me and Sam alone in this house. Great. When my dad left, we headed up the stairs. Hanging out with Sam at school or the rec center seemed fine, but to be here without anyone around somehow made me uneasy.

"Does the boyfriend know you're hanging out with me tonight?"

"He knows we're friends and he's fine with it," I said, but I wasn't sure that was even true.

"That didn't answer my question."

"I texted him," I said, as we entered my room.

Sam's eyes roamed the pictures on my wall until he settled on one of Mom when she was at university. "She played varsity football? Should've known by the football necklace in the other photos."

"Yeah. No one was able to find that necklace after she died," I commented. "It was her favorite."

"I didn't know you liked reading." He referred to the stack of books on my desk.

"My mom owned a bookstore when I was a kid, so I had a lot of books growing up."

He picked up a novel. "Good book."

"I didn't know *you* liked reading." Sam continued looking through a few other books. "What about your parents? What do they do?"

"I'm sure you know my dad co-owns the family company. My mum's a musician."

That's news. "Really?"

"Yeah," said Sam. "Toured the UK in her early days. Music's a big thing in our family. She and Aunt Liz would make everyone in the family play instruments growing up."

"You play an instrument?" I asked.

"A bit of guitar." He turned a book over in his hands. "My little brother—"

"You have a *brother*?" Clearly, I didn't get the memo about a lot of new information dropping tonight, but the Cahills definitely seemed to have a lot of boys in their families.

A small smile played on his lips. "His name is Gregory—Greg. He's twelve. He plays piano."

I hesitated before asking my next question. "What about your sister? Did she play an instrument too?"

Sam's hands stilled on the cover of one of my books. He leaned against my desk. "She liked singing. She went to an art school."

"She must've been really talented."

"She was."

An awkward silence fell upon us, which was understandable. Sam didn't like opening up. And I was a little stunned that he had. I think he was too.

Sam jumped on my bed, landing on his back. He took his jacket off and settled his arms behind his head. "Comfy bed." He winked at me. "Care to join?"

Even though he was joking, I hit him with my pillow anyway. "Care to shut up?"

He tossed a pillow at me and I swatted it away, ready to hit him with my pillow again when he grabbed my arm and pulled me down. He tried taking the pillow away from me only to end up getting hit in the face, almost falling off my bed. He grabbed my arm as I laughed, lifting himself up to stabilize himself.

I detached myself from him. "Let's find a movie."

When Sam and I were in my basement, he looked through the cases of movies we had in a box. "For a girl who doesn't seem to like romance, you sure do have a bunch of romantic comedies."

"Andrew and I make fun of them." Sam grabbed a DVD and held up one of Dad's horror movies. I was *not* good with horror movies.

A mischievous expression crossed his face. "You won't be scared of this movie?"

"Nope." I knew he wasn't buying it but he put the movie into the DVD player.

Not even an hour into the movie I was clutching the armrest beside me. The music was so suspenseful—I hated the fact that you knew something was going to happen but couldn't hide. Sam kept eyeing my reactions as the movie progressed.

His knee pressed against mine, our arms not touching because I was leaning forward. The suspenseful music got louder and louder and I grabbed Sam's arm. "It's just a movie, Hazel."

I paused the movie. "Based on a true story, it says."

He took the popcorn bowl. "I'll go get more. Don't start the movie without me."

I'm not even planning on finishing this movie at all.

He ran upstairs as I turned on my phone to check messages, unease coming over me. The feeling didn't help as my leg bounced up and down and suddenly a voice said, "*I'm going to get you and we can play forever and ever and—*"

I screamed and jumped, turning around to find a laughing Sam behind the couch and popcorn on the ground. Moving past him, I made my way upstairs and to my room, my annoyance growing.

"Hazel!" Sam knocked on the other side of my door. "Open up."

"You're such a dumbegg," I yelled back but he didn't cease. In a flash of anger, I opened the door to see him holding himself up by the opposite wall. "You're ridiculous," I hissed.

"*I'm* ridiculous? *Dumbegg?* I can't take the insult seriously." Then Sam sighed, his delight in my mood fading. "Hazel."

"No."

"I didn't mean to scare you. You were just sitting there with your back to me, and it just seemed so easy, and . . ." His tone had no sense of apology in it, only amusement. "Look, I'm sorry."

That surprised me. He wasn't the type of person to apologize. "Okay."

"What? That's all I get?"

"Were you expecting me to hand you flowers and shower you with kisses?"

"The flowers part, no. The kissing part? Go ahead." He grabbed my laptop from my desk. "What do you want to watch? I promise no horror movies this time. I mean, not after a whole hour and thirteen minutes of the other one."

"Do you always do that?" I asked, sitting cross-legged on my bed. "The time thing. You said the same thing at the park when we met. That our conversation was fifty-four seconds or something."

"I don't know." He shrugged. "I've always had a thing in my head that estimates how many seconds have passed by. It's something I picked up a while ago."

He pulled out his phone, text message notifications pinging on the home screen. "Is that Caleb or your fans?" I teased.

Sam tossed his phone to the end of the bed, and sat next to me. "It's not my fault some of my fans find the need to message me."

"They probably run away after they see how small you are," I joked, and he glared at me for striking his ego where it hurt.

"Hazel, you can make fun of my face, my personality, and my attitude, but you can never make fun of him."

"*Him?*" Sam's cheeks turned a faint pink. "Oh my God, you've named it, haven't you?"

"His name is Benjamin Ian the Great."

A snort escaped me at the seriousness of his tone. "*Seriously?* You named it B. I. G.?"

The stupidity only entertained him, and I reached for my camera, taking a picture of him midlaugh. Sam reached for my camera and I held it out of his reach. "Delete it," he said.

He looked good when he was in a happy moment. "It's a nice picture. You're not frowning or brooding or being disgusting." He grumbled under his breath, placing the laptop between us. As we watched another movie, my eyes drifted to my soccer ball. "When did you start playing soccer?"

Sam got up from my bed, looking at one of the video games on my dresser. "When I was six. I started off like Phillip, playing house league until I began playing competitively. Never had time for the school team back home."

"Why don't you play now? On the school team or a rep team here?" I asked.

"Sometimes you lose your passion," he mumbled, before holding up a video game. "I'm going to win this."

"Against me? Definitely not."

The way he changed the subject reminded me of Jasmine. Both never talked about what bothered them.

11

CAHILL FAMILY

Cedric looked handsome in his dress shirt and blazer as we pulled into his driveway on the sunny but breezy Saturday afternoon.

I smoothened the simple violet dress Jasmine had told me to wear when I had called her last night in a panic that I didn't have anything to wear. It was a dress I had received as a present from my dad's mom one Christmas years ago that surprisingly still fit. My fingers tugged on my cardigan sweater as Cedric and I stared at the numerous cars lined up in the Cahill driveway and outside the Cahill house.

What kind of eight-year-old had a *ball* for a party? My confusion grew as people—mostly adults—stepped out of their cars.

We exited the car when I saw Caleb. "Charming." He fell in step with us. Like Cedric, he was wearing a dress shirt, blazer, and pants.

"Here you are looking like a princess." His compliment made me flush. As he acknowledged Cedric, nicely dressed people walked by us in the front yard, chatting the afternoon away. Caleb must have sensed my awe. "They know a lot of people."

"You got that right," I muttered. We stepped inside, people everywhere, buffet tables filled with pastries and plates. Waiters in sharp outfits carried trays of full champagne glasses. When we headed toward the living room, there only seemed to be more adults.

"Cahill parties are a matter of connections," Caleb said. "Networking and lots of gossip."

"Caleb?"

Caleb winced, taking a deep breath before facing the older woman who'd called his name. "Mrs. Mattias, it's a pleasure to see you again."

She giggled. *Oh God.* She turned to Cedric with the same expression. When she looked at me she frowned. Caleb, in his most charming way, held her hands. "We have to get going but it was lovely seeing you again."

Caleb pulled us out of the living room to the corridor. Cedric whispered, "There're plenty of people like Mrs. Mattias. Wedding rings are forgotten at the door."

"She used to be at every event during the summer," Caleb added. "Let's go find the birthday boy."

Blue streamers, blue balloons, and plenty of entertainment meant for kids filled the entire backyard. A large tent was set up which waiters streamed in and out of—it was no doubt where food was going to be served later. Most of the adults were standing near the garden beds, talking as children ran around.

Phillip wasn't hard to find, a blue mask on his face as he ran toward me. "Macy! I'm Leonardo from Teenage Mutant Ninja Turtles." He put his hands on his hips. In the blue long-sleeved shirt he was wearing along with his bow tie, he didn't look cold on this breezy day. "I'm eight now!"

I handed him his present. "Here's what I got you."

"Thank you." His eyes were joyful. "I can't wait to open it."

"I thought you didn't like surprises."

"Dad says to open it later when everyone goes home so people don't get distracted." *What?* "Hey, Caleb."

Caleb fixed Phillip's lopsided blue mask and straightened his shirt. "Little man, you've got to impress the ladies. You don't want to look messy."

Phillip pointed at a girl talking with a bunch of other kids their age. "She said I looked nice."

Caleb leaned over to me, sounding accomplished. "Eight years old and already flirting."

"You're a bad influence."

"I'm a good role model," he said proudly.

Cedric grabbed hold of his little brother. "Anyway, show me the rest of your ninja turtle crew."

As he and Phillip headed toward the kids, Caleb got in my face, putting on a fake dramatic voice: "He's so cute, right? How did you land a guy like him? I'm *so jealous.*"

I playfully shoved him. "Shut up."

"Macy, now you're being rude."

"That's *my* job," a voice said behind us. Sam wore clothes identical to Cedric's, with a different colored shirt. He had a blazer over his dress shirt and, for once, wasn't in his leather jacket, which surprised me. His hair was messier than usual, as if he had run his fingers through it multiple times.

He looked good—and he knew it. "You cleaned up nice," Caleb said to him.

Sam shrugged, surveying the scene. "You too. Did you run into Mrs. Mattias?"

"Of course." Caleb groaned, starting to move ahead. "Everyone's probably at the pool house."

Sam turned to me. "Nice dress." His lips twitched as if he was about to smile. Or smirk.

I wasn't going to stick around to find out. "Thanks."

Cedric took my hand as I approached him. "I should probably give you the insight into the family—most of us are here." Cedric led the way, walking in the direction of the pool house. He nodded at a woman leaning outside of the pool house, talking to a bunch of people. "That's Natasha, Ivan's fiancé."

Whoa. "Ivan's engaged?"

"Wedding's in November. She's in school for music. Violin."

"You giving her the memo?" Sam caught up to us. Cedric ignored him.

In the pool house, groups of young adults stood in every corner, their conversations loud. No matter how extravagant their clothes were, they looked relaxed, happy to be away from the adults on the outside. Eyes were on us—no, on Sam and Cedric. They both disregarded the stares, and Sam gestured for two people to come over. "Hazel, this is Lucas and Joey. Cousins."

Like Cedric and Sam, they were wearing similar outfits; in fact, from my observations, most men were following the same dress code, every one of them related. Lucas and Joey were identical twins with very different hairstyles and personalities, judging from the way Joey looked around the room like he didn't have a single care in the world and Lucas's shyness.

"Do you guys live in town?" I asked.

"Yup," Joey said. "We go to the arts school downtown."

"Hamilton Academy of the Arts, right?"

Lucas nodded. "I go for art and Joey's there for music."

"Macy!" Another voice called out and Ivan slung his arms around the twins. "I see you've met some of my cousins."

"I didn't know you were engaged," I said.

The girl came up beside him. It wasn't hard to miss the delight on his face at the sight of her. "This is Natasha. Nat, this is Macy, Ced's girlfriend."

Natasha greeted me. She had bright-red hair and blue eyes. "It's nice to meet you."

Ivan looked around. "I'm always reminded of how much alcohol is needed every time one of us has a birthday and our parents decide to use it to—"

"*Exploit* us?" Sam suggested. The familiar smirk rose to his lips when he caught sight of a girl across the room talking to a few others.

"Not exactly the word I was looking for," Ivan mumbled as Sam sent the girl a two-fingered wave before he frowned at Ivan. Ivan glanced at Cedric and me. "Is he pissed off or something? Another fight with Dad? I'm telling you, buddy, it's all right to be pissed off. It's better to be pissed off than pissed *on*."

"What?" Natasha and I said out loud, and she hit him lightly on the chest, telling him to stop talking.

"You don't have your camera?" Sam asked me, ignoring his cousin. "I'm guessing you didn't delete any pictures from last night."

"You mean the pictures of you losing horribly?" I taunted. "It's not my fault you sucked."

Sam's attention went to another person. "Diana is here."

"Who's Diana?"

"Close family friend." He sounded displeased.

"Who's had a thing for Sam since we were kids." Cedric laughed and Sam shook his head, surprising me with their calm exchange.

"I'll see you all later."

"You guys hang out a lot?" Cedric asked as his cousin moved through the crowd. Sam always played soccer with me after my practices, the two of us speaking for hours; Caleb was there sometimes. Sam had also managed his way into my friend group, which I didn't mind because he and the boys found more things in common every day. I guess we did hang out a lot. The wary look in Cedric's eyes suggested he didn't like that.

"He's my friend," I said. Cedric's expression didn't change. When his eyes fell back on me, I leaned forward and kissed him chastely. "Nothing to worry about, okay?"

"Cedric!" a guy called, gesturing for him to come over and sit in a large, empty space on a couch.

"Macy, this is Peter," Cedric said. "Cousin from my mom's side."

"You're the girlfriend," Peter exclaimed, shaking my hand.

"Macy," one of the girls said. She had fake blue highlights in her hair and wore a dress that was so short I was grateful she was crossing her legs. "Where did you get your dress?"

"It was a present."

Cedric took that moment to whisper in my ear. "Diana." *Oh.*

"You're friends with Sam?" Her demeanor reminded me of Beatrice, and her condescending tone irritated me.

"Really?" Peter asked. "Because Sam doesn't have friends except that Caleb guy. He's always been a little distant."

Lucas and Joey joined the conversation, Joey pushing aside one of the boys on the couch. Cedric gestured to the other boy.

He looked familiar. He probably went to our school. "That's Christian. Another of the twins' brothers. Basically, my own. They're always at our house."

"Are all your cousins on your dad's side boys?" I froze when Lucas and Joey said yes at the same time.

"You two have got to stop doing that, geez," Ivan said. "You're freaking Macy out."

"Twins run in the Cahill family," Peter mumbled, glancing over at Sam.

Ivan's phone rang in his pocket and he pulled it out to answer it. When he raised his voice everyone's eyes fell to him. "That was Mum. It's time for lunch."

~

Caleb was devouring his plate beside me and it took everything in my will to not eat the same way. Instead, I focused on the fake elevator music in the air as adults spoke and kids ran around. Mrs. Cahill, in a nice white dress, stood next to Phillip. He took presents from people, grinning adorably and thanking them. I turned to Cedric. "When you said this was like a formal ball, I really didn't believe you."

"My family always kind of overdoes it when it comes to parties," Cedric explained. "It's a surprise that they used the backyard instead of renting out a ballroom. Doesn't stop people from acting like we're a royal family from the 1800s."

Sam showed up at our table, grabbing a drink from a waiter's tray and downing the glass in one go. "It's more like a way for their *daddies dearest* to network." Phillip ran over to him. "You all right, buddy? You having fun?"

Phillip nodded excitedly. "I want cake."

"Wait." Natasha stopped Phillip. "How much cake have you had? *Phil.*"

"It's *my* birthday." Phillip turned to me. "Can we play soccer later?"

Sam squeezed his cousin's shoulders. "*Football.*" He shook his cousin playfully by his shoulders, making Phillip burst into laughter. "We say football."

"Macy, can we play football later?" Phillip's excitement had me agree to his question. He pulled Sam down to tell him something and the smile fell from Sam's face.

Sam bent to his cousin's level, suddenly sad, and I had a good idea that what they had spoken about involved Sam's family. "I wish everyone was here too. Go back to your mum. Eat loads of cake."

Cedric tapped me on the hand. "Are you up for dancing or you want to go inside?"

"Inside."

I grabbed my plate, following him. Not many people were inside the large house as we walked through and up the big set of stairs near the front. "You'd better not forget me," Cedric said. "When you go off to university."

"Ced, I haven't even picked one yet," I said. "Besides, it's impossible to forget you. I can't forget the guy who almost blew up one of our chem labs last year."

"*That* wasn't my fault."

"Sometimes chemicals come together and release toxic gases?"

"Mace." He stepped forward to open his room door, then pulled me toward him and kissed me. As I kissed him back, the plate in my other hand almost slipped my mind. I set it on one of his dressers and he shut his door. "Believe what you want. I didn't blow it up."

"I said *almost*." Falling backward on his bed, I hit the soft duvet, and then his lips were pressed against my own once again. And as the kiss grew deeper, I was reminded that we'd done this multiple times, mostly in his car, and it had never been this intense before.

My heart raced faster when he took off his blazer and tossed it to the floor. And just as I realized what might happen next, the door opened. Cedric got off me, scowling at one of his cousins— Christian, who was standing at the threshold.

"Chris, get out," Cedric said.

His cousin was quick to close the door behind him. Cedric leaned his head back against the wall, his face scrunching up in a cute way. "Sorry about that."

"It's okay." Rugby posters hung on the walls, and there were pictures on his desk of his team. I picked up one with a lot of people in it, noticing the number of boys in one picture. "Is this your entire family?"

Cedric walked over. "Yeah, the Cahill side."

"So many boys."

"Four uncles and no aunts on Dad's side. Bethany was the only girl."

"The *only* girl?" I repeated in surprise. "Wow."

Cedric pointed at a person in the photograph. "That was her."

The girl in the photograph stood between Sam and Ivan. She was pretty, with straight, long, brown hair and a captivating grin identical to Sam's.

"My dad's the eldest. He and my uncle James, Sam's father, run the company that Ivan is going to take over."

"*Ivan?*" My eyebrows rose. "Seriously?"

"Years of battle between giving it to him and some of my family members, but it was decided he was the right man for the job if it came down to him."

"That's a lot of responsibility." I put the frame down. "I'll be back. I need to head to the bathroom."

After closing the door behind me, I moved along the hallway. When I turned a corner, I almost bumped into someone's chest, their hands on my arms the only things stabilizing me. "Always so damn clumsy," he said.

"What are you doing?" Sam's focus went over my shoulder. "Diana."

She was heading over with a group of her friends and Sam backed us against the wall, putting an arm up to block the side of my face.

"Just pretend we're busy," he mumbled in my ear. I swallowed hard, nervous about the feeling of his other hand on my waist bringing me in close, moving to the middle of my back.

Out of instinct I took a deep breath and that didn't help. Sam smelled good. The chatter quieted as Diana and her friends disappeared. "She's gone." I hoped he couldn't hear my rapid heartbeat as it thudded in my ears.

As if I was on fire, Sam yanked his hands off me and fixed his shirt. He looked everywhere but at me, and I didn't blame him. His natural confidence was shaken, and he ran a hand through his hair, mumbling, "Thanks."

He walked away from me, heading back down the stairs.

12
DIDN'T GET THE MEMO

The following Sunday evening, Cedric took a left in his car, heading in the direction of my house when I said, "You fell four times!"

Yesterday's party seemed successful judging by Phillip's cheery mood, and I hadn't spoken to Sam since what happened in the hallway yesterday. Cedric and I were coming home from an afternoon of skating, and bantered about the race we'd had on the ice rink.

"You *pushed* me!" he said. "Besides, you kept making other people fall too."

"They were in the way. We were racing—it's not my fault you're a sore loser."

"Instead you blaze past them and not look back to see them fall?"

"They obviously didn't get the memo," I muttered as he pulled up in front of my house.

"We've got company," Cedric said. I turned to see Justin's head by the window, an irritated expression clouding his face.

Why did he look so mad? My heart dropped at the realization of what day it was. It was Sunday. We were supposed to go get the game today. "I should go."

"I'll see you tomorrow?"

I agreed, kissing him once before exiting the car. When I got inside, I found my brother in the basement, his fingers aggressively clicking the buttons on a controller as he played a game.

The game.

Crap. "Justin—"

"I don't care," he said, eyes on the screen.

"I lost track of time."

"I don't care," he repeated.

"Don't be immature."

"*I'm* immature?" He paused the game and stood up to face me. "We've been waiting to play this for the longest time. We literally had a countdown and you decided that a date with your boyfriend is better?" He scoffed. "The Macy I knew wouldn't do shit like this. You're acting like it's not a big deal."

"Because it's *not.* We can play it right now. Dude, there's no way you can actually be this high-strung about it."

"Don't start acting like you suddenly know who I am outside that camera of yours. I'm not going to chill out."

"Where is this coming from?"

"You didn't show up."

"And I showed up *now.*"

"It doesn't matter."

"What? Justin, I'm sorry I didn't get the game with you and that I wasn't here to play it. Honestly, it completely slipped my mind."

"Of course, it slipped your mind," he muttered. "I didn't think you starting to date would turn you into such a bitch."

I took a step back at his bitter tone. "*Justin.*"

"Leave. I don't want to fucking talk to you." He sat back down on the couch, grabbing the controller again.

He meant it. When I reached my room, I took out my phone, my fingers hovering over Andrew's contact then Jasmine's contact before retracting. They were out together. Without thinking, I pressed a different name.

"Hazel?" Sam answered. "I'm surprised you called." I opened my mouth to give him a typical response but couldn't get the words out, tears blurring my vision. "Are you okay?"

"I'm fine."

"Don't lie to me." He hung up and as fast he ended the call, he was calling again, this time to video chat. "I'll be there in ten minutes." After he hung up, I changed, trying not to let my emotions get the best of me as I pulled on sweats. I made my way outside, turning on the porch lights and sitting on the front steps to wait. Sam's car pulled into the driveway a few minutes later.

"I'm certain you broke a few laws while driving," I mumbled when he walked toward me and pulled me up. And without any warning, I was engulfed in his strong arms, and for a moment, nothing else mattered.

"You're probably the first person I've hugged besides my aunt since I've gotten here." He was just trying to cheer me up but I laughed anyway. "There's that weird laugh I've grown accustomed to . . . unfortunately." I slapped him lightly on the shoulder. "And there's the Hazel I know."

"Why do you call me Hazel?"

"Your eyes."

I knitted my eyebrows in confusion. "They're brown."

He sighed. "When you're happy, they get lighter. Almost hazel. Especially when you're laughing. Now, what happened?"

As I recounted what had happened, Sam listened intently. "You and Justin are obviously very close. He didn't mean what he said when he called you that."

"He still said it."

"He didn't mean it," Sam repeated. "You made a promise and you broke it. That's what's bothering him—because he wants to spend time with you before you leave. Especially since you have a boyfriend now and postsecondary coming up. I think he's just scared. It's clear that you Andersons aren't big fans of change."

"It's been like that since our mom died," I confessed with a heavy heart. "We're actually going to see our grandmother, her mom, over spring break for the first time in years."

"I think your mum would be happy with the way you two turned out." Tears blurred my vision once again and I was quick to wipe them away. Sam's eyes widened as he reached out to do it for me hastily. "*No, no.* Hazel eyes only!" He paused. "Why did you call *me*?"

"You'd tell me what I needed to hear and not what I wanted to hear," I admitted, pulling the hood of my sweatshirt over my head. "Where were you coming from?"

"Caleb's. He doesn't live far from you. He was going off about an alien theory he'd read in a book. If anything, you kind of saved me." He smiled. "What would you have done? Call him a dumbegg?"

"Can you *not* make fun of me?"

"You're asking to be made fun of by saying *dumbegg*."

His relentless joking was an attempt to make me feel better and it was working. "Why are you like this with me?"

"It's *fun*," he teased.

"Why? Didn't have enough fun flirting with the girls today?"

"Didn't do much flirting today."

"It's because you don't have the motorcycle, right?" I teased.

"I don't need the motorcycle to get girls."

"Really?" I taunted him, my mood lifting at our banter. "I have yet to see this motorcycle. It's not snowing anymore. You're slacking on the bad-boy persona, Sam."

"I'm glad you're feeling *much* better." He took the two strings of my sweater and yanked on them. I groaned, loosening my hood as he laughed yet again.

~

"What's up with you and Justin?" Dad asked the following Monday after school, standing at the threshold of my door. "You guys aren't speaking?"

"He's mad at me," I admitted, closing my laptop. Dad knew about the game—Justin and I had been speaking about it every time we had dinner. But last night when my brother didn't say a word at the dinner table and breezed right by me when he came from the rec center after playing basketball with his friends, it was obvious what he was doing.

My dad disappeared and there was a brief murmur of chatter from Justin's room before my brother was pulled into my room. "I'm going to leave," Dad said. "When I come back, if you two still aren't talking then I'll get involved. Do we want me involved?"

Justin and I both grumbled no, and Dad seemed satisfied by our response, closing my door behind him. My brother's head hung low. "I never meant what I said when I called you a bitch. It was the last thing I would ever say to you."

"No, I'm sorry. I should have been there when I said I would be," I admitted. He sat down next to me on the bed. "We were looking forward to the game for months. But do you really think I have no idea who you are? Outside of"—I wiggled my camera hanging around my neck—"this?"

"You do," he insisted. "I don't know. I just think you're not going to when you're gone."

"Nothing is going to change between us," I promised. "Believe it or not, that's one of the only things that's stayed constant since Mom and Dad mentioned they were having another kid. Am I supposed to forget my brother who likes basketball more than the next guy? Or that you hate cheese-flavored chips because the color reminds you of when you threw up on your eleventh birthday when you had too much cake?" His face grimaced at the memory. "I love you, Patrick."

I pulled him into a hug, which he returned. "I love you, too, Sandy."

"Now, the game?" My brother pulled me out of my room, excitement in his eyes as he explained the levels he had played through last night.

~

Jon Ming, Andrew, and I stood at my locker on Tuesday between the first and second periods. I rushed to put my books in my bag as Jon Ming told us about how he was in the process of teaching himself Tagalog. Down the hallway, Sam leaned against a locker, a girl talking to him.

"Hey," Cedric said when he approached us.

"Hey." My eyebrows furrowed when Sam started doing exactly what I thought he'd do when he leaned toward the girl and kissed her. The kiss didn't last long because a teacher broke them apart.

"Not surprised," Cedric muttered as Sam, who started to get in an argument with the teacher, was handed a pink slip. Sam sneered as he took it and the teacher walked away. Sam waved in our direction, then made his way down the hallway.

"Shit," Andrew breathed. "I've got to ask Sam about calculus."

Irritation flashed in Cedric's eyes but Andrew didn't notice. "Oh, and I saw him at the rec center the other day and Mace, you're right. He's *sick* at soccer." Jon Ming hummed in agreement.

The two headed off to find Sam and I turned to Cedric, who was clearly annoyed by all the talk about his cousin. That was when I noticed the bruises on his arm. "What happened?"

Cedric pulled his arm away from my hold. "It was a tough rugby practice yesterday. Don't worry, Mace." He kissed me. "I'll see you later."

He walked away as Jasmine approached me, ready to walk to class together. Just then, a group of girls passed by. Ivy, one of Beatrice's close friends, eyed me up and down before turning her nose up at me. "Was that from Beatrice? Is she still harboring some idea that Sam and I are a thing?"

"Probably," Jasmine grumbled. "Ignore them and her. She's mad because he doesn't want her anymore."

"If Sam could do us all a favor and not get us involved in what happens when he can't keep it in his pants, that'd be great,"

I muttered, the image of him and the girl kissing moments ago still replaying in my head.

~

The ball soared into the air and hit the back of the net with ease. Brandon cursed under his breath from his position in the net but gave me a high five nevertheless. As I managed to score on the rest of my teammates during the scrimmage, Coach wasn't focused on the play. Instead, he spoke to Sam, who was sitting on the bleachers.

Whenever Sam watched practice, he'd make little comments afterward to me. The occasional "You should've passed it to so-and-so, they were open" or "I know you could have done that play better."

Talking to Coach was a first. I lingered behind at the end of practice, ready to play one-on-one with Sam. "What were you talking to Coach about?" I asked as he put on his cleats.

"He said he's seen me around here and asked why I wasn't on the team. Said if I wanted to play, he would give me a shot."

"Are you going to think about it?" Sam didn't answer me. "When was the last time you played soccer with a team?"

"Probably about two years ago."

"Do you ever miss it?"

"What's with all the fucking questions?"

My hands went up in defense at his sudden tone shift. "I'm just asking."

His expression softened. "Can we just—" He gestured to the ball at my feet and I moved over to the field.

He handled the ball with more aggression today, and when he missed a shot at the open net, I asked, "You okay?"

"Yeah," he mumbled, rolling the ball in my direction.

Leaving the ball behind me, I stood in front of him. "There's no way my question got you that mad."

"It's my uncle. I stayed at Caleb's last night."

"Have you and your uncle ever had a good relationship?" I asked warily.

"Things change," he said. "He just thinks I'm messing around now. And last night the fistfight didn't help."

"You hit your uncle?!"

"No, not my uncle."

The look he gave me suddenly gave away what he was talking about. "You had a fight with Cedric."

"He didn't tell you anything?" Cedric had said the bruise on his arm was from rugby, not from fighting with Sam. "Some of my cousins were over. We were talking about shit and suddenly we're on the ground fighting. Your boyfriend's too prideful to let anything touch his face. He probably only got a scratch with how quick Ivan pulled me off him."

"What the heck?"

He picked up the ball. "Don't start."

"Don't start?" I exclaimed. He couldn't be serious. "What's wrong with you?"

"Just like Uncle Vince," he muttered. "Thinking it's my fault and immediately siding with the asshole. You weren't even there."

"I don't have to be."

Sam looked at me like I had said the world was going to implode. "Do you even know him?"

"I know he's better than you," I blurted. "I'm sure he wouldn't start a fight, and he's not a player who's with a new girl every single hour of the day."

"Why are you acting like you love the guy? News flash: you haven't been going out for that long," he hissed. "And a player? Does it bother you? Seeing me with other girls?"

For the hundredth time today, the image of Sam kissing that girl in the hallway came into my head. It did bother me but I wasn't going to admit that. "*No*. Of course it doesn't."

My words were unheard. "Because Cedric has a girlfriend that makes him better than me?"

"Sam—"

"That doesn't even make sense."

"Cedric doesn't go around acting like you do. He doesn't have a reputation like you do."

Sam looked offended. "This is about my reputation?"

"Yes! You act like you're the best thing to happen to women because you're constantly flirting or you act like detention is your second home. Everyone says that you're nothing but trouble and they're probably right. I mean, look at the reason you were sent here in the first place."

I had understood that the topic of England was a sore subject. Maybe that was why the harsh look on his face turned to hurt as he realized what I'd said. I wanted to take back the words. "That's what you think of me?" he asked spitefully. "How ironic. He said something similar exactly last night."

"Sam—"

"I was at the wrong place at the wrong time with the wrong people." He shook his head. "That night, I didn't set fire to any building. One of the idiots I was with did. I wasn't involved, I told you that and yet you use it to form your opinion of me? You sound exactly like my uncle. It's one thing to hear it from him, but from you?"

"You've said it yourself. Trouble follows you. And you don't date and whenever I see you—it's who you are, Sam."

"It's who I am?" Sam muttered a curse under his breath. "That's fucked coming from you. What about you? The shit that Bonnie or whoever says about you. I heard her egging you on in the hallway that day and she's been saying shit around school. She keeps calling you names. Do her pointless comments define you?"

"Stop it."

"No," he taunted, the smile on his lips anything but joyful. "I'm the guy who messes around. A bad guy. And you're the fucking *tomboy*. Congratulations, you've succeeded in putting us into boxes we don't necessarily want to be in. Thank you for giving a shit about what other people think of you."

His sarcastic tone fueled my anger further and my fists clenched. "You clearly care what I think of you since you're reacting this way."

"Because you're my *friend*," he spat out. "I don't want to be seen negatively in any aspect by you of all people. Clearly that's how you view me."

"Am I wrong?"

"Does it even matter? For fuck's sakes, Hazel."

"It's not my fault that you're playing around and getting detention—"

"I'm not playing around with *anyone*," he sneered. "Any girl I've been with knows what they're involved in because my intentions are clear. Let me do what I've been doing for a while, all right?" Sam took a deep breath, his voice quiet. "I don't want to fight with you. I need you to know that one incident doesn't make me the bad guy."

He was right. It didn't and I shouldn't have brought anything up even in a moment of anger. "I don't want to fight with you either," I admitted. "And it doesn't. None of that was my business."

"Look, Cedric and I have never had a good relationship. I'm not even sure why but it is what it is." He threw the ball up in the air and kicked it and we watched it bounce down the other side of the field.

"I'm sorry. I really shouldn't have said that."

"I'm sorry too. I shouldn't have blown up at you like that," he muttered. "I'm not up to playing anymore." His green eyes lit up with an idea. "Let's go somewhere."

~

"You cheated!" Sam shouted. We were sitting at the edge of the cliff tops, overlooking the quarry below as Sam accused me for the hundredth time of cheating. Before we found ourselves here, he had driven us to the other side of town where there was a go-kart track, a place he went to all the time with his cousins when they were younger.

I had been there only once, for Andrew's eighth birthday party, but going now and realizing Sam was as competitive as I was—demonstrated by his loud cursing every time I passed him—made my entire month. Especially since he wouldn't stop talking about it. "I did beat you."

"Once after, like, three rounds."

Sam muttered dramatic curses that made me laugh. "A good hour of go-karting for me only to win once? You owe me lunch."

"What? No way. If anything *you* owe *me* lunch."

"You cheated at gaming too," he said, recalling the day we had played video games together, resulting in a lot of yelling from the two of us. "Just admit you cheated at the game at least and we can have a clean slate between us."

"I didn't cheat. I'm really good." I shoved a fry in my mouth. "You suck."

"Are you kidding me?"

"No." I took a picture of him with my camera. The picture sat in the gallery of my photos, beside one I had taken of him handing me my helmet earlier that day.

"Rematch," Sam declared. "Loser buys the other lunch."

"Might as well give it to me now." I grabbed the sunglasses sticking out of his leather jacket pocket and put them on as I continued eating. He gave me the finger again.

A loud burp came out of my mouth before I even had time to register it was coming up. Sam looked impressed, taking a swig of his own drink and pausing only to burp atrociously loud. "How was that?"

I grinned. "That was good."

"When you made that comment," Sam said, "earlier. Was it because of Blair?"

"*Beatrice* has made stupid comments here and there. To me and Jasmine. Now it's involving you. It's not your fault she's like that."

"I'll talk to her. Didn't mean to get you or Jas involved. Sorry about that."

"Thanks," I said as we finished eating and he looked through old pictures on my phone.

"Isn't this at the park? Where we bumped into each other?" It was a six-year-old version of me wearing shorts and a soccer jersey, my hair in a regular ponytail and a trophy in my little hand. My mom was hugging me, the two of us under a tree, smiling at the camera. Sam looked up at me then back at the picture. "I don't know what you've been saying. The more I see pictures of her, the more I realize you look like her."

"I don't see much similarity."

"Your hair too," he continued. "Your hair's really long. It's nice."

Trying to ignore the flush creeping up my neck, I gestured at the picture. "Justin and I would go to that park almost every summer. He'd force me to play basketball with him when his friends couldn't."

"You're tall," Sam commented, even though he stood a few inches above me.

"Yet I can't play basketball to save my life. I met you around there too."

"A good thing, right?" He looked at me warily.

"Definitely." The prior argument we had wasn't going to break our friendship. I hoped nothing would.

13
IT'S VICTORIA MARIE

I sat in school two days later, waiting for the bell to ring to signal the end of physics class. Last night, Cedric and I double-dated with Andrew and Jasmine at the movies.

The suggestion came from Cedric, and my friends were eager to join. Cedric loved movie theaters. However, for me, movies were better suited to home, where I'd lie down on my couch and react to what was on my TV with the person next to me. Cedric attempting to teach me the ropes of rugby or simply going out for food gained more of my interest than watching a movie surrounded by people. There was no commentary I could make without being shushed by someone nearby. He seemed excited about it, though, and even though it wasn't my favorite thing to do, I encouraged his plan.

The night had progressed and I grew restless, holding back my comments about how dull the movie was. Jasmine seemed to agree, but the two of us were entertained by how Andrew and

Cedric never took their eyes off the screen. Suddenly, my phone had buzzed with a notification from the group chat Caleb had thrown me into with Sam.

C: I have something to discuss

Me: Oh no

S: Hide your kids and pets, Caleb has another stupid theory
C: I honestly think the world will end in six years

Me: Dude

C: Mace, if it came down to you, me, and Sam and having to create a new human race, who would you choose?

Me: Neither

C: I believe the correct choice is me
S: Why would someone pick you over me?

"Macy!" I flinched at the sound of Jasmine's voice. Everyone else had already started filing out. The bell had rung. I gathered my things and as we walked into the hallway, we noticed Caleb and Sam talking. "Weren't you texting him last night?"

"Caleb was in the conversation. It wasn't just us." She didn't look convinced as we continued walking down the hallway.

After school, Cedric's larger hand tugged mine as we headed

inside his house. His mom sat in the kitchen, and Cedric grabbed a Gatorade from the fridge as we greeted her.

"Hi, honey." Her eyes fell on me behind the reading glasses she was wearing. "Hello, Macy."

Cedric said, "We're going to head to my room."

"Wait, Macy." She stopped him from exiting the room and turned to me. "It's come to my attention that Sam has been spending time with you lately. I understand you two are friends."

"We are. I hope that's not an issue." Next to me, Cedric bristled.

"Of course not. He talks about you and the rest of your friend group a lot. I'm happy to see him happy here."

Ivan entered the room, stopping in front of his mom. "Phillip's complaining about his outfit again."

"Again?" Liz sounded exasperated. "Cedric, can you get Phillip to settle down? You did it last time."

"I got it," Cedric agreed. "I'll be back." He followed his mom out of the room.

Ivan turned to me, reaching up to the cabinet and grabbing a couple of granola bars. He tossed one to me and I caught it with ease, mumbling a thanks as I sat down on a chair. "What outfit?"

"Phillip got these new shorts for gymnastics and he's decided he doesn't like them again." He leaned against the fridge. "How long have you and Ced been together?"

"A few weeks. Not long," I said.

As I finished my granola bar, Ivan asked, "Did he tell you about the fight between him and Sam?"

"Sam told me."

"That means he probably told you he and my dad had a little spat after that. Their relationship is complicated."

"Has it always been like that?"

"No, not always."

Phillip entered the room, picking at his gymnastics uniform. Another Cahill followed him. *Christian.* He pointed at me. "You were at Phil's party but I think I know you from somewhere else."

Christian stared at me a moment longer, and Ivan took that opportunity to smack his younger cousin upside the head. "Stop staring at her, dumbass."

Christian rubbed the back of his head with one hand. "You're Justin's sister. We play ball sometimes at the rec center."

That explained why he had looked familiar that day. Ivan turned to me. "And if you're looking for Sam, he will not be here tonight."

"What?" Phillip voiced my confusion. "Where is he?"

"Caleb's. Dad and Sam had another fight," Ivan said.

Worry overcame me and I pulled my phone out of my pocket, texting Sam to make sure he was okay as Phillip groaned. "*Again?* Did you hear it this time?"

Ivan shrugged. "Probably some nuisance he's caused. After the last fight they had? He was bound to get on Dad's nerves somehow."

Cedric appeared. "What are we talking about?"

"Sam," Phillip said.

Cedric frowned, obtaining a granola bar for himself and asked me, "My room?"

"Have fun, kids," Ivan teased.

"Shut up," I said, and the boys laughed as we exited the room. "You and Sam had a fight the other night?"

"Ivan told you?"

"Sam did." Cedric pushed the door open when we reached his room, then walked over to his closet to retrieve something. "You said the bruise was from rugby."

"It's fine," he assured me. "What happens between me and my cousin isn't as big of a deal as you think it is."

When my phone buzzed in my pocket, I took it out, reading Sam's response.

> Jerk: Just got out of detention, got into a little one on one argument with a teacher who marked my test wrong. I may have overreacted

> Me: Overreacted how and with which teacher?

He replied instantly.

> Jerk: Mr. Oliver

The same teacher who had given me detention.

> Jerk: May have broken his favorite pencils he keeps on his desk. Bought him a new set but he still gave me detention
> Jerk: I think detention would have been better with you there

The message surprised me. Sam flirted with me in an arrogant fashion but this time it sounded sincere. It probably wasn't even flirting.

Cedric finally located what he was looking for, pulling a thick blanket from the closet. "Found it." I reached out for the blanket, glad we shared the mentality that movies or TV shows were meant to be watched surrounded by comfort. He handed the blanket to me as he went over to his bed to retrieve pillows. I should take you to the music room after the movie."

Wrapping it around myself as I made my way over to a pile of video games on his desk. "I finally get to see your drumming skills?" I recognized the game on top. "You good at this?"

"Kind of. Have you played?"

Constantly. "Yeah."

"Really?" he said. "I didn't think many girls played it."

His assumption made me frown but I held the case up. "After the movie you'll see."

I sat next to him as he decided on a movie for us. How he didn't seem bothered by him and Sam's relationship confused me. While he remained as if the fight didn't even happen, Sam's actions that day on the soccer field proved something different. I texted Sam.

Me: You okay though?

Jerk: I'm fine. I'll see you soon

~

Andrew, Austin, and I passed the ball around after everyone on the team had left practice at the rec center the following day. Andrew took the ball when Austin attempted to pass it to me. "Dude." I playfully pushed Andrew.

"Foul."

"*Foul*," I mimicked, pushing Andrew again and grabbing hold of the soccer ball. Sam came over in his soccer gear and took the ball from my hands.

"Hey, man." Austin acknowledged Sam. "Always wondered why I saw you often."

Sam passed the ball to me. "Hazel could use the extra practice."

"That's *rude*," I chided, knowing he was joking. For the next hour we played two-on-two with ease and the boys were a little surprised at Sam's natural abilities. Austin's groan rang through the field as Sam scored again, and he took a seat where he was. We moved over to Austin, taking our seats with the ball between us.

Andrew flicked through his phone, putting it away as the doors opened and Jasmine skipped in our direction. She tackled me in a hug from behind before sitting between Andrew and me. "How was practice?"

"Brutal," I answered. "Coach made us—"

"Macy Marie Victoria Anderson."

"It's *Victoria Marie*."

"Whichever," she said, knowing she got it wrong on purpose every time she said my full name for emphasis. "I know nothing about soccer. I go to your games, cheer you on, you come to my games, cheer me on. When I ask how practice is, I don't want details. It's a system."

"System would work better if you understood the game," Austin mumbled.

Jasmine shot Austin a playful glare. "There's a party on Saturday."

Austin groaned. "There's no way I'm going to another party for a long time. Remember the last one we all went to? Where Macy basically got with Cedric? I cannot get that drunk ever again."

"Austin," Sam said. "You were out of it. Caleb and I had to hold you up at one point."

"Fuck." Austin ran a hand over his face. "That was a very interesting night."

"Didn't you kiss someone too?" I recalled. "That's what you told me and Cedric."

Austin frowned. "I told you?"

"Yeah, Sam and Caleb were helping you at that point."

Austin kept his eyes on Sam. "You saw."

"Caleb and I did," said Sam.

Austin's voice was quiet. "And you didn't tell anyone?"

"Not our position to," Sam said.

"What are you talking about?" Jasmine asked on behalf of me, her, and Andrew.

Austin looked down for a brief moment. Jasmine and Andrew waited for him to get to the point when I realized the golden tint of his skin had turned a very familiar pink.

"Did you kiss someone we know?"

"Was it Stevie?" Jasmine groaned. "I didn't think one of you boys was going to—"

"It wasn't a girl." His words were blurted out hoarsely, as if he had struggled to get that off his shoulders.

Oh. Silence fell upon our group.

"Okay." I spoke up first. "Who was it?"

"Oh my God, you didn't kiss David from physics, did you?" Jasmine made a face of disgust. "Because he was acting *gross* at that party."

Austin looked stunned. "You don't care?"

Andrew shrugged. "Did you think we would react badly?"

"Anything was possible."

"Does anyone else know?" I asked him.

"Jon Ming knows." He and Austin were best friends. "Now you guys and Caleb."

"All right," Jasmine said. "We're not going to tell anyone. It's a good thing Caleb or Sam didn't either."

"Thanks," Austin mumbled. When I ruffled his hair, he groaned loudly and pushed my hand away.

"Watch the hair."

"Play the game," I replied, grabbing the ball from Sam's hands and kicking it, watching it soar into the net.

~

Before the last period of the next day, I was hastily finding the binder for my next class in my locker while talking to Stevie, Andrew, and Jasmine. Jasmine and Andrew explained that they didn't have last period class because their teacher wasn't in and they were going to go on a date. Stevie asked me what I was doing after school and I replied, "I'm not doing anything."

"I'm surprised you don't have plans with Cedric," Jasmine said.

"He has a match," I explained.

"I was surprised when you two got together, to be honest," Stevie mused. "I thought you and Sam were together, not you and Cedric."

"Me and Sam?" I repeated. *Me and Sam?*

"Macy falling for someone in general is a little odd considering

how she used to cringe at any of us talking about relationships."
Andrew pointed at me. "*See*, that's the face. Before Cedric, Macy
never talked about anything involving love or boys. All she needed
was a soccer ball and she was set."

I pulled on the strings of my sweater, wishing this topic
would end. "Besides, I like Cedric, not Sam. Cedric's sweet and
I've known him for a long time."

"Did you say *sweet*?" said Andrew. "If having a boyfriend is
turning you into a total girl, can I break you guys up? This is
weird even for me."

Jon Ming approached us, looking frantic. He wasn't the only
one. People in the hallway were moving in the same direction,
and it was suddenly more chaotic than usual.

"Fight," Jon Ming said. Hearing that a fight had broken out
was always intriguing, but there was panic in his eyes.

"Between who?" Jasmine voiced.

"Sam's involved."

"What?" I shut my locker and followed the moving crowd
until we ended up in the parking lot. Pushing aside the crowd
of students in my way, I stopped moving when Sam shoved the
other figure away.

"Oh shit," Andrew mumbled.

There was blood on Sam's cheek and his lip was split. The
other guy was Oscar, a guy Jasmine used to have a crush on. His
face looked as beat-up as Sam's. And because this was a fight at
school, nobody was going to stop it because their phones were
recording it to share on social media.

"Admit it!" Oscar pushed Sam.

"She came onto me."

"Stop lying." He threw a punch at Sam's face. Sam tried backing up but still got caught, staggering back. He coughed violently, pity in his eyes.

Stevie gestured to where Beatrice was watching with her friends. *Of course she's involved.* "They got back together recently, her and Oscar."

Beatrice had a gleam in her eyes, probably hoping that her boyfriend would beat the heck out of Sam for ignoring her.

"It's not my fault your girlfriend's a conniving bi—" Sam's words definitely didn't help as he got shoved to the ground. Beatrice frowned at the insult. Sam got up, wiping the blood from his mouth. "I feel sorry for you."

"For me? I feel bad for you," Oscar spat out. "You clearly have issues since your parents shipped you off here."

Oh no. If Oscar knew that, then the rest of the school probably knew courtesy of Beatrice. The sore topic caused Sam to throw Oscar a harsh look. Like I'm-about-to-put-you-six-feet-under harsh.

Sam caught Oscar off guard with a punch across his face, and my jaw dropped at Sam's fast retaliation. And he didn't stop. Sam swung furiously and Andrew and our friends pushed by me to pull Sam away from Oscar.

"What is going on here?" a loud voice bellowed and everyone scattered in front of the authoritative figure. "My office now."

14
R-RATED

"Why are you going with him?" Cedric's question to me after school was filled with irritation.

I zipped up my windbreaker as the rain splattered hard against the front doors of the school. Although they were related, Cedric didn't care that Sam got hurt. The disinterest even though their relationship was strained annoyed me. He could have at least been concerned.

After the fight, Caleb had told me that he was going to drive Sam to his house. I offered to tag along because Sam could use the company. If this was any of my other friends, I would have done the same. "Because he's my friend and I'm going to check in on him. Besides, I'll still see you. What's the problem?"

"That you're going with him." *What?*

"If you're not going to give me a better answer, I'll see you later." Cedric didn't protest anymore and I pushed through the doors, rain hitting my jacket as I headed toward Caleb's car.

Oscar had been suspended for three days for starting the fight, proved by video evidence from a student. Sam got sent home to recover but was given two days of detention for being involved. Sam sat in the back seat, an ice pack on his cheek and a dark bruise forming around his right eye. "You didn't have to come," he said as Caleb started the car.

"I can't leave Caleb alone with your grumpiness."

Caleb sang along to the radio as he drove along the road, and Sam kicked his seat. "You're giving me a headache."

"One day," Caleb announced, "I want to write a song that will be known worldwide. Or an album."

"The title will be 'World's Biggest Douche Bag,' with your face on the cover of the album," Sam muttered.

"Sam, it's not good to talk about yourself that way," Caleb jested. "It can hurt your self-esteem."

"If I wasn't in pain right now I would do a lot more than hurt your self-esteem, Caleb."

"Prick," Caleb said.

"Dick," Sam mumbled.

"They're the same thing!" they said in unison, laughing uncontrollably—apparently a big inside joke I didn't even want to know about.

We pulled into the driveway and Caleb and I helped Sam out of the car. "It's like this house gets bigger," I muttered, pulling Sam up the steps.

Caleb shook his head. "Trust me, you'll get used to it in a few years."

"Are you used to it?"

"No."

"Aunt Liz!" Sam yelled once we were inside.

Liz appeared within seconds, sighing at the sight of him. "Let's get you to the kitchen."

Sam held on to Caleb and me as we reached the kitchen. Liz handed an ice bag to Sam, who put it on his swelling cheek, sighing in relief. "What happened?"

"High school drama," Caleb said, helping himself to the fridge.

"Yes, take whatever you want, please," Sam said dryly.

Caleb took out an energy drink then closed the fridge door. "I will! Besides, Mama Cahill loves me." He walked around the table to kiss Liz on the cheek, who patted him on the hand.

"You really shouldn't be drinking that." She pointed at the Red Bull as Caleb drank from the can.

Caleb offered the drink to Sam, who grabbed the can and took a sip from it. "Don't worry, Aunt Liz."

The concern on his aunt's face didn't slip as she inspected his face. "Sam, you're going to explain to me what happened when I return. I'm going to get Phillip from the bus stop but keep that ice pack on your face and rest, okay?" Sam nodded as Liz left the room.

Caleb and I helped him out of his chair and up the stairs. Caleb was accusing Sam of stepping on his toe purposely when Ivan stepped out of a bedroom, worry on his face as Caleb and Sam disappeared inside Sam's room. "What happened to him?"

"This girl, Beatrice. Her boyfriend found out that she and Sam . . ."

"Slept together?" Ivan suggested.

"Yeah, *that*. And he decided that beating up Sam was the answer to everything."

"It's reasons like this that makes me happy I'm not in high school anymore," he muttered.

"What are you doing now?"

"I finished university about a year ago. I'm shadowing my father at the company."

"You're going to take over a company *and* you're getting married soon?"

"That's the plan." We walked down to the kitchen while I waited for Caleb.

"That's crazy." Ivan was an interesting person—it was easy to see he had a wild side with that gleam in his eyes. To imagine him in a suit and tie like Vince Cahill, taking over their company and married?

"What's even crazier? Sam taking over the company instead."

No way. "You're lying."

"I had a few bumps along the way that led to my dad and uncle thinking I was unfit and the next best option eventually would be Sam. I cleaned up my act and suddenly I was the chosen one."

Caleb entered the kitchen. "He kicked you out?" Ivan asked as I sat down at the island.

"He kicked me out. He's getting changed," Caleb answered as Phillip walked into the kitchen, beaming at the sight of me.

"Macy," Phillip said.

"Hey." He took a seat next to me as Ivan retrieved a granola bar for his little brother.

"Are you here because of Cedric?" Phillip asked me. "He just pulled up with Lucas and Joey. He's coming in a second. You want to play soccer since you're here? You probably don't because you don't have cleats but you could borrow Sam's—"

"Phil," Ivan interrupted. "Just eat the granola bar."

"*Just eat the granola bar,*" Phillip mimicked.

Cedric entered the kitchen, stopping at the threshold when he saw me. "Can we talk?"

Cedric had given me the tour he had promised a while ago at Phillip's birthday party. He had shown me their personal library. I followed Cedric out of the kitchen, the two of us moving through the big house until we entered the library. He closed the door behind us. "Why were you upset that I went with Sam and Caleb?" I asked him.

"I didn't think you had to go with them. It didn't make sense to me."

"Ced, I wanted to make sure that Sam was okay," I explained. "He got hurt and I didn't have practice today. I figured he could use a friend or two."

Cedric crossed his arms. "I didn't know you spent that *much* time with him."

"He's one of the guys." I shrugged. That phrase explained enough. "We're friends."

Cedric sighed. "I'm just looking out for you. Sam's Sam. I don't want you to get involved in whatever follows him. You don't deserve that."

"I'm not going to," I promised him. "What Sam does is Sam's business, not mine. Don't worry, okay?"

"All right, I won't worry," he muttered.

"*C'mon*, Ced."

"I won't worry," he assured me.

We made our way to the living room where more Cahills were chatting—Christian and his two brothers, Lucas and Joey, who were wearing school uniforms, greeted me before heading into the kitchen. Sam was sitting next to Caleb, the ice pack no longer on his face. I took a seat next to Phillip on the floor and a foot lightly pushed against the side of my face. "Really?" Sam's sock-covered foot was in my face.

"Anything for you, Hazel."

Christian pushed between Sam and Caleb. "Macy, you know that blond girl who sits with you guys in caf?"

"Stevie?" I hoped he was joking. He was Justin's age. "I'm not sure you're her type."

That didn't faze Christian. "Let her know I'm available."

"What he means is to put signs up at your school that Christian is on the alert," Joey muttered and the boys laughed.

"Jacob and Brandon mentioned your birthday's coming up," Caleb said to me. "What do you want?"

"Be careful with your response," Ivan said. "A gift from Caleb could mean anything."

"And," Sam spoke up, "by *anything* he means *R-rated*."

"X-rated," Ivan corrected. "What day's your birthday?"

"The thirteenth," Cedric answered.

"Like Friday the thirteenth?" Phillip asked.

"Friday the thirteenth," Sam mused, and I knew where he was going with this. I grabbed the pillow and threw it at him. It hit him smack in the face and he groaned. "What was that for?"

"We don't speak of that day," I said, knowing that he was definitely going to share something I had told him.

"What about that day?" Cedric's eyes flickered between me and Sam.

A mischievous expression crossed Sam's face. "I don't know if any of you know this, but Hazel here is terrified of horror movies."

Caleb looked surprised. "I've seen you play the most graphic video games."

"Not the same thing,"

"She's right," Lucas agreed, and I grinned at him, glad a Cahill was on my side.

"She was going to a park to celebrate her thirteenth birthday with some friends but before they got there they watched *Child's Play*," Sam said. "Hazel felt fear course through her entire body. Her soul was shaking—"

"Leave the storytelling to me, please," Caleb muttered, but Sam continued.

"Because her birthday was the thirteenth and she was turning that very same age, she had the idea that the doll was going to appear. Her friends decided to buy her a present for the next day. When she opened it, she cried and ran all the way home. There's video proof on her laptop. I've seen it."

He had taken my laptop and locked himself in my bathroom for an hour trying to find it. A part of me regretted ever letting this idiot in my home.

Caleb headed toward the kitchen. "I know what I'm going to get you now."

"We agreed on something PG," I yelled, but my voice went unheard. I tapped Sam. "You sure you're feeling better? No need to go to the hospital?"

Ivan snorted behind me, then handed an acoustic guitar to Sam. "Sam and hospitals? Not a good mix."

Sam positioned the guitar, picking at the strings. Caleb, water in his hand, took a seat on the couch again. Conversation ceased; the boys who were standing took seats on the floor or in the empty spaces on the couches as we watched what was on the TV.

Cedric's hands played with my hair as mindless humming came from Sam's direction. Sam and Joey mumbled to each other as Sam played. But when Sam sang a familiar song quietly, I was surprised by how good he sounded.

His cousins and Caleb weren't fazed. "You're good," I said.

Sam shrugged. "It's nothing."

"He has a voice, right?" Ivan said. "He was so annoying when he would constantly sing when we were younger. Cedric wanted to shove a sock in your mouth whenever Aunt Liz would force us to go shopping together, remember?"

My head tilted up to look at Cedric, who kept his eyes on the TV, not wanting to engage in yet another conversation about his cousin. The rest of his cousins and brothers agreed, telling different stories about growing up with Sam.

If it wasn't for Cedric's cousins, who were all practically brothers, this house wouldn't seem full. All of the extended family together in one place made the Cahill house more lively and joyful.

My phone buzzed in my pocket and I took it out, reading Jasmine's contact name as I answered it.

"Don't freak out," she said.

"Why would I freak out? Are you okay?"

"I'm fine. Andrew isn't."

"*What?* What happened?"

Despite my panic, Jasmine was calm. "You know how Andrew and I didn't have class last period? We decided to go climbing at that place downtown. It was crazy, the rope slipped, and he fractured his ankle when he landed the wrong way on the mat. Never seen anything like it—those places are usually safe. We're about to leave the hospital right now. We're heading to his house."

"I'll be right there." Hanging up the phone, I stood. "Andrew hurt his ankle. Ced, can you give me a ride to his place?"

Cedric agreed and before I followed him out of the living room, Sam tapped me with his foot. "Don't panic. He'll be okay." Of course he would be, but after many years of being best friends, Andrew was a person I knew like the back of my hand. A significant portion of Andrew's injury would bring his concern to one thing: soccer.

15
ENTER YOUR ROOM

Andrew's right ankle was covered with a walking boot. He finished telling the rest of the team before practice about how he had broken his ankle during an indoor rock-climbing incident on his date with Jasmine. "I'm happy you're okay," I said for the hundredth time since I'd first rushed to his side a few days earlier. "I'm just sad that I won't have you by my side this year."

He playfully punched me on my side. "Don't get emotional on me now, Anderson."

Disappointment fell on Andrew's face when Jon Ming passed a ball to Jacob. "This sucks," he whispered.

"I'm sorry. If it's anything, Coach says you can come to every game of the tournament and be right here with us. It's a good thing you're in the team photo—" My words weren't even helping me much less Andrew. "You might be able to play during outdoor season."

"True." Andrew cursed under his breath. "I wanted to take down Michael."

"You and me both," I said.

"You still can."

Coach's whistle broke through the chatter in the air and we made our way over with the team to the center of the field, all eyes on Coach. "Andrew is not going to be able to play for a while. However, even with the loss of a strong player we're going to pull through." A murmur of agreement went through the rest of the team as Coach continued, "After some discussion, I'd like to announce that we have recruited a new player to our team."

Andrew and I exchanged confused looks, our eyes following Coach's to the person emerging on the field. *No way.*

The new player on our team stood beside Coach, clad in familiar athletic wear, clean cleats, and shin pads. He was all ready to practice. Sam inspected every single player on the team with his overanalyzing eyes and when they landed on me, he winked. *Idiot.* "This is Sam Cahill."

As practice started, the boys didn't say much to Sam, possibly due to their unease about his recent fight. People at school hadn't stopped talking about it. The shiner around his eye didn't help.

"Why didn't you tell me?" We had jogged over to set up for another drill. He was doing well with the drills, and the guys were warming up to him. It was easy for him to read the next move another player was going to make and act quickly with each play.

Sam shrugged. "Coach asked. I wasn't sure how you were going to take it and I told him not to tell you. Andrew said it was okay. Besides, it was kind of worth it to see the surprise on your face."

I was still shocked as I sat down in the back seat of Caleb's car after practice. I was used to us messing around with the ball after practice, but then Caleb showed up, and before I knew it, we were all in Caleb's car to drive to his house.

Caleb sang terribly at the top of his lungs as we arrived at an apartment building. I followed the guys out of the car, slinging my backpack over my shoulder as we made our way up to Caleb's floor in the elevator. The apartment was big and really nice, decorated with pictures of Caleb with different people, some of them Sam when he was younger.

"I was a cute kid," Sam said.

"Yeah, what happened?" I joked and he shot me a look.

"Tia!" Caleb yelled. "We're home!"

A short woman appeared from the living room, an apron around her waist and a frown on her face. She looked angry at Caleb, who was grinning at his aunt like a ninny. Tia Maria walked over to her nephew, a towel in her hand—and then she whacked him with it.

"Ow, ow," Caleb complained, putting his hands out and grabbing the towel. "What did I do?"

Tia Maria snatched the towel back, scowling. "How many times have I told you not to yell? My ears are sensitive."

Caleb only grinned. "Love you."

"Love you too." She turned to me, tucking the towel into a large pocket of her apron. "You must be the princess Caleb talks about."

"I prefer Macy," I said.

"She's a pretty girl." Caleb's aunt's compliment made me blush. "Why is she friends with you two?"

Caleb put his hands on my shoulders as I laughed, leading

me down the hall as he shouted, "We're taking her away now. Tell us when dinner is ready!"

"Caleb Romero," Tia Maria exclaimed. "What have I told you about yelling?"

As we made our way down the hallway, I saw a painting on the wall: a book with words coming out of the pages, delicately drawn with precision.

"My cousin Lucas drew that," Sam said.

"It's amazing."

"Yeah," he concurred. "I'm gonna go use the bathroom. Maybe check up on Andrew? Caleb, you're helping me with that stupid essay."

As Sam walked off, Caleb said, "You just want me to write it for you."

Caleb brought me to a brown door, a contrast from the white walls.

"You do realize I'm about to enter your room, right? I'm kind of scared of what I'll see."

Caleb pulled me inside the room. He loved writing and reading, but the number of books he had on his shelves was jaw dropping. His desk was filled with papers. "Working on something?"

"This is where I have my ideas." He pointed at a black leather-bound notebook. "I write them out here and start out my story lines."

There was writing on the edge of his ceiling. "Those are a few inspirational quotes," he explained.

Picture frames littered his desk: one showed a woman in a hospital bed holding a newborn in her arms. "Is that your mom?"

"Yeah. She died of complications from childbirth a few days after I was born," he said. "My dad had a heart attack a couple of years later. My sister always said that he never let us know how sad he was after our mom was gone, but then he was just . . . gone." I'd lost one parent. Caleb had lost both, and barely remembered them. "Isn't this the part where you give me a hug? Most girls do that when guys tell them their sob stories."

I hugged him, his arms wrapping around me too.

"That's the hug."

At his messy desk, amid all the papers, sat another photograph. Caleb was in midlaugh, standing next to Sam in what looked to be the Cahills' backyard. However, Sam was in the middle of play fighting with a girl, his eyes bright. The girl's brown hair blocked her face but I could see the glint of green eyes as she tried to look at the camera.

The familiar green eyes made me walk toward the picture frame. Caleb followed, "This was taken a while ago."

"That's her? Bethany?"

"Sam told you about her?" He sounded surprised. "He doesn't talk about it. No one really brings it up around him."

"Did you know her well?"

"I met Beth the day I met Sam," he explained. "We were all really close. Inseparable. Even though we mostly met up during summertime. When she passed"—he cleared his throat uncomfortably—"it was hard to accept."

I reached up to squeeze Caleb's shoulder in comfort when he took a deep breath. I was opening my mouth to speak when Sam entered the room. "Tia's making food."

As if he wasn't upset, Caleb feigned enthusiasm. "Let's get started on that essay."

"You mean *you* can get started on that essay." Sam tapped me on the side. "What do you say, Hazel? Want to watch a movie?"

He fetched Caleb's laptop and the three of us forgot our homework as he searched for a movie, the topic of his sister pushed away.

~

"Let me give you some pointers," Andrew told Sam in the busy cafeteria at lunch on Tuesday afternoon.

"On football?" Sam questioned.

"On *Macy*," Andrew clarified. "She hates left side even though she's good at it."

"I'm not," I said.

"You are," Andrew argued. "If she doesn't have a Pop-Tart for after a game, she's not motivated. Tell her that one will be provided and I'll be the one who'll give it to her because I'm the only person who can calm her down after a win."

As Andrew continued to talk to Sam, Austin, on the other side of me, typed rapidly on his phone. "What's up?" I asked him as everyone at the table fell into their own private conversations.

"I'm talking to someone."

"Talking to—*oh*." If I'd been having this conversation a while back, before I even had a boyfriend, I would've cringed at the topic of dating, but now I was intrigued by the smile that came to Austin's face.

"Yeah, *oh*," Austin joked. "I told the twins."

"And?"

"Same reaction as you guys."

"We won't break your trust, Austin," I assured him. "Never."

"I know that." His eyes snapped up to Stevie. "She's new to the group. That takes time." It was understandable. Jon Ming asked him a question about a class and my focus moved to Andrew, who was now engaged in a conversation with a girl who was in our calculus class, Olivia. She was asking him about an assignment we had due in a few days. Jasmine was talking to Caleb about another one of his weird theories but her eyes kept darting over to Olivia, a frown on her face.

Sam must've noticed too—the moment Jasmine excused herself to go to the bathroom he leaned into my ear and whispered, "She's jealous?"

I jumped back in surprise—Sam was closer to me than I'd realized. "You okay?"

"Yeah," I said, bewildered by my racing heartbeat. "I think she is."

"She has nothing to worry about," he assured me, his other hand playing with my camera strap. "Has she seen the way Andrew looks at her?"

"Jasmine jumps to conclusions sometimes," I said.

I was right. She did it whenever we watched a movie, predicting the ending. She did it when she decided that she and Andrew weren't going to work out before they had even gotten together.

The thought stayed in my head later that evening, when Cedric was in my room after officially meeting my dad over dinner. The two had hit it off, with Cedric being as polite as he'd ever been. With a quick warning from my dad to keep the door open—which made me turn red instantly—I dragged Cedric up to my room to do the homework we needed to do. I was snacking on a Pop-Tart as he went through his phone, showing me different posts from social media.

A loud knock came from downstairs. Justin was at the rec center playing basketball with his friends and my dad was most likely in his study. Pulling myself out of Cedric's arms, I headed downstairs to the door. I opened it to see Jasmine, her braided extensions up in a bun that I'd rarely ever seen her wear. Her eyes were puffy and red, and her cheeks were stained with dried tears.

Cedric, standing on the stairs behind me, wordlessly went back to my room and came back a few seconds later with his things. "I'll leave you guys to talk."

"Ced, I'm sorry," Jasmine said roughly.

"It's all right." He turned to me and kissed me briefly. "I'll call you later."

When he headed out, I grabbed Jasmine by the arm, closing the door behind her and immediately pulling her up to my room. "What happened?"

She lay on my bed. "Sometimes I hate going to school."

"You have us—"

"I know." She wiped a hand at her eyes. "You guys make it worth it, but there's so much shit."

"What are you talking about?" I sat in front of her, waiting.

"You and Drew have been friends for long," she said. "And you're like siblings with each other and I don't think you'll understand what this feels like. I was jealous."

"Why?" No one was stupid enough to not see that Andrew was in love with Jasmine with every atom of his body. For her to feel jealous must have been from a misunderstanding, but the upset expression on her face told me otherwise. Jealously over a boy was something I'd never experienced. I never understood why girls would put themselves through trouble for a guy. Nor would I ever understand why they would think they weren't good enough for them.

Jasmine let out a huge sigh, putting her hands to her face

before taking them off again. "I mean, look at Stevie, she's pretty and blond. And Olivia? She's pretty, nice hair, and they're both—"

"White. They're both white." I realized now what was happening. "Has Beatrice been saying stuff like this to you?"

For a moment Jasmine didn't speak. I thought she was going to brush off the topic but then she said, "When I explained to you that Beatrice makes me feel like I don't belong in Port Meadow, I meant that."

"But you do." I shifted on the bed, placing myself next to her.

"Sometimes I feel like I don't," she admitted. "Even before Beatrice started saying things to me at school. Remember sixth grade? You and Andrew were in the same class and I wasn't . . ."

I nodded.

"I kept my hair in braids like these during the school year so it was rare for me to show my natural hair unless it was summer. I didn't have braids for about a month, and other kids kept touching my hair. Constantly. Without asking. It almost felt like I was a zoo animal or something. I never told anyone."

Her dejected tone made my heart sink and I grabbed her hand as she continued. "And that just reminded me that not only is my hair different from everyone else's, I'm different. I think I became insecure after a few incidents. Especially about the way I acted around people who weren't you and Andrew. I got used to hearing micro-aggressive or generally racist comments growing up. Most of the incidents I would report and nothing would happen to the other person."

Beatrice's *Oreo* comment to Jasmine came to my mind as Jasmine spoke up again. "After meeting the guys and a few other people at Wellington, I saw myself a lot better. I used to tell myself 'Yeah, so what if I don't look like everyone? Neither does Jon Ming or Austin and that's okay. Because I like being myself.'"

"I like it when you're yourself too," I said, and she gave me a small teary-eyed smile.

"But sometimes Beatrice's comments make me feel like I really don't belong anywhere," she said quietly. "That I'm too black for white people, so she tries to provoke me into a stereotype to give everyone the reaction she wants. And then with the *Oreo* comment, it's like she wants to remind me that I'll never truly fit in. Sometimes her comments are worse. Sometimes I believe her."

"I wish she didn't say things like that to you or make you feel that way," I murmured, failing to suppress my anger about how one person could make Jasmine feel this. "You don't deserve that. No one does. Has Beatrice been saying that Andrew should be with a white girl instead?" Her silence confirmed my answer. "Andrew dating someone of a different race is no one's business. Same for you. Beatrice needs to—"

I took a breath before my frustration got the best of me. I stopped talking for a moment, pondering my words before I said, "I hope you know that Andrew is with you for *you*. Not Olivia. Or Stevie. Or anyone else. The guy loves you. A lot. I mean, he'd sit and watch every single movie you love with you. And you love a lot of weird movies." Jasmine nodded, a faint smile on her face as she grabbed my laptop and turned on *Star Wars*.

Her favorite film usually put her in a good mood. Yet her entire posture was slouchy, her shoulders hunched; a complete one-eighty from the Jasmine I was used to. During a moment of transition in the film she said, "My mom and dad are getting a divorce." I paused the movie, unable to hold in my gasp at the news. "Dad was having an affair with some woman at work.

"Drake called me," she continued. "He'd suspected for a while. I mean, it used to get bad. Dad would throw shit. He could've told her that he didn't love her anymore but instead he . . . I—I can't face him knowing what he did."

"You can stay here tonight if you want."

She rested her head on my shoulder, closing her eyes. "Thank you. I mean it."

"Anytime," I whispered to her, watching my best friend fall asleep even as the movie played on.

16
INFATUATION

"You coming to watch practice?" Austin asked Stevie the following day after school as we walked down the hall.

"Cute boys in shorts, who could pass that up?" she said.

"Who, them?" The team was my second family. Stevie wasn't exposed to their conversations and antics. "Cute? Gag me."

"Which are the cute ones?" Austin asked. "If I'm not an answer—"

"Austin, you don't need me to feed your ego," Stevie said as we passed by Cedric, who was in a conversation with his friends but who waved, telling me he'll see me later. "Cedric plays rugby, right?"

"You're into rugby players?" Austin asked.

"It's just a question!" she exclaimed, knowing Austin was teasing her.

"You're probably into Cahills," Austin said.

"The entire Cahill family is gorgeous. Have you seen all of

184

them? A few of them go to school with my sister and—" Stevie cringed. "Except for that one Cahill who hit on me a few days ago."

"Christian?" I asked. The young Cahill had approached her at our table the other day. His pickup lines failed, but Stevie wasn't really annoyed by it, more so entertained.

"He's *so* annoying," she said dramatically before turning to me. "Anyway, look at Sam and Cedric. You know your boyfriend's cute. And Sam is—"

"A *friend*," I reminded her. Besides, she and Sam spoke, but it was never in a flirty way.

"Yes, we're friends," Stevie repeated. "Am I not allowed to admit when someone's attractive? Sam's attractive as hell. Macy, back me up."

"I don't see Sam that way," I said.

Stevie shot me a dry look. "Have you *met* him? Tell me you don't think he's the slightest bit attractive."

Down the hallway, Caleb stuffed his binders inside his backpack as Sam spoke to him. His curly hair framed his face and his pink lips moved animatedly as he talked, hands gesturing all over the place to prove his point. His build was strong yet not overly muscular. His emerald eyes squinted whenever he laughed and grew brighter when he smiled. Those same eyes met mine. He waved in greeting and I returned it.

"Yeah." My voice was soft. "He's attractive."

"Even if you weren't dating his cousin, you would stay friends with him?"

My heart was beating in my ears. My hands gripped the strap of my backpack. "Definitely."

~

"Andrew!" I yelled once I entered his house after practice. Andrew's dad waved at me as I headed upstairs. Andrew was lying on his bed, his foot propped up on a pillow as he scrolled through his phone.

I dropped my backpack and duffel bag as he said, "I think I'm coming down with a cold."

"Did you take something to help with it?" Moving past his dog, Freddy, I climbed onto his bed beside him.

"Yeah, but a broken ankle and a cold?" Andrew groaned. "Anyway, what's up?"

"How did you know you at first liked Jasmine?"

He put his phone down. "I guess it was that feeling you get. Heart beating faster when I saw her. I got really nervous around her. I had to choose my words carefully to get on her good side. Even when I got on her bad side, I wanted to be the one to make her happy and I still do. Why?"

"No reason." I hastily retrieved my backpack. Some of his points about how he felt for Jasmine did seem applicable to my situation, but I didn't want to think about it any longer. "Want to work on homework for a while?"

A couple of hours later, as my mind was distracted by a word problem, the door opened to reveal Jasmine. "I texted you three hours ago," I said, and she shrugged and closed the door before settling down on the bed.

Andrew looked down at the paper in front of him. "Why do I have to do this? I'm impaired for a while. Don't people know that?"

"You fractured your foot, idiot," I pointed out. "Not your fingers."

Jasmine explained the homework to him but I must have been fidgety because Andrew stopped working. "What's wrong?"

"Yeah, what's up?" Jasmine asked.

"I think—" I paused. Admitting it out loud was harder than I thought. The realization hit me like a truck. "I like Sam."

For a moment it was quiet. Too quiet.

"You like Sam?" Jasmine asked slowly.

"I said I *think*," I clarified.

"Cahill?" Andrew echoed.

Jasmine put her hands up to her temples. "I can't believe it."

Andrew cleared his throat. "If you think you like Sam then what about Cedric? His cousin? The one you're supposedly dating."

"I'm pretty sure it's a small infatuation." My words formed a pit in my stomach. "It'll end soon."

"What are you going to do about it?"

"*Nothing*," I said abruptly to Jasmine's question. "Absolutely nothing because I have Cedric, who is nothing like Sam. I'm fine and happy."

"Then why do you have feelings for Sam?" Andrew mumbled.

"The sexual tension should be killing the both of you," Jasmine muttered.

"There is no tension!" I exclaimed.

"You shouldn't deny it. Plus, he's a bad boy. He has some type of tension with everybody."

I shot her a look as Freddy hopped in my lap. "He doesn't have tattoos or piercings."

"He's charismatic," Jasmine pointed out. "Good looking and dangerous."

"I wouldn't exactly call Sam dangerous."

"This is Samuel Cahill," Jasmine continued. "Ultimate player, gets all the girls who have the nerve to walk up to him. Even after the fight people are buzzing about how he's had twice as many girls coming up to him. Him rejecting even one girl besides Beatrice is bound to make some news."

"Honestly, I think it's nothing. Just a little infatuation, nothing more."

"Seriously? You're turning redder the more we speak about him," Jasmine said.

I instinctively moved my hands up to my warm cheeks. "It's nothing more," I repeated.

"And Chewbacca is Luke Skywalker's father," Jasmine muttered dryly. I lay back beside Andrew who cracked a grin, Freddy crawling between the two of us.

~

Jasmine and I stood at my locker on Thursday morning before the first bell, when she nudged me. "Here he is at ten o'clock."

I turned, thinking she was talking about Cedric, but Sam approached us, his duffel bag over his shoulder and soccer ball in his hand. "Ready for practice today? We get to play together. We'll finally understand each other through this sport. The whole two peas in a pod bit."

"Like understanding each other, right?" I asked.

"Whatever you want it to sound like," he said with a grin.

"That was flirting," Jasmine whispered to me as Caleb came up and started talking to Sam.

Behind her Cedric was approaching. "And *that's* my boyfriend."

"Hey." Cedric kissed me on the cheek.

He put an arm around my waist. As Caleb continued talking, Sam's eyes were on his cousin. I waited for either of them to say something to the other when thankfully, the bell rang and everyone went to their classes.

Sam? Cedric. Sam? Cedric.

As I walked to my class, my muddled thoughts cleared when Jasmine suddenly called my name, falling into step with me. "Where did you stay last night?"

"Stevie's," she murmured as we entered the classroom and approached our desks.

"Your dad isn't at home anymore, right?"

"No, but I don't want to spend time at home."

"You're avoiding your mom?"

"I'm avoiding the house," she corrected. "If I face the house, I face the reality that my parents aren't together anymore."

"You're going to have to sooner or later."

"I prefer later," she quipped, taking her binder out of her backpack.

Loud chatter came from the hallway and I walked back to the threshold to see Caleb throw a soccer ball at Sam. Sam stopped the ball and Caleb hit Sam lightly with the familiar notebook in his hand just as a teacher approached. Sam took charge, feigning seriousness as he issued a fake apology that satisfied the teacher.

Sam caught my eye after the teacher left, then he rushed down the hallway. He latched on to my arm, his warm touch freezing me in place. "My place after practice?"

"I'm surprised you didn't get detention."

"I'm on the team," he reminded me. "Can't get in trouble now."

"I can't. I have plans with Cedric. Go to class, dude, the second bell's about to ring."

"I will. I'll send you a video. Phillip had an idea to prank Ivan. It involves exploding powder. I was going to try it out at school but I don't want to risk expulsion, suspension, or words from my dearest uncle."

"You're crazy." It didn't help when I reciprocated his smile.

"I've been told," he teased, tossing the ball to Caleb before walking away.

17
THE DOUBLE C CUP

Later that day, I was grabbing my duffel bag from my locker when I spotted Sam talking to Brandon down the hallway. This little crush needed to end.

The entire day consisted of me waiting for when he would talk to me, visit my locker before last period, or if he would pass by me in the hallway. *It needed to stop.* I had closed my locker when Beatrice's condescending voice spoke up, "You know you'll never have him, right?"

The dirty looks she had thrown my way weren't enough anymore and now she was resorting to trying to talk to me again? I sighed, turning to see her with her famous follower, Ivy. "What are you talking about?"

"It's obvious you like Sam since you can't stop hanging around him."

"Guys and girls can't be friends?" She gave me the familiar once-over. At my hair, at my clothes, at me.

Ivy scoffed next to her, her own eyes pointed in his direction. "Not with Sam Cahill."

How does Beatrice not notice that her own friend is interested in the one she "claimed"?

"He wouldn't be with Jasmine either," Beatrice said. "She knows that Sam would never go for someone like her so she gave up. A word of advice: you should give up too."

My grip on my bag tightened. "We're friends," I hissed at her. "Jasmine has a *boyfriend*. If you want him go ahead and try, but after that fight? Leave me and Jasmine out of it. And leave us alone."

I moved over to the boys, not wanting to engage in any conversation with Beatrice for longer than I needed to. By practice that afternoon, I was still angry about it.

Passing the ball to Jon Ming, I ran far down the field where the rest of the team was doing other drills.

"Now!" I yelled and Jon Ming kicked it. I caught the ball with the side of my knee just as a whistle cut through the air.

We jogged over to the side with the rest of the team. "How about a little game?" said Coach before splitting us up into teams. A lot of my teammates glanced over at Sam. This was our second practice with him. Sam's soccer skills were outstanding, and everyone was curious about how he played.

Sam nudged me. "Jon Ming needs to practice."

"What he means," I said, noticing Jon Ming's frown when he overheard, "is to keep trying those long shots." I suggested to one of our teammates, Liam, that he practice with Jon Ming by the side.

"How about Malcolm takes Liam's place at center midfield," Sam suggested and I agreed. "I'll take forward with Anderson."

Anderson?

As the game progressed, I dribbled the ball, watching it go through Jacob's legs and he grumbled, attempting to catch up to me. I passed the ball to Sam, the two of us rallying until we were close to the net. When the ball came to me, I faked a kick at Tyrone in goal, tipping the ball to Sam, whose foot touched the front of the ball, directing it into the net.

Sam squeezed my shoulder. "Nice job."

My breath caught in my throat at his touch. Nodding, I jogged back over to my spot. Tightening my ponytail, I wiped my clammy hands on my shorts. Until a few days ago, Sam was just my friend. What was happening to me?

~

I sat on my bed with a plop later that evening after Cedric and I had gone out to eat. "I think I ate a lot."

Cedric lay down next to me. "I don't understand how you finished all that."

"I think I'm going to take a long nap." I was about to roll onto my stomach when I saw a thoughtful expression on Cedric's face.

"I was watching you guys at practice before I picked you up. You and Sam play like you've been by each other's side for years."

"Sam and I practice together. We want to win." Cedric wasn't letting up, looking bothered. I was too. There was no way I could act like that around Sam again: flustered, awaiting his next move. Cedric was here and yet Sam constantly came to my mind. *I hate this.*

Cedric was the right guy. Not Sam. *Focus on Cedric.*

I steered the conversation away from Sam and when Cedric left, I let out a loud groan that led to Justin yelling outside my closed door. "Did Cedric leave? Because if you guys are being inappropriate, let me warn you, Sandy, Mr. Krabs is coming in about ten minutes."

"He left," I shouted.

Justin opened the door, then came over to sit next to me on the bed. "What's wrong?"

I covered my face with a pillow. "Nothing."

"I'm fourteen, not stupid. Is it boy trouble? Now that you're in a relationship, I can guess that it's boy trouble this time."

"What do you know about relationships?"

"I know *some* things." He stood, taking my camera from around my neck with some difficulty and turning it on to record. "Let's talk about your relationship with the infamous Cedric Cahill. The rugby star CC. The double C cup." He looked pleased by his joke, turning off the camera and lying down next to me. "What's the problem?"

"Have you ever been confused about your feelings?"

"What feelings?" I hit him with a pillow. "I don't know. Just follow your heart or something. If you do that, then you can find an awesome way to proclaim your love for *Sam*!"

"I wasn't talking about Sam," I lied.

"Okay." Justin got off the bed, unconvinced. "Once again, I may be fourteen but I'm not stupid."

~

In the parking lot of school on a cloudy Friday morning, someone rapped their knuckles on the window of Cedric's car, making Cedric and I spring apart. Caleb grinned on the other side, opening the door. "Get a room!" he shouted.

Jon Ming was standing next to him, wiping fake tears away. He gave me a dramatic hug once I got out of the car. "I'd never thought I'd see the day that Macy Anderson would be locking lips with someone in a car. They just grow up so fast!"

Pushing him away with a scowl, I caught sight of Jasmine walking toward the front of the school. "There's Jasmine. I gotta go."

Cedric pecked me on the cheek before I ran to catch up with her. "Jas!"

My lips parted at the sight of her. She looked extremely tired and worn out, with bags under her eyes and cracked lips that she usually would've fussed over but didn't seem to have the energy to do so.

"What happened?"

"Can we talk?" Her voice was raspy and hollow, as if she had been screaming. "Not here."

"We'll go to Andrew's, okay?" He was still sick with a cold, and his mom had insisted he stay home. We were about to crash his fun by skipping school along with him.

I grabbed her keys from her purse and made a beeline for her car, Jasmine hurrying along behind me. "Macy, you haven't driven in months and are you seriously going to skip school for me? You barely ever miss school."

I jumped into the driver's seat. "It's fine."

Minutes later, we entered Andrew's driveway and I texted my dad to call the school to say I wouldn't be in today. *Jasmine family emergency*, I added, grabbing the spare key under the plant.

"Mom, that you?" Andrew yelled when we entered.

"No it's us," I shouted back as Jasmine and I kicked off our shoes and joined him in the living room. He sat on a pile of pillows in the middle of the room, his foot raised on a separate pile, with a game controller in his hands, his eyes glued intently to the screen. A box of tissues was on the coffee table while a bunch of used ones littered the floor around him.

He paused the game and looked at us, an arm raised in Jasmine's direction for her to sit next to him. "What happened?"

I sat on the floor in front of them as Jasmine coughed, trying to clear her throat. "What happened to your voice?" Andrew took her hair out of the bun, using the elastic to tie her braids into a low ponytail instead.

"Yesterday I came home and he was arguing with Mom and a woman was standing beside him." Jasmine's voice was a harsh whisper, her eyes trained on the ground. "Turns out the woman was the person he was having the affair with, and he had the nerve to bring her to our home. He said he was leaving. Mom was crying and I just . . . I found out the woman's pregnant."

She was on the verge of tears now, and my heart sank as she started to cry. "She was probably in her midtwenties, having a kid with a guy who is thirty years older. If Drake was there he would've known what to do or say. Dad left with her."

Jasmine sniffled and wiped her eyes with the heels of her hands. I reached over to the coffee table to get her a tissue, which she gladly used to blow her nose. I couldn't fathom how she must've been feeling for the past weeks about everything happening to and around her.

"How about we all have a peaceful day? No dads, no Sams," Andrew suggested. "Just us three. How it used to be."

Jasmine wrinkled her nose. "Have you showered lately?"

Andrew shrugged. "When you feel like completing missions on a variety of video games and you feel like the walking dead, showering is the last thing on a person's mind." Andrew handed each of us a controller. "I'm going to kick both of your asses."

"With that injury? How?" Jasmine snorted at my words, her spirits lifted a bit. I reached over and grasped her hand. "Wait, how are you feeling, though?"

"Honestly, I feel betrayed by everything he did." She raised the controller. "Let's go?"

"Jas." I stopped her with my hand on her arm. "You sure you don't want to talk about it any further? We're here if you want to talk."

Jasmine objected, eyes on the television. "No more talking. Let's just play."

~

The one Saturday I didn't have to volunteer at the rec center and Cedric was sleeping through the afternoon, I stood outside of my house with my group of friends, arguing about where to go, when Sam nudged me. "Let's go skydiving."

He was too close for me to think clearly about his joke. Caleb pointed at me and Sam. "You know I still can't believe that you two went go-karting without me," Caleb muttered and Jasmine's eyes went to me. She'd been staying over at my house. Her voice was less raspy, and she was a little more upbeat.

"Let's go to the mall," Stevie proposed.

I groaned loudly. "No. Not the mall."

Justin came out of the house and onto the porch with Christian Cahill, who spotted Stevie. "Stevie, I didn't know you came around here," he said.

"I didn't know you came around here either," she said, sounding displeased. Sam chuckled behind me at the interaction. "Anyway, who votes for shopping?" Almost everyone raised their hand.

Caleb grinned, everyone piling into cars before I had a chance to protest. Justin and Christian went back into the house and Sam grabbed my arm, pulling me over to his car. *Out of all people.* "No Caleb this time?" I asked.

"He has a new topic to discuss and I'm not ready to get into another debate with him about it."

"What's it on?" I pulled the hood of my sweater over my head as I got into his car.

"Something about food," he muttered. As we drove away from the house he nudged my camera bag. "What? No picture? I expect at least ten pictures of myself whenever I'm with you, Hazel."

Pulling my camera out of the bag, I turned it on, the first photo staring back at me was, of course, a picture of him. *Stop. Looking. At. Him.*

I cleared my throat. "Just ten?"

"A hundred, thousands, take as many as you like," he teased, reaching over to poke me with one hand. I squirmed, pushing his hand away. "Don't lie. You like spending time with me."

He wasn't wrong.

~

Whenever we hung out as a group outside of school it was always good time. That was probably because the boys planned it and I went along with it. Usually, it resulted in food and my basement. When Jasmine and Stevie planned outings, it was usually the mall or a clothing store. They picked places I wasn't ever fond of going.

"It's just a store," Jasmine said like always.

"I'm not setting foot in it," I said, wishing I was anywhere but here. Even Cedric couldn't save me. He had texted me the night before after he had come back from a rugby game about how tired he was. And when he slept, he slept like the dead. "I can't handle the whole '*You have to buy this,*' and '*You have to try this on.*' I'm not a shopper."

I mimicked her voice and she hit me lightly on the arm. "I don't sound like that."

Sam threw an arm around my shoulder. "Buy one thing."

There was no way he was going to know how much he was starting to affect me. Or how overwhelmed I became at our proximity. "You guys do what you want to do, and I will go see a movie." Jasmine was ready to protest but my hands went to her shoulders to stop her. "Remember, Jasmine, you're you and I'm me. There's a big difference."

Sam pointed at one of the mannequins in summer clothing. "You'd look great in that."

He needed to stop. The whole complimenting and flirting thing used to be funny, but now it was making my head spin. "I'll meet up with you guys later. Have fun."

"Macy." Stevie and Jasmine both grabbed my arm and I sighed.

"Fine, but if the guys make a suggestion for me to try something on like last time then I'm out."

I didn't last three seconds.

The second we set foot into the first store, Caleb sauntered over with clothing in his hands and I rushed out, hitting him away. I walked toward the movie theaters as a last resort.

"Hazel." Sam's voice had me stop in my tracks as I pulled the hood off my head. "What movie are we watching?" He followed me onto the escalator. *We?*

"I don't know." I couldn't imagine sitting next to him in a dark theater. He'd make comments like I usually did but it'd be too tense; he'd notice me acting strange.

"You're not watching a romance."

"No, I'm not."

"How about a scary movie?"

"*Sam.*" I scowled, knowing he'd suggest that to spite me.

"Let's go somewhere else if there's nothing you want to see here."

"Where to?"

"I don't know," he muttered. "I wasn't planning on going to the mall but we're here now."

"What were you planning? Go-karting again? Or are we going to get food?" For us, food was habitual. "Or were you going to fly us all to England?"

"The gang in my hometown?" He shook his head at the thought. "Might cause a riot."

"Bookstore?" I dashed into the bookstore in front of us.

Heading to the teen section, I let my hands skim along the bookcase and spines of books. "Macy Anderson," a voice behind me said.

Oh. God. *Michael.* One of his teammates stood next to him. "What are you doing here?"

"It's illegal to be at the mall?"

"What are you doing here?" I repeated.

"Picking a present for my sister." *How nice for someone so rude.* "Are they allowing you to play in the tournament?"

"Why wouldn't they?"

He got in my face and his friend pulled him back before he could start something with me. "It's the *male* tournament."

"And I'm on the *male* team," I snapped.

"Hazel." Sam appeared, taking note of my annoyance. His gaze grew harsh at the sight of Michael.

"You two?" Michael looked stunned. "You're dating Cahill? You sure you want to do that?"

"Michael, go," I demanded. He didn't say another word, glaring at us before he and his friend walked away.

After getting my books, we went to a bakery. By the time we had paid for our food, and were sitting down, his phone started buzzing. "Your fans?" Sam chuckled but my curiosity didn't stop. "Why don't you actually connect with one of them? Have a relationship? There's bound to be a girl you like, right?"

He raised an eyebrow. "We're really having this conversation? Okay, let's pretend that I'm dating you."

"Excuse me?" My heart skipped a beat.

"Only pretending." There was a smirk on his face. "You're nervous." My fidgeting fingers proved him correct. "You're scared what would happen if my cousin wasn't in the picture? As if none of the girls on my phone existed?"

I avoided his green eyes. "I'm not scared of that."

"I don't deserve to have a girl who would waste her time with me. She could do much better than be with a guy who consistently gets in trouble. Who doesn't know what the hell he's doing. When all he wants to do is go to the past and change things but he can't. The same way you can't prevent your mum from getting into that accident and the same way he couldn't stop the accident that killed his sister."

Sam glanced at my camera hanging around my neck in its sling. "Because we live in the present and your camera holds memories we can go back to when we can't go back to that moment anymore."

My phone buzzed in my pocket and I recoiled in surprise, blinking frantically. I put a hand over my bouncing knee as I read a text from Jasmine telling us to meet them in the food court in a couple of minutes. Sam's attention went to his phone as if our conversation never took place. Did he say that because he sensed that I felt something for him?

Draining my lemonade in record time, I reached into the mini donuts Sam and I were sharing and touched his hand. My hand moved his away, "Give it to me. It's the last one."

"No." He pushed my hand away. He yelped as I pinched his muscled arm.

Sam looked behind me. "What the hell is Andrew doing?" I turned to look but Andrew wasn't there—only some people in line to get coffee.

A victorious Sam chewed on the last donut. "You're a jerk," I uttered, stealing his lemonade.

"Tell me something I don't know."

18
FLYING LEMURS

Sam barely spoke to me during practice or school. On Wednesday, Caleb said Sam was at home. I had a feeling the conversation at the mall had something to do with it.

After school, Cedric and I headed over to his house, and now we were in the music room as he showed off his talent on drums, his feet tapping along with the beat.

"Why weren't you in band?" I asked from where I sat on the ottoman.

"I wanted to play my own thing on the side. We all play a bit of something in the family, I guess." I stood up as he handed the drumsticks to me, as if I could get in touch with some nonexistent musical abilities.

At the side was the guitar I had seen Sam with one day, along with an electric one on its stand. The other side of the room was an open space with a drum set, a bass guitar hanging on the wall, and a keyboard standing in the corner. By the time Cedric had agreed that drums were most definitely not my thing, I told him I was heading to the bathroom. I went upstairs but my feet took me to the door that, like Cedric's door, had the occupant's name on a plaque.

The door flung open after I knocked, revealing a shirtless and confused Sam. He was sweaty, breathing irregularly with a skipping rope in his hands. My eyes dropped to his abdomen as a smirk played on his lips. "If I'd known I could get that reaction, I'd have shown up to school like this."

"I need to talk to you."

His relaxed posture irritated me. "We're talking."

I pushed past him. Soccer posters and a few musical artists in smaller photos hung on the wall. Trophies he had accumulated over the years were placed upon a bookshelf that also held several books and video game cases. His room wasn't clean, his big bed wasn't made, and the couch parallel to the mounted TV had a bunch of clothes on it.

"Why are you ignoring me?"

He went over to his dresser and pulled out a shirt. "I'm just giving you some space."

I furrowed my eyebrows. "Why?"

"With my reputation around school and stuff, I didn't want to influence you."

Huh? "You think this *now*? After all that time you spent on becoming my friend? Was this because of our talk at the mall?" Of course it was.

"Hazel, I didn't mean to give you the impression that I was ignoring you. I just needed to think things through."

"Why weren't you at school?"

"I was in a bit of pain and my aunt suggested I stay home. At least this black eye is leaving." He pointed to the fading discoloration around his eye.

"Noted," I murmured. If I stayed in his room any longer, near him looking like that—I didn't know what to think. "I'll leave you to whatever you were doing before I came."

"You want to see me working out? You can see me shirtless all you want." I gave him a lighthearted shove. "I'm joking. A couple minutes of talking and you're already mad at me?" *Couple minutes? No. Sam has been estimating the minutes we've been talking since I stepped in the room.*

"You don't influence me in a negative way." Sam's humorous mood faded at my serious tone. "Nor do you cause trouble around me. We *are* friends. No matter the reputation you have."

"I know."

I stepped back, allowing him to close the door. My shoulders slumped at the wooden barrier between us. Just as I reached the top of the stairs, a head of red hair came bobbing up: Ivan's fiancé.

"Hey, Natasha."

"Hey." Her eyes slid to Sam's door. "Ivan says you and Sam call yourselves *friends*."

"Yes, friends."

Natasha leaned against the railing, crossing her arms. "Ivan also has this weird idea that Sam's in love with you."

A snort escaped my lips and I headed down the stairs. "He's not."

Cedric appeared in the corridor at the bottom, a confused look on his face. He was no doubt wondering what I'd been doing upstairs.

"Everything all right?"

I nodded, saying good-bye to Natasha as I followed Cedric back to the music room.

Sam was worried he was influencing me, and I needed to convince him that he didn't have to pull away now. Not when I didn't want him to.

~

When I entered the cafeteria the following day, I could see that Caleb was the first at our table. "Happy birthday!" I was wrapped in a strong hug as the rest of my friends filed in, taking their seats. When Caleb let go, I bent over to catch my breath but his energy added to my cheery. "Don't be dramatic. It wasn't that strong of a hug."

"At least you didn't attempt to punch me like my brother and Andrew did this morning," I said, rethinking my birthday traditions with those two.

"That doesn't sound promising," Cedric said behind me as he pulled me into a gentler hug. "I'll see you after school, yeah?"

"It's a date," Caleb responded on my behalf, knowing that it was just meant to be a good time with him and my friends at my house.

Cedric shot me a grin and headed over to his friends. As my friends discussed tonight's plans, Sam tapped me on the shoulder. He nodded for me to follow him out the doors.

"Get your sweater." He didn't allow me to say another word as we exited the cafeteria. "You'll be back for third period, I promise. Meet me at the front."

~

Tightening the strings on my hoodie, I exited the school doors. The sun hidden behind the clouds on this March day would've saddened my mood if Sam hadn't held two helmets in his hands. He was excited, judging by his restless nature, while I was confused by his state. He grabbed a hold of my hand, pulled me farther down the front of the school, and there it was, parked by the curb. "Told you it exists."

"No way." I was in awe, and reached out to touch his motorcycle. The material was smooth against my skin as my hand glided over the seat before moving to the handles.

Sam handed me one of the helmets. "Want to go for a ride?"

"You're joking with me?" I put it on as he grinned at my excitement. "Holy—"

"—flying lemurs?" he suggested.

"Does it have a name?"

"BS." And like Benjamin Ian the Great, I realized what BS stood for. Sam put his helmet on, getting on the bike. I followed, my hands on his shoulders. Grabbing my hands, he pulled them around his waist, making sure I was hugging him tightly from behind. "Don't let go."

A scream left me when we moved—I held on to Sam as he gripped the handlebars. The scenery whipped by us as we rode through the less busy suburban streets. The gust of cold hair was constant as it went through my sweater, only egging me to hold on to Sam tighter each time he made a turn. He was focused on handling the vehicle yet I felt exhilarated every time he accelerated the motorcycle, leaning in with the motion. My eyes fell shut for a moment, and I didn't want this to end. Then we stopped suddenly. He patted my arms around him and I opened my eyes. "You okay?"

"That was sick." I took off my helmet and got off when I realized he had circled us back to the school area, down the street from the diner. "Dude, bring it around tonight. Wait, you're coming over, right?"

"I'll be there." He took his helmet off and got off the bike.

"Cedric's coming too," I reminded him.

"I know. Don't worry. Nothing will ruin your day," he promised. Sam opened the storage compartment of his motorcycle. A wrapped medium-sized box was thrust in my direction. "Happy birthday."

I took off the wrapping paper and opened the lid of the cardboard box. Inside was a camera. A very *new* camera. The box dropped as I took it out, staring at it with awe. "I know you like forest green and I got it customized. You don't have to like it—I mean . . . there's a receipt."

The tight embrace I give him released a shaky laugh from his lips and he reciprocated, wrapping his arms around me. "This wasn't that big of a deal, Hazel."

"Are you kidding me? Thank you."

He let go of me, rubbing the back of his neck. "I have something else."

He reached into his pocket and drew out a velvet box. A silver necklace was inside, the pendant a glittery soccer ball. The white and black parts were held together tightly by beads. It was a similar pendant to the one my mom wore in every picture I had with her in it.

"You said you never found the necklace after your mum died. I thought you would like to have your own, or at least a necklace that was similar."

No words could express my gratitude for his generosity.

He knew that when he removed the necklace and turned me around. Placing the cool metal against my collarbone, he clicked the clasp, pushing my hair over my shoulders to expose the necklace, the action itself making my head hazy and hands clammy.

I turned around, fully aware of his hands on my arms. His eyes looked conflicted, flickering down then back up. He moved closer. Or I moved closer.

I didn't know what would've happened if a group of people hadn't suddenly come out of the diner. My heart seemed to thud harder as I stepped away from him, picking up the camera box and putting the velvet case inside. Tucking the box under my arm, I said, "Want to grab food to bring to the group?"

Sam looked confused but nevertheless, he agreed. Even as we made our way inside the diner, a part of me hoped that he knew he wasn't the only one who regretted the interruption.

~

My friends and brother crowded my basement later that evening. Dad was prepared for me to have "the best night ever" and we stood at the foot of the basement stairs listening to my friends argue over what movie we were going to watch. Stevie groaned, stopping Caleb and Jacob from trying to control the laptop connected to the TV.

"Macy, you got to pick a movie," Stevie said.

My arms went up in defense. "Nope, you guys decide."

"You're the birthday girl," Andrew said from where he and Austin were playing air hockey. "Pick a movie."

"Okay." Justin was sitting between Sam and Jasmine on the couch. I forced myself not to look at Sam, focusing on my brother. There was no mention between Sam and me about what happened earlier today. Maybe that moment didn't happen the way I thought it had. Maybe we didn't almost kiss. "Justin, you pick."

Justin took over the laptop as Dad went upstairs to answer the doorbell for the pizza delivery.

Sam and Cedric hadn't acknowledged each other and I still felt the tension between them. There was no sight of a potential fight, and how civil they were despite being in the same room with each other for the past hour made me relax.

"Can we talk?" Cedric asked me.

"Yeah." The two of us headed upstairs, leaving my friends, who were still arguing about the movie. As my dad was paying the pizza man at the door, I pulled Cedric up to my room.

Closing the door behind us, I said, "More privacy. My friends can be extremely nosy, like my dad and brother. Whatever you want to tell me, make it quick before they find out we're gone."

Cedric reached into the pocket of his sweater and handed me a box. "Happy birthday."

The action made me freeze at the similarity between him and his cousin. I took the box from Cedric, opening it up to see a charm bracelet inside. Small silver stars dangled from the bracelet and that made it more beautiful. He put it on for me and as I moved my wrist, we watched it jangle. "I love it. Thank you."

When he kissed me, for that moment before the nosiest people in my life, Jon Ming, Austin, and my brother, attempted to burst into my room, I knew that with Cedric in front of me, there should be no reason for me to think about Sam. At least, that was what I tried to convince myself.

19

THIS ISN'T SOME WRESTLING MATCH

The following Tuesday, I was standing at my locker after school talking with Jasmine, who was about to go to one of her student club meetings. Caleb and Jon Ming were next to us practicing Spanish when Austin, Jacob, and Brandon came up to us, looking ready for practice. "What's everyone doing during the break?" Jacob asked.

Everyone was listing their plans when Sam appeared beside me, startling me. "Stop doing that," I said, my hand over my heart.

"Did you know that Sam was on a math team back in England?" Caleb mentioned. Sam scowled as the boys entertained the topic.

"They're idiots," Jasmine said.

I shot her a grin. "They're *our* idiots." She linked her arm with mine as we headed in the direction of the gym, passing a group of people. Beatrice was among them, and her eyes lingered on Jasmine's for a moment before she continued her conversation. I hadn't seen Beatrice and Jasmine interact since that day weeks ago. I nudged Jasmine. "You okay?"

"I'll see you at your place." She unlinked our arms and headed down the hallway.

The interaction was still on my mind later that day as Jasmine ran a comb through my hair in my room. Or at least tried to. "Do you brush this thing?" she asked.

"This *thing* is attached to my head," I defended myself, wincing. After practice today, Jasmine had come over, a duffel bag of clothes indicating that she was staying the night.

She huffed, dropping the comb on my desk I was sitting in front of. "I'm done. I can't work like this."

I pulled my long hair around my shoulder, my bracelet jangling on my wrist. "I should get a haircut."

"With a haircut you need to get layers," Jasmine advised as she lay on her stomach on my bed. "Untangle those knots, get rid of the many split ends, and maybe you can get highlights."

"Jas, we agreed that you can comb my hair," I said as I went through my closet. "Not make suggestions for me to find a way of ruining it."

"You're *not* going to ruin it," she groaned. "You're stubborn."

I grabbed a large sweatshirt, throwing it over my T-shirt as Jasmine objected. "I'm not allowing you to leave the house, let alone have your boyfriend see you like that."

She stood and ransacked my closet before throwing over some different clothes. Staring at the outfits she picked, I sighed, the sudden memory of the way Beatrice had looked at me, the way she and her posse had looked at me for years appearing in my head. "Jas, I know a lot of things are going on but—"

"No," she said abruptly. "Don't talk about it."

"You can't let Beatrice get to you."

Her eyebrows furrowed as she stood. "That's hypocritical."

"How?"

"You let her get to you all the time," Jasmine exclaimed.

"*No.*"

"*Yes,*" she argued. "She makes you feel insecure when it comes to you being yourself, but what she says to me? Especially when you're not around? When *no one* is around so it's my word against hers and I know I'll lose every time? It's not the same, Mace. Don't let her get to me? Don't let her get to *you.*"

"She doesn't."

"Yes, she does," Jasmine continued. "Every single time she calls you names and says bullshit. She's obviously wrong but you still let her get to you."

"Okay, what about you? What about what she says to you?" I countered, taking a step toward her. She sounded frustrated, which made me frustrated as I continued, "Dude, there's a lot of stuff going on with you right now. From her to your dad—"

"*Stop.*"

"No." Jasmine had been trying to push everything away for a long time. "These things are clearly affecting you and you never want to speak about it. I was shocked that you even told me what was happening with Beatrice because you always do this. From why you and Andrew kept fighting to your parents—don't you think it's an issue?"

"You're not going to understand anyway, why the hell would I even tell you?"

"Because we're best friends!"

"Best friends don't push people into doing things they don't want to do." Her tone was rising but her hypocrisy set me off.

"You do it to me all the time! From the second I started dating Cedric you've been making me wear clothes I hate wearing—"

"*Not* the same thing," she stated firmly, getting up and packing her things.

"Jasmine, you're doing it right now."

"I don't care."

"Fine, leave then," I huffed. "You always do anyway." Jasmine didn't waste time as she grabbed her things and left the room, and a minute later the front door slammed.

~

Jasmine and I avoided each other for the remaining days until the break. Andrew didn't take much notice, unaware of the tension between us even though she never sat with us or came near me, saying she was busy.

The other guys didn't notice either—except for one. When Austin wondered aloud where Jasmine was, Sam immediately shot me a look, but he didn't pressure me into telling him what had happened.

When the doorbell rang on a dull Thursday evening, I opened the door to find standing on the other side the only person who would definitely know what had happened. *Drake*. "She told you."

"You guys are better than this." Drake had seen us get into arguments over the years over stupid things. Not one like this.

"*She's* the one who's not talking."

"Have you ever thought that maybe she needs her friend while everything is happening around her?"

"She keeps pushing me away," I said. "Why are you here? Don't you have school?"

"I came to visit Jas before she went off to our aunt's because I have Fridays off. Macy, she doesn't know how to deal with all the shit that's happening in our family—"

A familiar motorcycle pulled up in front of the house. Sam took his helmet off as he got off the bike and walked toward us. However, when Sam's eyes fell on Drake, his good mood dropped. I'd never introduced them to each other but I guess I didn't have to.

Drake cleared his throat nervously. "Sam."

"Why are you here?" Sam asked him.

"I should be asking *you* that question," Drake answered dryly, his confidence rearing up.

"I don't have any reason to answer you."

Drake's eyes looked up to the sky before locking again on Sam. "I haven't seen you in over two years, Sam."

"What?" My question was unheard, the boys too caught up in whatever tension they had with each other. "How do you two even know each other?"

"Drake dated Bethany two summers ago," Sam muttered. *Oh.* Although Drake and I were close, he never shared who he was dating. "And then he broke her heart."

"Sam," Drake said. "It was long ago. She was going back to England. I wasn't going to do long distance when I was going to leave for university anyway."

"Yeah, but she loved you. A lot, and you led her on."

"You think I felt nothing for her?" Drake sighed. "Sam, you have to—"

Sam's fist curled. "What you're trying to say doesn't mean shit."

"*Okay.*" This was escalating, and I was getting scared about where it could lead. "Sam, back off."

Drake kept talking. "Yes, I admit, I didn't end things on the right note but—"

"Stop talking, Drake," Sam urged.

"Even I—" That's when the curled fist connected with Drake's face, knocking him to the front lawn.

Sam jumped on him, furiously punching him in the face multiple times. My feet were frozen, my mind in a state of shock at the scene before me. Drake eventually found the upper hand and pushed Sam off him. Drake's lip was split, and Sam was breaking free of his grasp. I suddenly came to my senses just as Sam turned the tables again, and ran over, trying to pull Sam off Drake.

"Sam, stop, you're hurting him! Dude!" I managed to push Sam off Drake but Sam tried to get at Drake again. "Would you *fucking* stop?!"

Sam's lips parted, his shock apparent at the word that had come out of my mouth. Both of them immediately stopped fighting.

"Get off him." My voice was shaky, trying to comprehend what I had witnessed.

Sam got up carefully. "You don't understand."

"You're upset. I get that, but that doesn't give you the right to beat the crap out of him. This isn't some wrestling match." I stopped him from moving closer to me. "Leave."

His eyes widened. "Hazel."

"*Go.*"

"You don't mean that." He tried to move closer to me but I pushed him back with both hands.

I didn't mean that. "Give me space, okay?"

He hesitated. "I'm sorry." He walked past me and down the sidewalk to his bike. He put the helmet on, inserted the key in the ignition, and rode off.

Regaining my stance and ignoring the drops of blood on the grass, I went back inside my house and headed to the kitchen, where Drake was sitting on the counter, wetting a paper towel to wipe off the blood. I left the room momentarily to get antiseptic from the bathroom. When I returned, I handed the bottle to him and he opened it up, putting the liquid on a paper towel.

"I hope you don't have to get stitches." Drake was cleaning his lip, hissing at the pain.

"I'm okay," he assured me. "I'm not calling the cops or anything."

"You dated his sister?"

"For a short time one summer," he explained. "It didn't end well—the breakup didn't go well. She was upset and in turn that got Sam upset. He's never really forgotten about it."

"He didn't have to do that."

"I haven't seen him since that summer. Or her. That was the last I heard of her before, you know, the accident." He sighed. "I'm going to head out. Have a good break, Mace."

Drake left, the conversation about Jasmine apparently forgotten, and I went to my room.

Later that night, I was texting Cedric about his upcoming trip to Bali when someone knocked on my bedroom door.

"Macy?" Dad opened the door and walked in, still in his

work clothes—a gray suit but sans his black shoes—and plopped down on the bed beside me. "You had a rough day?"

I told him what happened. My dad looked amused. "You swore?"

I sat up. "*That's* all you got out of that story?"

"I'm sorry, it's just hard to believe. You made a vow when you were eleven that you would never swear. This is *gold*."

"Because Sam wouldn't listen and he was being a jackass."

My dad raised his eyebrows at my second slipup. "Sam hurt Drake, huh?"

"He should have spoken with Drake instead of lashing out," I said. "I don't even know what that was about. I can't forgive him for that."

"Eventually, you will."

"Why do you think that?" I asked before he stepped out the door.

"Because I know you will," Dad said. "And because you haven't taken off the necklace he gave you."

20
DO YOU HAVE WI-FI?

I didn't get my height from my mom's side of the family.

Justin, Dad, and I stood in the suburban neighborhood of my maternal grandmother's house on Saturday morning. My brother and I both held large duffel bags filled with clothes for the week. Our grandmother treated us to a smile, her hazel eyes bright.

Nonna hugged me. "Macy, you look tall from down here!" She moved to Justin, grasping him in a hug. "I haven't seen you two in so long. Macy, last time I saw you, you were dressed in the most boyish clothing for a girl."

"Good to know some things haven't changed," Justin muttered as I swatted him on the back of the head.

We stepped inside the comforting house with its wooden floors and beige walls, some adorned with photos. The air even smelled like lavender. Nonna grinned at Dad, who lingered on the threshold. "Nick, how have you been?"

"I've been good." They exchanged a hug and I struggled to recall the last time I had seen them in a room together. "How about you?"

"I've been great." She held him at arms' length. "It's good to see you."

Dad's grin softened. "It's good to see you too. When you play board games or card games? Don't go easy on them."

"I never will," Nonna promised. "They're my grandkids."

Dad laughed, turning to us. "Be good to your grandmother, all right?"

"We will be," I promised him.

After Dad left, Nonna turned to me and Justin. "Have you two eaten? I'll make food. But first, let's get you to your rooms."

We climbed the stairs and Justin spoke up. "Nonna, do you have Wi-Fi?"

Nonna waved a hand. "I don't need the internet. I have cable."

My brother gasped. *Drama queen.* "I have to go a week without internet?" Nonna and I ignored him and she gestured for me to open my door.

The walls were a neutral beige color. From the double bed to the desk to the bookshelf to the pictures in frames and posters of bands, anyone could tell that the person who'd owned this room had been organized.

"This was her room," Nonna said behind me. "There were some days Lauren barely left it, and just sat reading on that window seat."

Lauren Jessica Anderson. There was a picture of her on the desk, in which she was dribbling a soccer ball on a field. Nonna picked it up and held it for a moment before setting it down. She shot me a comforting smile before leaving and closing the door behind her.

I found a scrapbook in one of the drawers. There were multiple pictures of her and my dad before they'd gotten married. Suddenly, Justin opened the door, eyes wide as he surveyed the room. "Wow. It's like she's right here."

Justin opened the drawers one by one, grabbing the first thing he could find and lifting it to his nose, inhaling.

"What are you doing?"

"Shh, I'm trying to make this moment last—I think I can smell her on this T-shirt." I snorted and Justin looked at me, confused. "What?"

"You're smelling a sports bra."

My brother dropped it like it was on fire.

"Kids, I've got your dinner ready!" Nonna yelled from downstairs.

Looking down at my phone as Justin left the room, I saw Sam's name was near the top of my text messages. I shouldn't feel anything for him. He was too impulsive. There was no way I should want to be with someone like that. I was supposed to be giving him the silent treatment, but all I wanted to do was talk to him.

~

"That was good." I fell back in my chair, hands on my stomach.

"I could tell since you wolfed it down." My face grew warm and Nonna laughed even louder. "Don't worry about that. Your grandfather would have eaten this every night if he could have. He never got tired of it."

The mention of my grandfather reminded me how much the house had probably changed for Nonna since he and Mom passed. I couldn't fathom how much grief she had endured for the last decade. Once we were done eating, I took the dishes and washed the plates. Justin wandered into the kitchen, grabbing an apple from the fruit basket on the counter.

"What's that you have there?" Nonna asked as I dried my hands.

She moved her glasses from the top of her head to the bridge of her nose, her eyes on my necklace. Justin answered. "It's a gift from her *friend*."

Nonna examined the pendant. She'd recognize the similarity to the other necklace. "If he gave you something like this, I'm guessing he's more than a friend."

"He's just a friend," I said. "Nothing more." She looked at me like she no more believed that than I did.

~

On Sunday afternoon, Justin, Nonna, and I sat on the porch in thick sweaters playing card games. "Do you have any threes?" Justin asked me.

"We're not playing that game. No wonder we call you Patrick."

"I wasn't listening." He pointed to his earphones. I yanked them out of his ears and he yelped. "That's why we call you Sandy, except you're not a squirrel that loves karate, you're a violent sister."

The revving of an engine grew louder as a car entered the small driveway. Two girls got out and walked toward the steps. I took note of how one was definitely older than the other, possibly around my age, and the other was probably Justin's age. They were clearly sisters, with olive skin, brown hair, and brown eyes. The younger one walked ahead, far friendlier than her sister. The older one carried herself as if she was better than everyone.

I didn't like her.

"Emma, you're here!" Nonna exclaimed. "Nice to see you, Alexis. These are my grandchildren, Macy and Justin."

"What do you think of town?" Emma asked us.

"We haven't seen much yet," Justin said.

Nonna clapped her hands. "How about Emma and Alexis show you guys around?"

Emma perked up. "Yeah, we can show you around."

Alexis's conceited eyes were on me as she scanned my sweater. "You sure you don't want to change first?"

She wore a brown leather jacket, combat boots, and leggings. Grabbing my phone and camera bag, which held my camera and wallet, I wasn't going to let her get to me. "No, I'm good."

As Alexis walked toward the car, Emma sighed. "Sorry, my sister is just—"

"I know her type, trust me," I assured her.

In Alexis's car, Emma told Justin and me about the area, pointing out her favorite stores along the way. There was a tiny mall Emma wanted to show us—the second we got out of the car in the not-so-busy parking lot, Alexis walked off.

"You and your sister don't get along, huh?"

"We do, she's just a major drama queen," Emma explained. "It's getting worse because this guy has just come back and she wanted to see him, then found out she had to spend the day with me. Since her plans changed, she's going to be in a bad mood."

"Let's eat," Justin proposed once we got inside. He and Emma talked as I flicked through photos on my phone. Alexis joined us once again, taking the seat across from me. Emma offered to show Justin where the bathrooms were, and the two of them left as I found a picture of Sam I had taken at the quarry. I pulled up another picture I had taken of Cedric after one of the matches I had attended a while ago. He was in his rugby uniform.

"Stalking a boy you'll never have?" There was a smirk on Alexis's face. I locked my phone and placed it on the table, glad my brightness was on low.

"It's my boyfriend."

"You have a boyfriend?" Now she was getting on my last nerve. "How would you know what it's like to have someone fall in love with you?"

"Why don't you focus on the guy you think loves you instead of *my* business?" I suggested. "I can tell that he probably doesn't."

I got my answer from her offended expression. "Yes, he does."

"Then how come he hasn't told you that?" I guessed, knowing that I was right.

"You don't know what you're talking about."

Her obvious denial fueled me to keep talking. "You have no idea about how he feels about you. We both know that."

Justin and Emma came back to the table. Justin gave me a look as he took in Alexis's flustered face. Once we were all done, Emma and Justin didn't stop talking on the way back.

When we get to the familiar street, over at a house near Nonna's, someone was getting out of their car. A car I knew. The door of that car opened and Alexis parked next to the sidewalk, jumping out. She ran over and Emma said, "That's who my sister is desperately in love with."

Sam.

He closed the car door, pocketing his keys. Alexis caught him off guard, wrapping her arms around his neck in a tight hug. He returned the hug equally eagerly. Then his green eyes locked with mine through the window, and my heart dropped all the way to my stomach.

Even so, Sam didn't look fazed. He let Alexis go and walked toward me. But I got out of the car and headed straight into Nonna's house. I didn't want to see or talk to him. Locking my mom's bedroom door behind me, I took a deep breath. "What the hell?"

What is he even doing here? How the hell does he know Alexis—no, why is he here?

The realization hit me. Cedric said his grandmother lived in Redmond. Redmond wasn't as big of a city as Port Meadow, but it was a pretty freaky coincidence that our grandmothers would live on the same street.

This week was meant for me to have space from Port Meadow—from him, especially. I was going to forgive him for what he'd done to Drake, but now was too soon.

~

A few hours later, there was a knock at my door. "Macy Victoria Marie Anderson"—well at least *someone* got it right—"you've been cooped in that room all day. Get out now."

My grandmother sounded like she would kick the door down. Not taking any chances, I opened the door. Her eyes softened at my tired appearance. "We're having dinner with Lucy."

"Lucy?"

"Lucy's my friend. She wanted to meet my grandkids."

"I'll wear something decent."

The doorbell rang moments later as I came downstairs. Nonna's voice yelled from the kitchen, "Justin, can you get that?"

"Macy, can you get that?" Justin shouted.

I opened the door to see a motherly woman who was around the same age as Nonna, but taller. Her face looked familiar. "You must be Macy."

"You must be Lucy. Nice to meet you." She entered the house and she and Nonna greeted each other as best friends do. As Nonna was taking her coat, the doorbell rang again.

I opened it to see Sam standing in front of me, wearing his leather jacket unzipped and dark jeans, his necklace tucked under his plaid button-up. His green eyes were wary, as if I was about to attack. *What is he doing here?*

Sam walked in, closing and locking the door behind him before he took off his leather jacket and hung it on the coatrack. "Sam," I stammered. "You can't just . . . why are you . . ."

He ignored me, walking instead into the dining area where my grandmother joyfully greeted him with a hug. "Sam! Looking as handsome as ever. I was just telling your grandma that I couldn't wait to see you again."

Again? Sam winked at her. "Look at *me*? You're looking as young and fit as ever."

"Sit, sit, how are your cousins? The family? Your brother, Greg?"

Sam and I sat down, with him across from me as Nonna fetched him a plate. "They're all fine; Dad and Mum send their love. Mum said this summer when they come to Canada, they'd definitely like to meet you." They became engaged in a conversation quickly. Too quickly.

I barely talked through dinner, watching Sam interact with

my brother and our grandmothers easily. Justin kept giving me confused looks across the table. He was probably wondering if I'd known Sam was coming. I tried to convey that I was as surprised as Justin was.

When we finished, Justin and Sam volunteered to wash the plates and I trudged upstairs to my room. I changed out of my jeans into sweatpants and sat at Mom's desk, completely perplexed.

Sam let himself in, closing and leaning against the door.

"I thought you'd be in Bali with your family. Why are you here? *How* are you here?"

"Bali would just mean tension with my uncle," Sam said. "I decided to spend spring break here with my grandmother instead."

I sat there, saying nothing.

"I came up here during Christmas break in December with Caleb for a few days," he continued. "I met your grandmother a few times. She's really nice."

That made sense. "And Alexis?"

"Emma and Alexis are old family friends. Every summer, we Cahills come here for at least two weeks to spend time with our grandmother. Emma loved giving her company and they live in the area. We all spent time together growing up." He ran a hand through his hair, taking a deep breath.

Our grandmothers were friends. Living in Redmond and only a few houses from each other. "How coincidental," I mumbled.

"You're mad."

"At your grandmother for living close by? No."

Sam huffed. "At me being here and what happened between me and Drake."

I sat forward. "I was shocked by how violent, especially when—"

"Especially when I knew you were there," he whispered.

"I understand that you were upset, I just . . ." I trailed off, not knowing how to end that sentence.

"I'm sorry you saw me like that."

"If Drake wants me to forgive you then fine. I'm doing it for him, not for you."

The bruises on his knuckles were purple. He sighed heavily, pushing himself off the door. He grabbed my hands, pulling me from my seat to lead me to the bed. When we sat down, he asked, "You were scared, weren't you? I'm sorry."

"I know." Our arms pressed against each other as I continued, "Every time I've seen you like that, you've had a reason. It's not like you're going to end up hurting your family or your friends, but you've got to keep yourself in check. And Drake is my friend."

"I know," he mumbled. "I just—I don't want to hurt you."

"I don't think you would do that," I said. "You need to control yourself the way you control a soccer ball."

"Football."

"It's the same thing." When he shifted to face me, his eyes were twinkling with amusement. A part of me tried to deny that I was happy he was here. The good feeling didn't fade even when his grandmother called his name from downstairs.

Sam sighed. "I'll see you tomorrow?"

I nodded and he took one look at me before leaving, closing the door on his way out.

"*Fuck*," I muttered.

21
COMPLICATED

The doorbell rang the following morning as Justin and I were finishing breakfast. My brother raced to the door and a moment later he and Emma entered the kitchen. "Hi, Macy. I'm guessing you know Sam?"

Before shoving another piece of bacon in my mouth, I said to Emma, "We go to school together back in Port Meadow."

"Emma, show Justin that game system we have in the basement," Nonna said.

When they headed downstairs, Nonna sat down opposite me. "Is Sam the 'friend' Justin was talking about?"

"Yes."

"Who gave you that charm bracelet hidden under your sweater?"

"His cousin, Cedric, gave me that."

She got up and I exhaled at the end of her questioning. "Lucy called me to say you should go over and wait for Sam to come down."

After closing the front door behind me, I held my camera bag close as I made my way down the street to Sam's grandmother's house, lifting the hood of my windbreaker over my head as light rain fell from the sky. I was about to knock on the door when it swung open and Sam appeared. "Did you decide to wear the same color as me or are we becoming one of *those* couples?"

We were both wearing the same shade of blue. But he shouldn't have used that word. My face was probably red when Sam said, "How can I help you?"

"Didn't you say you wanted to hang out today?"

He smirked. "I knew you wouldn't last a week without me."

"Please, you're the one begging for me to talk to you."

"You're right, I would beg all day if I had to. Doesn't mean you wouldn't either."

"What are—" I cleared my throat, suddenly shy. "What are we doing today?"

"Sam!" a voice called behind me.

We both looked at Alexis, whose hair was in a high ponytail and who was wearing a light jacket and jeans. Wedges clomping up the steps, she walked up to him, ignoring me completely. "Hey."

"Hey, Lexi." *Of course there's a nickname.*

"We were going out today, remember?"

Oh. "Oh shit," Sam mumbled.

"I'll see you later then," I said.

"Are you sure?" He didn't budge until I assured him I was sure.

"I need to get my phone then we can go," he said to Alexis, turning back inside the house. Alexis smirked, ready to comment, but I was already walking down the steps.

Nonna was sitting on the porch when I returned. "I thought you would be with Samuel."

"Alexis has him captured in her petty little claws," I muttered, my hand tightening on my camera bag.

"Let's have a day to ourselves then."

I ran my fingers through my hair, feeling it fall near my waist. "Is there a hairdresser around here?"

~

Nonna and I sat inside a little coffee shop that rainy afternoon. I played around with the straw in my lemonade, which had a slice of lemon perched on the rim of the glass.

My hair was now above the middle of my back, layered, trimmed, and washed. I felt a little exposed from the haircut, but I liked it. "You look like your mother," said Nonna. "You act like her too."

"What was she like?" I asked.

"Lauren wasn't as tall as you are." Nonna pointed and I chuckled at her teasing. She'd been mentioning my height since we'd gotten here. "She was a soccer fanatic like you, though. She spent one summer attempting to break the world record of kicking a soccer ball without it touching the ground. There's a name to that, what's it called?"

"Keep-ups," I said. "I'm going to assume that she didn't break the record."

"No, but she beat her personal best," Nonna said. "Your grandfather took her to get a new bike because of all the time she spent practicing. She was dedicated to anything she put her mind to. I'm going to assume you're the same—all your dedication to practicing since your dad mentioned something about a scout?"

"I have a tournament for a few days after the break," I explained. "They're coming from a university I applied to."

"You can be recruited for their team? Scholarship too?"

"That's what I'm hoping for. I'm kind of nervous about the idea of someone coming to an event for me. It makes the tournament a bigger deal than it originally was."

"You know your mom played soccer in college, right?"

I nodded.

"When she was in high school, we didn't know if we had enough money to send her where she wanted to go. She was relying on scholarships. She worked hard but she knew that soccer was where she was going to get most of the money. When she found out that she could be given that opportunity and that the college had an eye on her stats, she was terrified of messing up her chance. She thought she wasn't going to be good enough."

"What did she do?"

"She talked to me and your grandfather about it one night. We told her that it didn't matter how she played as long as she did her best and she loved being out there, on the field. I'm sure you can relate to that."

I knew exactly how Mom probably felt walking onto a field, determination coursing through her as she was ready to play the game. "I can."

"Just do your best, Macy," Nonna advised. "It'll be enough. I'm sure your mom would've said the same thing."

"Thanks, Nonna." The pressure on my shoulders lessened. "Can I ask you a question? Why did you leave Redmond in the first place? After Mom's funeral?"

THE BAD BOY & THE TOMBOY 233

Nonna's expression saddened. "After Lauren passed not long after your grandfather . . . sometimes home can get too much. All the memories. I went back to Italy for a while. Other places. I always knew I was going to come back. I'm glad, because I get to see you and Justin before you leave for university."

"I'm glad you came back too," I confessed.

"There's a soccer ball in the basement that your mom had," she said. "You can pump it up. There's also a few videos at the house of her old games if you want to see."

"That'd be great."

My grandmother smiled at my hopeful tone before she took a sip of her tea. "Now tell me what's going on between you and Sam."

I swirled the straw before looking up at her. "It's complicated for me."

"You two are friends?"

"Good friends."

"Lucy tells me he hasn't had many friends growing up. He and Caleb came by during the Christmas break when I was visiting Lucy. Now *that* is an entertaining young man, with all his theories, but something tells me you and Sam might be more than friends?"

"I don't know," I admitted.

"It's your decision, Macy," she said. "To decide whether you want to open your feelings toward him or ignore them until they *possibly* go away."

How easy is it to ignore them when he's closer than I expected him to be?

When we returned home from the coffee shop and the rain stopped, I grabbed the soccer ball in my mom's room, pumping it up and playing outside on the front lawn. I kept my focus on the ball I was kicking up in the air, doing my best to prevent it from touching the ground.

"You cut it." Sam stood on the sidewalk, wearing a thick hoodie. I stopped the ball. "Your hair. When? Why?"

"Earlier today. I wanted to."

Sam sat down on the grass. "It looks nice."

I continued kicking the ball up. "Isn't Alexis in your house? Your lover is probably waiting for you."

Sam looked amused. "Lover?"

"She seems infatuated with you." *She thinks you're in love with her.*

"Alexis and I have known each other for a long time. It's nothing serious."

I grabbed the soccer ball. "You might want to tell her that."

Sam followed me to the porch. "I'll see you tomorrow? It was kind of boring without you around. Who else am I going to argue with?"

"Caleb?"

"He ends up taking my side after a couple of words." He tilted his head. "So . . . tomorrow?"

"Tomorrow," I agreed. "'Night, Sam."

"'Night, Hazel." He walked down the front porch steps and to his grandmother's.

22
LIKE A HORMONAL PREGNANT WOMAN

Andrew called on Tuesday afternoon. Andrew, who'd been texting me repeatedly for the past few days. "Sorry," I said. "I've been taking a break—"

"From *everyone*? Just because you and Jasmine had a huge blowout?" At least he knew.

"I don't want to talk about it." My stomach rumbled. I had been so caught up in doing as much homework as I could in the morning that my body had decided that I should eat now that it was afternoon.

"Mace, it'll be okay," Andrew said. "Talk to her when the break's over." He didn't allow me to respond, changing the subject to prevent me from arguing. "Caleb says he has a short play he wants to show us." The mention of Caleb's name brought me back to the topic of Sam and I sucked in a breath. It didn't go unnoticed by Andrew. "What's wrong? What happened?"

"Sam's in Redmond," I explained. "Turns out our grandmothers are good friends and she lives down the street."

"That's a shitty coincidence. I don't know if the universe is on your side or not."

"I'm not sure either."

Andrew's mom's voice rang out in the background, calling his name. "I'll talk to you later," I said.

After we hung up, I went downstairs to find Justin and Emma talking on the couch in the living room.

"You missed breakfast," Nonna said. "I saved you some pancakes." She handed me a plate of pancakes and a bottle of maple syrup as I headed for the table.

I shot her a look of gratitude, and was eating quickly when she said, "I'm concerned about your digestive system."

"Dad's been saying that for years."

After I finished eating, the doorbell rang and I opened the door to Sam. "Hey," I said as I closed the door behind him. He entered the living room where Justin and Emma were talking.

"Emma," Sam said.

She turned to look at him and leapt off the couch to give him a hug. "My sister's been hogging you."

He reciprocated the hug. "It's good to see you too."

Nonna walked in and pointed at me and Sam. "Try to get home early. Rain's coming later on."

"Do you like being here?" Sam asked me once we were on our way to wherever he was taking me.

"Yeah, we used to come here all the time when we were kids, and Nonna's really cool." Sam nodded, keeping his eyes on the road. "What about you?"

"I like it. It's quieter than Port Meadow." His eyes flicked over to me. "It's kind of strange how our grandmothers happened to become friends—what are the chances?"

"Yeah, it's strange."

Sam rolled down the driver's side window. I rested my head against the window on my side, looking at him from the corner of my eye. The corner of Sam's mouth raised when he saw me looking at him but he didn't say anything. My cheeks burned and I took out my buzzing phone, answering the call. "Yup?"

"Why can't you say hello like a normal person?" Austin asked.

"Hello, Austin, what do you want?"

"I'm bored," he whined.

"Then go to Jon Ming's or something." Placing the phone between my ear and shoulder, I took out my camera. When I pushed the button, the window on my side of the car rolled down and I took pictures of the passing scenery.

"All the guys are busy until later."

"Then you're screwed," I said.

"What are you doing?"

"Sam's taking me somewhere."

"*Oh.*" He paused and I stopped taking pictures to bring my phone away from my ear at a safe distance.

"Yo, Sam!" he yelled through the speaker.

Sam chuckled as he turned onto a street. "Hey, Austin."

I brought the phone back to my ear in time to hear Austin say, "You and Sam are spending the break together? How? Is this why Jasmine gave you that look in the cafeteria the other day?"

"What *look*?"

"As if you had a thing for him or something. Do you?"

"Bye, Austin."

"Wait—"

I hung up on him, hoping Sam hadn't heard what Austin said.

"We're here," Sam said.

We got out of the car, slamming the doors shut. "You brought me to a café?"

"It's like the diner. Remember detention?"

"Mr. Oliver still gives me weird looks like I'm going to scream in homeroom." Sam chuckled, holding the door open for me. The place did remind me of the diner back home. Same atmosphere of teenagers talking, but with the smell of bread and coffee.

"Let's get something to eat, yeah?" Sam suggested.

"I just ate breakfast."

"You had *brunch*. It's about one o'clock, Hazel." I punched him lightly on the arm. "Plus, we always get food. It's tradition."

When we sat down at a table after getting our food, a voice asked, "Sam?" *Oh. My. God.*

"Hey." Alexis took a seat beside him. "I had a great time yesterday. We should do that again." She twirled her brunet hair and batted her eyelashes. I almost puked. Sam agreed and Alexis's eyes flicked over to me with distaste. *Don't worry. I'm looking at you the exact same way.* "Mabel, right?" she said snidely.

If she was trying to insult me by forgetting my name, she needed to try harder. "It's Macy. Hazel to some."

Sam cracked a smile. Alexis turned to him, looking at the drink in his hands. "You always get that drink."

"It's the only one I like," he said.

"It's the only one you've picked for so long." She giggled. "You have to choose a different drink."

Sam looked over at me. "What do *you* think I should get?"

Alexis pointed at a drink on the menu for him to try. They spoke naturally, with their banter and inside jokes. Sam excused himself to go to the bathroom and moments later, Alexis said, "Did you know Sam sings? He used to sing all the time when we were younger. Played soccer well too."

"We're on the same team."

Alexis's eyebrows pulled together in confusion. "You're on the *boys'* team? That explains a lot."

When Sam came back, she acted like she hadn't said anything. I wasn't having it.

My hands fished out my phone and I ignored the notifications, pretending to read a text one of the boys had sent to the group chat. "Nonna wants me back home for something. Any chance you can give me a ride?" When Alexis protested, I spoke faster. "Or I can find my own way back. I'll see you later."

I left the diner quickly, irritated at people like Alexis, like Beatrice, who always attempted to make me feel less than I was. To make things worse, the light rain Nonna had warned me about started to fall. I was pulling out my phone to call Nonna when a hand clasped my elbow. "You think I'm going to leave you stranded? C'mon."

I followed Sam to his car. As he started the engine, he looked worried. "You okay?"

I nodded as he backed out of the parking space and drove down the road. My thoughts moved from Alexis to Beatrice to Jasmine to Sam. My knee bounced up and down. I leaned against the door, my head on the window. The houses and trees blurred around us. Suddenly, the car rolled to a stop at the side of the street. The car engine turned off as Sam twisted the key in the ignition. He turned to me, "What's wrong?"

"Nothing's wrong," I muttered.

"You're a horrible liar. I'm not leaving until you tell me."

"Fine." Unclipping my seat belt, I got out of the car and slammed the door behind me.

I was mad. At Alexis and Beatrice for the way they were. At the fight Jasmine and I had had before this. At Jasmine's dad for doing what he had done to their family. I was mad at Sam for being here when I needed distance to think things through. I was mad at stupid Mother Nature who wanted it to rain today.

"Hazel, stop," Sam yelled, grabbing my arm. "Why are you so mad?"

I whipped my head around to face him, my hair moving in wet locks. "Leave me alone."

I tried to pull my grip from him, failing. "Hazel, tell me what's wrong."

"Nothing's wrong, it's just . . ." I paused. ". . . your taste in women is very questionable."

"Are you talking about Alexis? Wait." His eyes widened and he let go of my arm. "Were you jealous?"

"Why would I be jealous of her?" I exclaimed, walking away.

"Would you talk to me and stop acting like a child?"

He bumped into my back as I stopped in my tracks. When I turned around, I poked my finger in his hard chest. "I'm *not* acting like a child. If I was a child I wouldn't notice these stupid things about you."

He stared at me with disbelief. "What stupid things?"

"I don't know. Your stupid hair and stupid face. How you talk in that stupid accent of yours and whenever you say Hazel it sounds weird but fits because your voice is . . . you know what, I'm just sick of it. Right now I hate you."

A lock of his hair fell into his puzzled face. As I got wetter, I got even angrier, my fists clenching and heart thudding hard inside my chest.

"What could I have possibly done? I didn't hurt you in any way."

"You didn't, I'm just . . . I'm just mad at myself for having feelings for someone like you." There. I'd finally had the guts to tell him I felt like a hormonal pregnant woman, my emotions all over the place.

Sam froze. "You can't have feelings for me."

"Give me one reason why." Determination replaced the hurt I should have been feeling over what he'd said.

"For the past two years all I've done is hurt and disappoint people—my parents, my brother—and I can't hurt you, Hazel. I can't hurt Cedric either." His eyes grew dim. "I'll give you space again, and that might help whatever is going on here."

"Don't you realize I've been trying?" I pushed my hair out of my face in frustration. "And it hasn't been working. Then Alexis comes by and you guys are friends and she clearly wants more too."

He took a cautious step toward me. "This conversation is not about Alexis. It's about you and me. You're mad at me and I get that. It's what happens when you bottle up emotions: you explode."

"I think I know what happens when you do that." My voice was tight. "Like when you hurt Drake. Or Oscar for what he said to you." Sam suddenly looked agitated. He was getting angry and I was happy he was experiencing what I was feeling. "And what I'm feeling *sucks* because I know how you are with other girls. I mean, when was the last time you slept with a girl?"

"Beatrice. Every other girl you probably heard about after her is a lie."

No part of me wanted to believe him. "You're lying."

Sam closed his eyes for a moment before opening them. "Why would I ever lie to you?"

"Why *wouldn't* you lie to me?" He looked conflicted. "Why, Sam?"

Then he kissed me.

Sam fricking Cahill kissed me.

His arms wrapped around my waist, pulling me to him, and my response was quick. My hands on his shoulders, my mind hazy as my eyes closed. *This isn't happening.* But the intensity of the kiss and the way my heart was pounding begged to differ. I met his intent with my own and his hands moved from my waist, trying to get lower, and I slapped his shoulder softly. He laughed against my lips and I found myself grinning back as he deepened the kiss.

When his tongue touched mine, a sound escaped the back of my throat and I coiled my hands in his soft hair. A meteor could have crashed and I wouldn't have noticed in that moment. When we pulled away from each other, my eyes flew open. I didn't know how to feel, but somehow it was happiness—and shock—at what Sam had done.

23

SPARK, SPARK, BANG, BANG

I laughed.

Most likely because this moment occurred with the most unexpected person and I didn't know how to feel. Sam looked at me, puzzled. Then thunder echoed in the sky. He tugged on my hand. "C'mon."

We ran back to the car then headed straight for Nonna's house. Shortly after, I sat in the living room, a couple of pillows and blankets surrounding me. Nonna had left a note for me on the fridge saying that Justin was at Emma's house and she was over at Lucy's. I got up and looked out the window as the rain got worse, trees blowing frantically in the powerful wind.

I sat back down on a blanket, covering myself with the other one and leaning back against the couch. Sam came downstairs from the bathroom and sat next to me. My heart heaved in my chest and guilt coursed through my entire body.

"Look at me."

Tears pricked at my eyes and he slid an arm around me, pulling me into an embrace. "We kissed," I said.

"I know." He sighed. "You should stay with my cousin. I mean, I want to be with you, Hazel, but . . ." My heart felt like it was going to explode out of my chest. "I think we both—I don't want to lose you because I could mess up what we have. We can't be together. I don't want to do that to you."

His words only reminded me of why I hadn't wanted to feel this way about him in the first place. "Do we just forget about it?"

"I don't know. You obviously still have feelings for Cedric, and he doesn't have to know about the kiss." Sam sounded like he was trying to convince himself. Convince both of us. "He isn't here right now; it's only me," he added.

After a couple of moments, he cleared his throat. "I have an idea."

"What is it?" I ask cautiously.

"We have a few days together before we go back."

"And . . . ?"

"It means that we could try something out here and then everything could go back to normal when we go home. We need to get each other out of our systems and move on."

If we were back in Port Meadow, his proposal would've been dismissed. In Redmond, this was our bubble, away from the worry of home. "That sounds complicated."

"Maybe it does. I know that you have feelings for Cedric. We may have our fallouts but as strange as our relationship is, he's a good guy, and you deserve somebody good for you. If we have these days together then we can say we had this time. And then we'll go home, you can go back to my cousin, and I will go back to being the . . ."

245 THE BAD BOY & THE TOMBOY

"The player, the bad boy, as the school calls you?" I suggested.

He shook his head. "I'm not that. I'm just Sam, Sam Cahill. Do you want to go along with this? We could try. Think of it as just our friendship with the couple shit added on."

I couldn't think properly with him sitting so close to me. The brief conversation I had with Justin back in Port Meadow about feelings crossed my mind. Like my brother had advised, I went with my heart, which was pounding so erratically. "Okay."

"Okay?"

"We do whatever this is and forget about it after the break. We'll be good." I didn't know how I would forget about it, but I didn't care about that now.

"We'll be good," he echoed.

Then a tickle in my throat caused me to cough into my arm. "I'm pretty sure you got me sick."

"You're blaming me for kissing you?"

"I'm *not*."

"I don't regret it." He pressed his lips against mine again. At this point, my heart was doing a full-out gymnastics session. I allowed myself to get lost in him. Was this what falling in love felt like?

The growl from my stomach made me pull away from him.

"What's wrong?"

Cedric's face flashed through my head. "Nothing, I'm starving," I lied. "Come on, Nonna has lasagna in the fridge."

Sam turned the oven on, setting the timer and the temperature before sticking the lasagna in the oven. I grabbed a chair and sat behind the tiny island in the middle of the room. He brought out a cutting board, then grabbed some vegetables from the fridge. I took out my phone and found a message from Caleb. "Do you think tomato sauce is a jam?"

"What?"

"*What?*" I mocked Sam's accent. "Caleb's asking stupid questions."

I pressed my finger against the screen to call Caleb. He optioned to video chat me instead and I accepted. He was lying down on his bed holding his phone above him to reveal his face. "Hi, princess."

"Hey, Charming. Tomato sauce?"

"Do you think it's a jam? Because I think it is."

I let Caleb see the both of us, leaning my phone against a fruit basket and he said, "Look who it is. Mister *I'll-hang-up-on-my-friend-because-it's-fun-to* Samuel Cahill."

"Tomato sauce is not a jam, Caleb," Sam said.

"Tomato is a fruit," Caleb explained. "Therefore tomato sauce should be considered a jam."

Sam put the vegetables into a pan while I grabbed some ice cream from the freezer. "Applesauce isn't a jam," Sam pointed out.

"I'm going with my theory," Caleb said as I took a spoonful of ice cream out of the carton.

Sam suddenly grabbed my hand and put the spoon in his mouth. He removed his hand from the spoon as Caleb spoke up. "What just happened?"

"Nothing."

Caleb's brown eyes widened like those of a squirrel with rabies. "Pupils slightly dilated. Macy's kind of flushed. Sam, you have that stupid smirk on your ugly face and something new in your eyes. You two have that spark, spark, bang, bang thing going on." Sam and I were unfazed by his description until he added, "Oh my God, you guys have kissed."

Oh no. "Excuse me?" Sam asked.

"You locked lips, got to the first part before the action, you both had a spark, spark, bang, bang moment and *you*, Samuel Cahill, didn't bother telling me." Sam tried to intervene but Caleb continued, "Don't pretend it didn't happen. I'm not stupid."

Neither of us said anything and Caleb groaned. "You guys aren't going to tell me what happened? I could write a book about this." He held up his familiar notebook. "I should call it something stereotypical and lame like *The Bad Boy and the Tomboy.*"

I made a face. "That's basic. And neither of those labels are true; that title doesn't even make sense."

Caleb waved his notebook in front of the camera. "C'mon, this story isn't going to write itself."

Sam looked up above the screen. "Hazel's grandmother's here. We've gotta go."

"I want to say hi."

"Maybe later. Bye." He ended the video chat and we both exhaled loudly.

"When you said this relationship would remain only between us, you definitely didn't mean Caleb, right?"

Sam sent me a dry look and I headed back to the living room with my ice cream and phone. "Caleb's not going to say anything," Sam assured me. "Find a movie."

Five minutes later, we were eating ice cream and talking together. The sound of the movie was drowned out as we talked about anything and everything. About different soccer (football) teams he thought were bad and could use a trade. About the stupid ideas that Caleb had cooked up for reality shows. The movie played in the background as we chatted the night away, eating the lasagna. Eventually, it got late and I yawned. Sam stood, and was collecting the plates when the front door opened.

"Macy?" Nonna yelled.

"Here!"

Nonna entered the living room, Justin right behind her.

My brother plopped down next to me on the couch, grabbing the remote to flick through channels. "It's pouring out there."

"What did you do today?"

"Emma and I hung out then her dad dropped us off at Lucy's. You missed a mean game of Monopoly."

"We'll play tomorrow," Nonna promised as Sam came out of the kitchen. "Sam! Did you two have a good time today?"

"Yeah, we did." Sam grabbed his jacket. "I should head out. I'll see you guys tomorrow."

"You'll be by tomorrow?" Nonna asked. "Come early."

"I will," he promised, saying good-bye to her and Justin before gesturing for me to follow him to the door.

Sam put his shoes on then shrugged on his jacket. In the living room, Nonna told Justin to turn down the TV and in the hallway Sam stared at me. "What?" I asked.

He reached out, intertwining our fingers. The action itself was more intimate than it needed to be. "Are we okay?"

With this? With this week? "We're okay. I'll see you tomorrow."

Sam leaned forward and pressed a quick kiss to my lips. In that moment before he left, I forgot about Cedric and Jasmine. Just for a moment.

24

UNTIL WE LEAVE

A knock on my bedroom door woke me up. I groaned as I opened my eyes. I had forgotten to close the curtains last night, and the bright morning sun streamed into the room. Sam peeked his head in. "Don't tell me you just woke up."

"You woke me up." I laced my fingers and lifted my arms up in a stretch as he entered the room, closing the door behind him.

"Your grandmother said to come early." Sam removed his jacket, putting it on the dresser before walking toward me as I sat up. "She's been attempting to make me and Justin wash her car for an hour."

Still groggy, I reached for my phone on the nightstand. "It's 11:03. Why did you wake me up?"

"How are you *still* asleep?"

"I value my sleep."

"I would like for you to value your time with me," Sam teased.

When he leaned in to kiss me, I stopped him with a hand on his mouth. "Disclaimer for the morning: *I* have morning breath. Gimme a second."

Once I had finished brushing my teeth, I returned to my room to find Sam scrolling through his phone, sitting on the bed. This was happening. Granted, only for less than a week, but this was happening. *Oh my God.*

"This was your mum's room, right?" asked Sam as I dug through my duffel bag for clothes to wear.

"Yeah. Nonna mentioned a few things about her when we went out. It feels good being in this house, like it was when Justin and I were kids. We're going to look through some of Mom's things in the attic tonight and watch her old soccer tapes tomorrow."

"Was she as good as you?" Sam pulled me down to lie beside him on the bed.

"She was probably better." His fingers played with my hair as I placed my head on his chest. "Taught me everything from the beginning. I used to watch old videos of her with me at the park when I was three—"

"The one next to the rec center, right?"

"And she'd try to get me to kick the ball we had, and I just kept missing the ball so at one point she said in the background of the video—she was recording—'You're going to look back on this and laugh.' I was *so* bad."

"You were three," Sam said. "You had to start somewhere."

Humming in agreement, I tilted my head up to find him looking down at me. He leaned in first and my lips met his halfway. His hands never seemed to rest in one place, constantly moving as he removed his mouth from mine, his lips moving against my neck. His tongue went over the place his lips had been and my hands slipped under his shirt.

Sam's eyes were hazy as he took off his shirt, tugging it from the back and throwing it to the ground before kissing me again. I loved the feeling of him, close and against me. I didn't even stop him as his hands slowly found their way up my shirt, skimming my stomach.

"*Holy shit!*"

I pushed Sam off me and he fell on the floor with a thud, getting tangled in the sheets that he took down with him. "Fuck," he muttered as Justin slammed the door closed and ran back down the hall.

Regaining my senses, I rolled over to see Sam kicking the sheets off himself. He got up and put his shirt on. "This is going to be interesting."

Putting my hair up in a ponytail, I went down the stairs to find Justin sitting in the living room. I took a seat next to my brother, and he didn't waste a second. "Why did you and Sam decide to do *it* in the morning?"

"We weren't doing *it*," I said.

"It was leading to *it*, was it not? Why were you kissing him anyway? Aren't you still dating his cousin?"

The charm bracelet on my wrist jangled. I didn't even know how Cedric was. There wasn't any cell phone service where he was.

"He left a mark," Justin muttered, and I ran to the mirror in the bathroom. There it was. On my neck. Something I'd seen many times on my sexually or romantically active friends, but never on me.

Sam was frowning as I marched back into the living room. "What's got you all worked up?"

I grabbed one of the throw pillows. "You." *Hit.* "Gave." *Hit.* "Me." *Hit.* "A stupid." *Hit.* "Hickey!"

"It's not that dark. Makeup?" The dry look I sent him answered his question. Sam looked at my brother. "You're spending time with Emma?"

"Yeah, why?"

"Did you try anything on her?"

"No!" Justin glared at the two of us. "Are you two together?" Sam and I didn't answer but Justin didn't care. "I'm going to Emma's. We're going out to a movie." He looked at me, begging with his brown eyes.

I walked over to my wallet in my camera bag near the door, and gave him fifty dollars.

"I'll drop you off," Sam said to Justin, before turning to me. "I'll be back in a couple of hours. I want to show you something."

He kissed me before he left and when I turned around, Nonna stood in front of me with her hands on her hips. Even with her small stature, she somehow towered over me. "When did *this* start between you two?"

"It's only a thing until we leave."

Nonna frowned. "I hope you both know what you're doing."

No. I don't think we do.

~

"You're being annoying."

Sam handed me a napkin for the spilled lemonade, indulging in his need to annoy me. It wasn't my fault—all he had done since picking me up was look at me in a way that made me nervous. We were back at the café that afternoon and, thankfully,

Alexis wasn't here. "You didn't hand it to me properly, you jerk."

"We've only been here for nine minutes." *There's that time thing again.* "I'll get you another one."

He was at the counter ordering another drink when my phone rang in my pocket, and a video-chat call came in from Austin. When I answered, he was combing his hair, looking at himself in the camera. "What's going on with you?"

The guy I've been pushing away my feelings for kissed me yesterday and decided that we should basically date for a few days behind his cousin's back and explore our level of attraction toward one another to get it out of our systems. "Not much, what about you?"

"Hanging out with the guys and Stevie. Why is Caleb asking everyone if tomato sauce is a jam or not?"

"We never know what's going on in his mind," I admitted as Sam gave our order at the counter. The girl taking his order was obviously interested in him but he didn't look like he cared.

"Austin, I'll call you tonight."

"It's a plan," he agreed, before hanging up the call as Sam came back.

Sam handed me my lemonade in an exaggeratedly slow way, causing me to snatch it from him. I glanced over at the girl. "She seemed friendly."

Sam's eyes scanned my face. "You're not jealous, are you?"

"No. I'm a little surprised, that's all. I'm used to you reciprocating attention, not ignoring it."

"It's not the attention. It's who it comes from."

Warmth crept up to my cheeks and I broke eye contact. "That was cringe." His phone rang: Alexis.

He answered, putting the phone against his ear. "Yeah? . . . I can't . . . I'm at the café . . . with Hazel . . ." Irritation flashed in his eyes before he looked at me as she spoke to him. "I have to go."

He hung up. My face was probably red as I got up. "I'm going to get another cinnamon roll."

"I'll buy it," Sam offered.

"*Dude.*"

Sam gently pushed me back in my seat. "*Dude,*" he mocked me and I stuck my tongue out at him. "I'll pay."

He returned with my food and I gladly dug in. "Do you get a big allowance or something?" I asked, looking at the bills in the black wallet he put back in his pocket.

"No. I don't like asking for money. It's usually saved up from presents and this job I did as a kid."

"What was it?"

"I was a model, okay?"

Modeling was a great job, nothing to be embarrassed about. But Sam as a model? I slapped my hands over my mouth. He tilted his head in annoyance and I dropped my hands back down. "Sorry, that's . . . cool. It's not that big a deal."

Sam shrugged. "It wasn't. One summer, Aunt Liz had a new clothing line and my mum offered me up. That led to another, and another, then a photo shoot when I was fourteen, and I'm going to stop talking because you seem to be picturing me as a model."

I was. He scowled and threw his drink in the garbage.

~

Later that day, we got out of the car after a short drive. It was a bright day in Redmond but traces of winter stayed. "This is the second time you've taken me to a place surrounded by trees."

Sam went over to the trunk of the car and pulled out a full plastic bag. He held the bag in one hand, then slung an arm around my shoulders. "I take you to places where I like thinking."

His warm hand pulled me deeper into the forest. "You'd better not be planning to take me to a cabin and kill me. Or blindfold me so I can't find my way out once you leave me. Or—"

"Your imagination is so vivid. I don't know whether that is a good thing or a bad thing sometimes."

We continued walking, listening to the branches and pinecones crunching under our feet. His white Converse shoes were getting dirty but Sam didn't seem to mind as he stopped at our destination. "Here we are."

Past a tiny clearing, I could see the blue water of a lake stretched out before us, and Sam led us to the shore. Bending down in a crab position, I ran my hands through the bright water. "It's not warm enough for anyone to go into that water."

"It's practically spring."

"It's *pneumonia*," I argued, and he shook his head, probably at the memory of my words, bending forward to look at the water.

Why was this guy into me? I worried that, when we went back home, I wouldn't get over him. That I wouldn't have gotten him out of my system enough to fully focus on his cousin, the one I was in a relationship with, especially since Sam was looking at me the same way as before, with that smile reserved solely for me on his face.

I pushed him and he stumbled enough to almost fall into the cold water. The look I received was playful. "I don't think that's what girlfriends should do to their boyfriends." He walked toward me and I backed away.

"How would *you* know?"

His hand grabbed my arm, and he started to drag me toward the water. I screamed as it seeped into my shoes and he flung some water, splashing it in my face.

Later, we sat on grass, watching the water move ahead of us as we ate the food Sam had in the plastic bag. Two containers were filled with pasta he claimed to have made with his grandmother earlier today, along with another tub of assorted fruit. I shoved another forkful of pasta into my mouth from the container he'd brought, marveling at the taste. "You should cook for me every day," I said.

He took a napkin and wiped the corner of my mouth with it. The area was quiet, the water moving ahead of us as I set the container beside me. This reminded me of swimming with Andrew and Jasmine as kids at the public pool back home. We were so happy, it wasn't hard to remember the joy we felt back then.

I whipped my head toward Sam when the sound of my camera cut through the air. "What's wrong?" he asked.

"Jasmine and I aren't speaking." I told him about most of the argument and that Jasmine has been facing family issues but was careful not to say anything more than that. "I messed up. I shouldn't have tried to force her to talk about something she didn't want to."

"We all mess up. You're going to fix this. You and Jasmine have been friends for a long time and there's a reason. You have to look at it from Jasmine's perspective: she, along with Austin, Caleb, and Jon Ming, is one of the few minorities at our school in Port Meadow. There are a lot of people out there who are going to say horrible and bigoted shit to Jasmine, and you can't tell her to suck it up."

"She doesn't deserve to be treated like that."

"No one does," he agreed. "Be there for her for that, for her family situation, for whatever it is. Anything involving family can be rough: she's going to need you and Andrew." He took my hand. "I don't think she meant to change you either. It wasn't her intention."

"It wasn't," I agreed.

"I mean, you could be a little less annoying and stop eating all those Pop-Tarts." I scowled. "Kidding. I wouldn't change you for the world."

"Can't relate," I jested, squirming out of his hold before he ran after me.

~

That night in the attic of Nonna's house, Justin and I sat on the wooden floor and went through scrapbooks that had been in packed up boxes. Nonna was sorting through other boxes when my finger landed on a picture of Mom when she was a baby. "She looked like you when you were a baby," I said to Justin.

Justin looked surprised when he looked at the photo. "She did. That's so weird."

He flipped through a few pages in the scrapbook he was holding before showing me a picture of our parents. "They were in university. That's where Mom and Dad met, right?"

"Yup," Nonna answered from where she stood. "They met in their second year of university, then a few years later had the tall one over there."

I groaned. "*Nonna.*" We all shared a laugh.

Justin was still staring at the photo. He pointed at the familiar necklace around her neck in the photograph. His eyes flicked to my own. "Hey, Nonna," Justin said. "Do you know where Mom's necklace is?"

"Which necklace?"

"This one." Justin pointed to it in the picture.

"One second." She made her way downstairs and when she came back up, she handed Justin a box. "The last time Lauren visited here with you all, the pendant was broken and I offered to fix it. When Lauren passed, I had never gotten the opportunity to give it back to her after it was repaired, and I took it with me when I left years ago."

Justin opened the box. "Who gave it to her?"

"Your grandfather," Nonna answered as he took the necklace out of the box. "After her first year on her university team." The soccer-ball pendant was smooth, the chain of the necklace silver. After years of seeing it only in pictures, tears burned my eyes. While my family thought it was lost, it was truly with the right person.

"You know," Justin said after a moment of silence, "she should've played basketball. I think she would've been really good."

I snorted at Justin's words but he only continued. "A basketball necklace sounds really good. Macy, take notes for my birthday present." Nonna and I burst into laughter at Justin's remark and he put the necklace back in its box then handed it back to our grandmother.

25

I DON'T SMELL LIKE A FRUIT

"Royal flush," Nonna gloated, taking the chips all for herself. That Thursday, we continued bonding over card games, with Justin and Nonna becoming more competitive the more we played.

"You cheated." Justin glared at Nonna.

"I did not. It's all about the probability."

"Did you spend a year in Vegas or something?" Justin muttered.

My phone buzzed in my pocket and I read the message.

> Jerk: Grandmother's making me tag along to a func-
> tion of hers
>
> Jerk: I'll come over tonight

This week was going by fast. We were returning home on Sunday. Home made me think of Jasmine, of Cedric, of how Sam and I would be after this break. How I would react seeing him flirt with other girls. In fact, I didn't know if he expected me to act like one of the girls he had been with back in Port Meadow while we were here.

Later that evening, I was playing in the small backyard, counting the passes I made with the soccer ball against the wall of the house. Getting past only fifty, I stopped the ball when the backyard gate opened.

"Miss me?" Sam asked.

I must've taken too long to answer as I stared at his gray suit, black tie, and nice shoes, because a conceited expression overcame his face. "How do I look?"

Then his expression softened. "You can say it, Hazel. *I* know I look sexy but it would sound better if *you* say it." *Always arrogant.*

"You are not letting me get a word in edgewise," I said.

"You wouldn't believe the day I had. The least you could've done was give me an award. I couldn't even text you because my grandmother took my phone."

"You missed me?" I teased.

"I did. I'll be back in a bit." He leaned in and kissed me, but my worry from earlier distracted me. When I pulled away, his hands were still cupping my face. "What's wrong?"

"Nothing."

"Don't lie to me." I focused on the grass underneath us when he sighed. "We'll talk later. Wow, here we are acting like a married couple."

The thought of me married to Sam made me roll my eyes. We couldn't even stick to being an actual couple. Sam's lips pressed against my forehead. I indulged in the feeling even as he pulled away. "There's the Hazel I know."

~

Sam returned to Nonna's house a few minutes later in his leather jacket and jeans. "How was the event, Samuel?" Nonna asked him.

"Most boring thing I've ever had to attend."

Sam laid his head on my lap, facing the TV. I played with his hair as the night progressed. Nonna excused herself. "I'm going to make a call."

Justin was typing on his phone, chatting with Emma. Sam and I grabbed throw pillows and launched them in my brother's direction. He grumbled under his breath and left the room.

"Now can you tell me what's wrong?" Sam asked.

"I know you said we were in this 'relationship' because we needed to get each other out of our systems," I said. "I just want to know if you're expecting what you usually do with other girls."

Sam paused. "I wouldn't do anything you're not comfortable with. Besides, you should have your first time with someone special to you. I don't think I'm that person."

Think. The way Sam viewed himself an undeserving person bothered me but I didn't press the matter, instead running my fingers through his hair. "What kind of conditioner do you use? You smell like apples."

His puzzled expression made me laugh as he said, "I don't smell like a fruit. We were having a normal conversation literally eight seconds ago."

With Nonna and Justin no longer here, I asked, "Want to come upstairs?"

Sam bolted upright. "Hazel, if you wanted me in your bed then you should've been blunt about it." We entered my mom's old room as his phone rang and I lay down on my bed. Sam lay down next to me as he answered the video chat. "What do you want, dude?"

Caleb was in his kitchen, eating a bowl of cereal. "Are you two still doing the spark, spark, bang, bang thing?"

"Shut up," Sam muttered.

"*Ooh*," he exclaimed. "I see that the spark, spark, bang, bang is now spark, spark, lock."

"What are you talking about?" a voice said behind him, and Jon Ming looked at us over Caleb's shoulder. "How did you two end up together on break? Wait, why is he talking about locks?"

"Not locks," Caleb said. "They kissed."

"They did *what*?" Jon Ming exclaimed.

"Are you two dating? I need an answer," Caleb asked. "What about the cousin?"

"Did you break up with Cedric?" Jon Ming looked shocked at my lack of response, my stomach in knots at a reminder of home. "Mace."

"Is this thing you and Sam have only temporary?" Caleb interjected.

"Yeah," Sam answered.

"This isn't going to affect anything when you guys get back, is it?" Jon Ming asked.

"No," Sam and I said in unison.

"Does the rest of the gang know about this?" Caleb asked, and Sam said no.

Jon Ming's eyes were on me when he sighed. "Not even Andrew? Our lips are sealed then. We'll let you guys go. Bye."

The video chat disconnected and Sam put his phone on the nightstand, almost knocking off one of the scrapbooks from the attic I had been looking through last night. He picked it up, glancing at me for permission to look through it. I nodded, attempting to push the guilt away as he opened it up. "Have you watched her soccer tapes yet?"

"I was going to watch them tonight. Want to join?"

"Yeah. Where'd you get the scrapbook from?"

"Justin and I raided the attic yesterday. We found so many pictures of Mom," I said, wishing we could stay here longer for me to find out more. "I don't want to leave."

"I don't want to leave either."

"Are you trying to be romantic?"

"No. I was joking," he said dryly. "I can't *wait* to get out of here."

As I whacked him with my pillow, he blocked the playful attack with his hands. "I'm kidding. I don't want to leave—ow." Sam tumbled off the bed and onto the floor, taking me down with him. I landed on his body as he groaned. "That's the second time I've fallen off this bed because of you."

I lifted my head from his chest, beaming. "You're welcome."

As I helped him up, the door opened. Nonna stood at the threshold holding a phone to her ear. "If you two are in here, this door had better be open." My face grew hot with embarrassment, and I looked out the window at the setting sun. "And Sam? Lucy wants you back in thirty minutes."

Sam's phone rang once Nonna left; the plain ringtone I knew to be Alexis's. He waited for the ringing to stop before powering down his phone. "I'll call her back later. Alexis doesn't like you."

"Of course she doesn't," I said. "Because she's in love with you."

"She's not," he assured me, sitting down on the bed.

I sat down beside him and swung my legs over his lap. "She said that you were coming here so that you both can finally be together."

"She's just a friend." He dismissed me. "I've known her for a long time. Alexis is not someone you should worry about. No one should be." He was right. I hadn't seen Alexis since that encounter in the café. "I have thirty minutes. Show me the tapes?"

Sam made his way downstairs and I ran up to the attic to get the videos Nonna had shown me. Justin wasn't in his room, leaving me to assume that he was out with Emma but would soon be returning. Heading to the living room where Sam was settled on the couch, I placed one video in the old VCR Nonna had yet to get rid of.

The first video showed a sunny day on the field. Mom was with her team, in her high school soccer jersey. The game started off slow but then she had the ball, sprinting on a breakaway. She took the shot and it went in the net. Sam chuckled next to me at the sight of my mom's excitement in the video as she was surrounded by her team.

"Knew she would be good," he commented.

"Are you the only soccer fan in your family?" I asked.

"No, my dad," Sam said after a moment. "He played a bit when he was in secondary school."

"Your siblings weren't into it?"

Sam's eyes cast downward. "Beth wasn't a big fan but she came to all my games. Greg despises football."

"*Despises?*"

"He hates it. He could not kick a ball to save his life." Sam twiddled his phone in his hands. "It's why I was happy that Phillip got into football. Greg plays tennis and he likes it."

"Do you talk to him often?"

"Every day." For once, he seemed okay with talking about something connecting him to England. "Do you want to see what he looks like?"

"Sure." Sam went through his phone and pulled up a picture of his family. His little brother's arm held the phone to take the selfie, his family surrounding Greg. They were outside, in nice clothing, with big smiles.

At the sight of Sam's father, I said, "When my dad said you were the spitting image of your dad, he wasn't kidding." The main differences were that his dad's eyes were brown, his hair was wavy instead of curly, and he was older, but they looked very similar.

His mom was pretty, with straight brown hair and green eyes. Even just looking at the picture of her, I could tell that Sam shared her confidence. His little brother had similar curly hair but his dad's brown eyes. In the photo, Sam stood next to his sister. The Sam I met in Port Meadow only smiled on rare occasions but the way he was with his family in England was brighter. Before everything changed for him.

My hand covered his, squeezing. "You really miss them, huh?"

"Yeah, I do." He cleared his throat and put the phone back in his pocket to focus on the TV.

~

Friday was spent with Nonna, Justin, and Emma, who'd come over to play board games with us. Sam and his grandmother, Lucy, eventually joined and it was fun. It reminded me of when Justin and I were kids and the game nights Nonna had held with us, Mom, and Dad.

On Saturday, Emma and Justin were playing video games in the basement. I gave her a high five when she killed Justin's character. "Justin, when Macy said you suck, I didn't think she meant it."

"I was letting you win," he defended himself lamely.

"Three times?"

Justin cursed under his breath, reloading the game and digging into the popcorn next to him. Sam came down the stairs and pointed at me. "I'm taking you out on the best date of your life."

The sight of him in a great mood provoked me to kiss him, which didn't last long as pellets of popcorn assaulted us. Justin scowled, scooping another handful of popcorn. "Do us a favor and play tonsil hockey somewhere else."

I picked the popcorn out of my hair as he and Emma resumed their game. Sam brushed the popcorn off himself. "What was that for?" he asked, referring to my spontaneous kiss.

Because after eighteen years, those romance books and movies I had made fun of with Andrew finally made sense.

Shortly after, Sam and I made our way up the stairs, passing by Nonna, who was seated on the couch in the living room, her phone hovering by her ear. "Nonna, we're going out," I told her.

"Might be back around ten or eleven," Sam added, and my grandmother didn't object, shooting us a thumbs-up to show she had heard before the two of us left the house.

About twenty minutes later, Sam drove into the parking lot of a grocery store.

"You took me out to buy groceries? What are we going to do? Race shopping carts?"

Sam laughed and I decided that I loved this side of him—the

playful one that teased and made jokes every second. After he parked, we exited the vehicle. Sam then took a bag from the trunk.

"Let's go." He pulled me to a narrow alley. There was a dumpster against the wall. "Hazel, don't say something dramatic."

I kept my mouth shut, and we continued walking farther into the alley, eventually reaching an open gate. Sam pulled me through, shutting it behind us, and we were surrounded by graffitied walls. "*Whoa.*"

Sam rifled through the bag and then tossed a can of spray paint at me. I caught it as he took out more cans, placing them on the ground. "Can't we get arrested for this?"

"Life is all about taking risks, no?" he teased. "People use this wall as a canvas all the time, don't worry." Pulling us forward, he turned me around to face a brick wall. "Close your eyes." I did as he said, feeling only his presence around me. "Tell me what you feel right now."

I didn't think about it. "Happy."

"Open your eyes." I did. "Now write something that makes you feel happy. Like food or football."

We got to work separately, and after a few moments, I snorted at how bad my writing looked. Spotting what Sam was doing, my eyes widened as I hadn't expected to see my name. Sam cleared his throat, his cheeks a slight pink. I picked up another can. "Let's do another one. How about I write something that makes me feel confused? I'll write your name."

"I'm not *that* confusing."

"You change moods so fast. You're as confusing as Caleb's theories."

He pulled me toward him. "Like this?"

The can in my hand dropped to the ground.

~

Sam clamped a hand over my mouth as I attempted to sing, driving with one hand. "I think you ruined this song for me," he muttered, not entirely annoyed.

As he slowed down, people of all ages walked past the car, carrying drinks or bags full of popcorn. Other cars were lined up around us, some people sitting on the hood or staying inside, everyone awaiting the bright screen a good distance away.

"Ever been to a drive-in?"

"No," I said as we both got out of the car.

"Since it hasn't snowed since early January, they opened up early, recommending that people stay in their cars."

"You say that as we get out of the car."

"I was never really one for following the rules." He spread out a blanket on the hood of the car for us to sit on, then left and returned with food. As the movie started, his hands played with mine as I sat between his legs, my back against his chest.

"My family and I used to come here a lot when we were younger," he said.

"The entire family?"

"Usually. Mostly my family and Ivan's."

"Even Cedric?"

"Even Cedric," Sam said with a sigh. "Better days, I suppose."

His comments throughout the night made the film more interesting than if I had watched it alone. I was comfortable in his presence, but then a cold breeze whipped through the air. I shivered, about to get my thicker jacket from inside the car when Sam stopped me. Wordlessly, he removed his leather jacket and gestured for me to put it on. I stared at it. This was Sam's jacket. He almost never took it off. He probably slept in it.

"Are you serious? This is sacred. Like 'Thou shalt not wear Samuel Cahill's jacket' sacred," I said.

Sam rolled his eyes. "Just wear the damn jacket, Hazel."

As I put the jacket on I said, "I was right, you do smell like apples." Sam faked irritation, and I pressed a kiss to his cheek before leaning into him, playing with the soccer-ball pendant around my neck.

~

We returned to Nonna's house, but I had dozed off during the drive. Sam rushed over to the passenger side, opened the door, then hoisted me up into his arms, bridal style. I pretended to stay asleep, hoping to prolong being so close to him. He kicked the door closed with his foot before making his way up the front steps. "Hazel, you weigh a ton."

The front door opened. "Wow, I didn't expect you guys to come back here." *Justin.*

"Where's your grandmother?" Sam whispered.

"Sleeping. What's wrong with my sister? Did you kill her?"

"What is it with you Andersons and your imaginations?"

Justin walked away. Sam groaned under his breath as he made his way into the house. "How much does this girl weigh?" he repeated.

I hit him lightly on the chest, opening my eyes.

"I knew you were awake. I was kidding, by the way."

I got out of his arms and closed the door behind him. The two of us made our way up the stairs and into my bedroom, and

I took off his jacket, placing it on the dresser before tumbling onto my bed.

"Did you have a good time?" He didn't even wait for me to reply before he whispered, "Of course you did; you were with me."

"You're very arrogant and annoying today, aren't you?"

"You're very beautiful today, aren't you?" he teased. "Are we done pointing out the obvious?"

"Don't," I protested. "Don't call me things like that."

He furrowed his eyebrows as he sat next to me, and I pulled my legs up and hugged them to my chest. "I may be a jerk sometimes—"

"I noticed."

"And I may be obnoxious—hell, even annoying at times—but I always mean what I say."

His eyes. His stupid eyes that had to look right through me. "We have to get up early tomorrow and I'm a little tired."

A hushed, deep laugh came from Sam. "You don't take compliments well, do you?"

"On my footwork, yes. On my appearance, not so much," I admitted. "Are you going to head back to your grandmother's?"

Sam's eyes flicked up to me. "Do you want me to stay?"

This would never happen again. He would never be here with me after a great day like this ever again. "Nonna's going to kill you."

"Hazel, do you want me to stay?" he repeated.

This would never happen again. "I do."

"Okay."

We moved swiftly, me heading to the bathroom to change into sweatpants and a T-shirt and brush my teeth. Sam joined me a second later and I gave him a spare toothbrush I had found. Hurrying back into the bedroom, I tied my hair up into a ponytail as he closed the door. I dug through my duffel bag for anything that could possibly fit him. When I found a pair of sweatpants that were fairly loose on me, I tossed them to him. "Here," I whispered.

"Why are you whispering?" He asked quietly, taking his shirt off.

"Do you want to get caught?"

Sam moved to pull off his jeans, and I made my way to the bed as he slipped on the sweatpants. He turned off the light and crawled under the covers with me as I yawned, rolling to face him. We didn't say anything more, but at one point before I slept, his hand reached for mine under the comforter intertwining our fingers.

~

I shifted slightly as the voice got louder. "Wakey, wakey, eggs and bakey."

"What?!" I groaned, pulling the comforter away from my face.

Sam chuckled. He sounded happy this morning despite waking up at what must be an ungodly hour. "I don't know what you North Americans say."

"Are you going back home, to Bath, after graduation?" I asked as I opened my eyes. Sam's face was close, his body warm. Morning light streamed into the room, making me squint for a moment at how bright everything was.

"For the summer," he mumbled. "I don't know yet if I'm going to stay here after."

"Would you want to?"

"I'm indifferent. There are good schools here. A lot of my family lives here. Even though my cousins . . . we've always had issues, conflicts, but we're family." He didn't say anything more, sitting up. My phone showed me a time that suggested I could sleep longer but Sam protested. "You have to pack."

"*Sam.*" He laughed loudly at my tone, about to get up. "When are *you* going home?"

"Later today."

The door to my room burst open. "Samuel Cahill!" Nonna's voice made both of us jump. For the third time this week he fell out of the bed. "Why are you in this room? More importantly, why are you in that bed?!"

Justin stood behind her in the doorway, enjoying what was happening. My grandmother stood over Sam. "And wear a shirt, this behavior is unacceptable." She turned to me. "At least you had the decency to cover up after you two finished whatever it was you were doing."

"No," I yelped. "We didn't do anything, we just slept."

"Really?" My assurance was unheard as she looked over at Sam, who wasn't wearing a shirt. *What else is she going to think?* "Sam, get out."

Sam and I relaxed when she left. "She never fails to scare me." He pulled on his shirt then took the sweats off to pull his jeans on.

"Why are you awake?" I asked Justin, getting up from the bed and walking over to him.

"Couldn't sleep properly." He shrugged. "I kind of don't want to leave."

"Me neither," I agreed, running a hand over his hair and he

didn't protest, yawning. Patting his back, I gestured for him to go back to bed, telling him I'd help him pack before we left.

"I'll be back in a bit." Sam put his jacket on. "Almost got me out of your system?"

"Almost."

Not even close.

~

"Emma, talk to him, would you?" Sam said. We stood inside the front door while Justin, Nonna, and our duffel bags were on the outside.

"What am I going to say, Sam?" she asked, her voice clearly upset. "'It sucks that I like you but now you're leaving?'"

"Just *talk*," he urged her.

Emma walked out. She said something to my little brother and they walked down the street. Looking out the window, we saw a car pull into the driveway.

Dad got out of the car and Nonna engaged in conversation with him. "I'm going to say hi to your dad. I'll load the things into the car." Sam trekked toward the car with a duffel bag in each hand. I closed the front door behind me, and was making my way down the front steps when another person appeared beside me as Sam shook hands with my dad.

"Mabel."

I'm about to get a headache. "Why are you here?"

"I dropped my sister off, *idiot*. Thank God you're going back." She flipped her brown hair over her shoulder.

"You're mad because of me and Sam?"

She glowered at me. "He doesn't belong with someone like you."

"Someone like me?" I repeated. "*Seriously?*"

"You don't even deserve him. It's not like you were there for him when he was going through a rough patch."

"Alexis?" Sam asked as he advanced toward us.

"I was saying good-bye to her." *Yes, because he definitely believed that lie.* I walked past them, in the direction of Dad and Nonna.

"Hey," Dad said, and I stepped into his embrace. "How was your time here?"

"Really good." Nonna smiled at my answer, and she and my dad continued their conversation. As I watched Alexis and Sam talk, I saw Alexis frown, but then she hugged him. I stood still, waiting for the stupid hug to be over and when it finally was, Alexis planted her lips on his cheek.

I turned away to see Emma and Justin in conversation. Suddenly, Justin boldly hugged her. Sam walked over to me while Alexis stood by the side of her car, waiting for her sister to finish up.

Emma said her good-byes to Sam and me before she left, giving Sam a big hug, which I photographed as a nice memory. As she left with Alexis, I was leaning over to show the photo to Sam when he was suddenly pushed aside. My grandmother clasped Justin in a hug, his face turning a bright shade of red.

"Nonna," he groaned.

She let go. "You're almost fifteen—puberty must be hitting you hard if you can't even take your Nonna's hugs. Now just you remember: you will never beat me in any card game, got it?"

"I still think you cheat," my brother grumbled.

"Here are some cookies for the ride." Nonna took a small pile of wrapped-up cookies out of her small bag and handed it to Justin.

"Sam," Dad said. "How are you getting back? Do you need a ride?"

"I brought my car up, so I'm good, but thank you, Nick." His gaze slid over to me.

"I just need to talk to Sam about something," I said to my family. "We'll be back." Sam and I pushed through the wooden gate that led to the backyard. Closing the gate, I leaned against it as Sam shoved his hands into his leather jacket pockets.

"Are you okay?" I asked.

"I'm fine." When someone says they're fine, they usually aren't. Sam must've realized that was what it sounded like, and added, "I'm okay. This was a good few days."

"You're saying 'few' as if you don't know the exact number," I teased. "Right down to the minute probably."

"This was a good, counting today, roughly six days," he estimated.

My fingers fiddled with the strap of my camera bag, in which a multitude of pictures I was going to go through were stored. "We'll still be good friends, right?"

"You're one of my best friends," he said. "It's hard to earn the title of one of Sam Cahill's best mates. Caleb wears that title with pride. You should too." The smile began to slip off his face. "This is it, huh? The end of us?"

"The end of us," I repeated, failing to keep an upbeat tone.

"It's for the best," he whispered.

When his lips pressed against mine for the last time, it was different. Suddenly, I was overwhelmed, my heart lurching in contrast to the slow kiss that deepened with more passion than I could handle. My eyes fell shut, my fingers clutching his leather jacket. His heart mimicked my own, rapidly beating throughout the kiss.

Sam and I pulled away gently at the same time, his cheeks flushed and his eyes as bright and wild as ever. I took his hand in mine. "Around the time we first met, when you wanted to get to know me better, you said having you in my life would be exciting."

A smirk played on his lips. "Did I fulfill my promise?"

"You did. And you still are," I admitted.

His grip on my hand tightened. "You're welcome." His expression softened as he whispered, "You ready?" *Definitely not.*

I let my thumb move away from his on our locked hands. "Do you have me out of your system?"

Sam hesitated before he replied, letting our ring fingers remove their hold. "Yeah. Do you have me out of your system?"

"Yeah, I do," I lied. "I'll see you at school?"

"I'll see you at school."

We let our pinkie fingers go and pulled our hands back to ourselves, as if they were never together in the first place.

Sam left the backyard first, saying good-bye to my family. He hugged Nonna one more time before walking back to his grandmother's house. Nonna pulled me down for a hug. "You're going to do great in that tournament, okay? Now get going. Visit again soon, all right?"

"We will. Bye, Nonna." Justin gave her one final hug and we got settled in the car.

Justin and I waved at Nonna through the window, leaving her—and Mom's childhood home—behind. Justin leaned against the car door next to me. "Hey, Sandy?"

I grinned at the nickname. "Yeah, Patrick?"

"Before you leave for uni, we're coming back, right?"

His voice was quiet, eyes focused on the house. I ruffled his hair. "Of course we are."

26

WELCOME TO THE DARK SIDE

"Is Jasmine back yet? I know she was planning on staying a few extra days," I said to Andrew on Wednesday morning. We stood in front of the school bus we were taking to our tournament, most of the boys already boarding.

"She came back last night," Andrew said. "She can tell you about being at her aunt's when you two talk. How's Ced?"

"I haven't spoken to him but he's coming back on Friday."

The harsh reality settled within me: there were no romantic feelings anymore. What I felt for Sam wasn't even in the same category as what I felt for Cedric.

I hadn't told Andrew anything that was going on. During the past couple of days, my mind had been so full of confusion I hadn't even asked how he was doing, nor had I told him what I'd been dealing with.

"I have something to—" A car pulled up next to the school bus and I stopped talking immediately. I spotted Caleb and Sam in the car. The two of them got out. Sam and I hadn't spoken since my grandmother's; I hadn't seen him at school over the two days since we'd come back.

"You two scream relationship goals," Caleb said, looking at the similar track pants and sweatshirts we were wearing. "You guys excited?"

Andrew answered Caleb with a joyful yes. Sam's eyes moved over to me and he asked, "How are you?"

This was on the verge of an awkwardness I didn't think was possible between us. "Good. How about you?"

"Same. Funny how we kind of wore the same thing, huh?"

"You ruined it with your *Converse* shoes."

The strain between us eased a little when he said, "You ruined it with your *Jordans*."

"Talk to me when you get common sense," I mumbled.

Sam gave an exaggerated sigh. "I'm afraid I don't have any."

Andrew nudged me. "Time to go."

Caleb's shout of "Good luck" as I headed up the bus stairs made me wave at him before finding a seat. Andrew took the spot behind me, extending his leg out on the seat. Through the window, I could see Caleb and Sam talking. They shared a brief hug before Caleb headed to the car and Sam climbed onto the bus.

Sam walked down the aisle toward the back, where most of the seniors were sitting. His eyes traveled to me but another person sat down next to me. "Mace." Austin shifted into a comfortable position. "How was the break?"

"Good." Sam plopped down next to Brandon, and the two engaged in an easy conversation. "It was good."

~

"I'm starving," I muttered hours later as the entire team lined up in the middle of the healthiest fast food restaurant near the hotel we were staying.

Before Jacob could even attempt the "When are you not?" comeback, a familiar voice behind me said, "Look who it is, Wellington." I turned around to face him.

"What do you want?" I asked Michael.

Michael's lips quirked up when he spotted Sam. "You got matching outfits and everything."

His teammates enjoyed his lame joke. "Please shut up," I said.

Michael clenched his jaw. "When we beat you, Anderson, that's when you'll know girls can't play soccer."

Sam stepped in front of me and the two glared at each other. "Good-bye, Michael," I said, hoping to prevent a fight.

Michael slid his eyes over to me, his face taunting. "I'll see you later, Macy."

Austin slung an arm around my shoulders as Michael moved away. "He's only acting like that because he knows he's going to lose."

"I can't wait to kick their asses on the field."

Austin's arm dropped and my teammates turned to face me with wide eyes. The only people not in shock were Sam and Andrew, who snorted. "What?"

"You swore," Jacob and Brandon said in unison.

"You didn't say *dumbegg*," Jon Ming pointed out.

"Or *holy flying lemurs*," Austin added.

I rolled my eyes. "Is it that big of a deal?"

"Welcome to the dark side," Sam joked. "We've been waiting."

"Don't get used to it."

He snuck in front of me to order and I was unable to get his smile out of my head, even when we returned to the hotel after attending the tournament opening. I jumped onto the bed after dropping my luggage at the side. Andrew was hanging out with me for a bit before heading over to his room, which he was sharing with a few of the others—I was the only team member with my own room. "At least no one can hear you snore."

"I don't snore," I protested.

"Yes, you do. I'll probably hear you next door. I feel sorry for Sam, though. His bed is right on the other side of this wall; he won't get *any* sleep."

I yawned and Andrew took that as his cue to leave. "You should get some rest, bro, you're going to need it for tomorrow."

He left the room, and I changed for bed, my mind ping-ponging between Jasmine and Sam, one far away and one too close for my liking. I punched the soft pillow before leaning back and attempting to sleep.

My hand moved to the side of the headboard and up the wall, fingers clenched into a fist. I knocked softly against the wall mindlessly. My phone buzzed.

Jerk: Are you trying some kind of Morse code with me?

Me: I couldn't sleep

Jerk: It's only ten. Why would Coach want us in bed this early?

Me: Because we have early practice

Jerk: Nooooo

Jerk: Is it weird?

Was it weird going back to normal? Was it weird not having him beside me?

Me: Yeah. We should sleep. Night

Jerk: Night Hazel

~

The team was doing drills on the indoor soccer field where we would play our games the next afternoon when Sam came up to me. He nodded over to the high bleachers. At the top of them, a guy sat, eyes on the field. "That's the scout?"

"Coach was talking to him and he's going to be at our game tomorrow."

"He knows we're going to make it to the next round?" Jon Ming said.

"Way to be pessimistic, JM." Brandon nudged him.

"What are you all doing standing around there? Practice!" Coach yelled loud enough for the entire city to hear him.

The team scattered, and as he moved away, I caught sight of Sam's necklace. "Sam," He hummed in acknowledgment. "You have to take off the necklace."

Sam's hand reached up to the golden *B* pendant. "I need it."

"If you get caught with that or it injures someone, you could be out of the game. We can't risk losing you. Don't you think I want to play with mine?"

Sam reluctantly took it off and asked, "You're not worried about the scout, are you?"

"No," I partially lied. "What about you? What are your plans after high school?"

He shrugged, dropping onto one knee to retie his cleats. "I applied and got accepted to a few places. We'll see."

"You haven't decided."

"I haven't decided because I have time. You didn't decide because you're scared that picking a school changes everything. Now you have an opportunity to go to a school you want to go to." When he got up, he pointed a finger in my face. Pushing his hand down, I grew aware of our close proximity. He was too close. He knew it.

Andrew did, too, watching us from where he stood a distance away. Sam cleared his throat, dangling his necklace in his hand. "I'm going to give this to Coach."

Later that night when someone knocked on my hotel room door, I wasn't surprised to find my best friend on the other side. Andrew closed the door behind him. "What happened between you and Sam, idiot?"

"Don't call me an idiot, *idiot*."

"I want to know what's going on."

As I recounted all that had happened between us last week, Andrew didn't interrupt. He kept all of his thoughts to himself until I was done.

"You cheated on Cedric." There was disappointment in his voice, and the guilt in me was unnerving.

"I did."

"You guys dated? Like, you went out? And made out, and then you—"

"No, we didn't do *that*."

"Sam is . . . *kinda* known for that, remember?"

There was another knock on the door, and I opened it to Jon Ming and Austin. "How serious is the conversation we walked in on?" Jon Ming asked as they walked in, his eyes flicking between me and Andrew.

"I'm guessing an eleven," Austin said.

"On what scale?" Jon Ming sat on the carpeted floor. "Is it about Mace and Sam dating for, like, those few days?" Andrew's lips parted in surprise, but Jon Ming kept talking. "It was weird, man, you should've seen them."

My guilt grew as I turned to Andrew. "Can I talk to you for a quick second in the bathroom? *Please*."

He limped ahead of me and I shut the door behind us, my fist against my lips.

"You tell me everything." Andrew ran a hand through his blond hair. "Maybe I'm overreacting."

"You're *not*. If you were in my position I would want you to tell me what's going on. It's always been like that."

"Clearly, things are changing," he said dryly.

"I'm sorry." I closed my eyes for a second. "I should have told you and I shouldn't have said all that shit I said to Jasmine and I shouldn't have done what I did with Sam and I should've broken up with Cedric the moment I realized I didn't have feelings for him anymore. I'm sorry." I inhaled roughly, my hands over my face, and Andrew put his arms around me in a comforting hug—one that I didn't deserve but that he knew I needed. My eyes squeezed shut as I leaned my head against his shoulder. "I feel like a horrible person."

"You're not a horrible person," he said. "I think you just made a few decisions that could have been made differently. You need to resolve them."

Andrew let me go and I wiped my eyes. "I'm sorry I didn't tell you. By the time I was caught up in all of it, it was too late for you to talk me out of it."

"It's okay."

When we walked back into the room, Austin asked, "You're breaking up with Cedric, right? I mean, you and Sam confessed you like each other."

"Like a couple of middle schoolers," Jon Ming muttered and I glared at him.

"All that matters now is what you do next," Austin said.

"Macy, do you still have feelings for Sam?" Andrew asked.

"Yes," I said.

"Do you have feelings for Cedric?" Jon Ming questioned.

"No," I answered. "I thought that if I was still with him, what I felt for Sam would just go away, but it doesn't feel like that anymore. Why do we have to have hormones? Why couldn't humans be given superspeed or the ability to fly instead?"

"God didn't want us to be superheroes because not many people can pull off tights," Austin answered dryly. "Now break up with him."

"I don't want to do it over text. I have to explain it to him in person. When we get back."

"Wanna know the worst way to get dumped?" Jon Ming said. "Email. Happened to my cousin. I mean, through email? Who even *uses* that anymore?"

"This breakup will be good," Andrew said. "Even if you and Sam don't end up together, you'll have a chance to sort out your feelings."

"It will be good," I agreed. "But Sam and I won't happen."

"Why are you sure of that?" Austin wondered.

"Because he said it. He said that he would mess up. That he would probably end up hurting me. Sure, he's possibly changed and the break was . . . it doesn't matter. He made it pretty clear when we spoke about why we did what we did during the break. We did it because it was better for us to stay friends."

"You can't stay friends after something like that," Jon Ming pointed out. "Look at Andrew and Jasmine."

"Shut up, JM," Andrew told Jon Ming before turning to me. "You should talk to him about it,"

"I should focus on Cedric," I said. "On breaking up with him. At least once I do it, I won't be—"

"Cheating on Cedric?" Jon Ming said. Hearing it made my stomach twist because that was exactly what I had done.

~

Coach yelled from the sidelines. The scout stood next to him. I dribbled the ball with my feet. My heart was pounding. I'd been nervous throughout the whole game—not even the Pop-Tart I'd had an hour before had calmed me down.

I controlled my breathing as I ran with the ball, jumping up as a member of the other team tried to slide-tackle me. I'd hit the dirt more times than one could count in my eighteen years of life. I'd grown up with Andrew and Justin—when I shoved them to the ground, I naturally got pushed down too. Trying to find Sam, I dodged an opposing midfielder then passed the ball to Austin at a short distance. He got the ball, dribbling it up as I ran in for the clearing.

The score was tied with fifteen minutes left. Sam dribbled up and over a player's head, controlling it smoothly. He noticed me going for the run and shot it up.

Laying the ball down with my feet, I passed the defender. My heart was beating too fast, knowing that the scout was watching my every move. As I ran up, my foot struck the ball and shot it into the air. The ball hit the corner of the crossbar and went out. I inhaled sharply, anger rising within me as I trudged to my side. The ref retrieved the ball as Sam walked over. "Loosen up. You're doing well."

"I should've gotten that in."

"It's okay." He grabbed my hands, massaging the backs with his thumbs. "Calm down. Breathe."

I took a deep breath not just because of the scout but also because of the heat and nice feelings that came with holding his hands. "Thanks."

"Let's get 'em."

~

"I want ice cream," Jacob said, rolling onto his stomach. He, Brandon, Andrew, Jon Ming, and Austin were lounging on my bed later that afternoon, searching through my laptop for something to watch.

"We don't care," Austin mumbled, and Jacob stuck his foot out to hit Austin's face.

"There's an ice-cream store across the street," Brandon said, pulling a pillow over his head.

"I'll go get it," I offered, getting up from the crowded bed. "I need a break from the level of testosterone in this room." Grabbing my key card and wallet, I headed downstairs to the lobby.

We'd won, but my nerves had gotten the better of me, and while I'd assisted in every goal our team made, I'd failed to bring myself to take a shot on the net for fear the scout would see me miss again. I should have been happy that we won, but I was upset that I hadn't been brave enough to stand out.

Players from different teams were talking to one another in the common room as I passed by. Suddenly, my name was called, and it was Michael, flanked by two of his goons. "What do you want?" I muttered.

"You looked like you were having a meltdown at your game today."

Michael just *had* to pay attention to me. "Don't you have something better to do than taunt me?"

"I would have something better to do but as you can see, you're the only girl I like to bother."

"Leave me alone." My attempt to push past him was failed when he grabbed my arm. I was ready to push him again but he was suddenly on the ground.

Michael stood up, brushing off his friends' attempts to help.

"Don't bother her," Sam hissed.

"She came onto *me*, asshole," Michael said, and I gasped in disbelief.

"Where the *heck* did you get that idea?" I said.

Michael turned back to me. "Don't be such a bi—"

Sam's arm moved to punch Michael's face, but I grabbed him before he could connect, yanking him back. Michael laughed scornfully and walked away.

I pulled Sam through the lobby, passing by different rooms until I saw an unoccupied one and shoved him inside. I closed the door behind us and the small light in the ceiling dimmed the room filled with cleaning products. "You shouldn't have stopped me," Sam said.

"What I need you to do is calm down."

His nostrils flared. "He was harassing you."

I put my hands on his cheeks and he took a moment, visibly relaxing. "I can take care of myself and people like Michael. Thanks, though," I said. Once his breathing slowed, I turned to leave the room but Sam grabbed my arm, looking at me in a way I recognized from the days of the break.

"Don't do that," I said, pulling away from his grasp. "We can't do that. I need to talk to Cedric, and you aren't exactly showing that you have me out of your system. At least be straightforward."

"I am."

I prodded my finger into his hard chest. "Actions speak louder than words."

I didn't say anything more, leaving and finding my way back to my assigned room. I opened the door to see the boys arguing about what to watch on my laptop. Jacob's face fell when he saw my empty hands. "Where's the ice cream?"

27
FIT INTO A BOX

If Crenshaw Hills won their next game, they would be in the finals. And they were dominating each of their games. If we won this one, we'd be their opponent. This game would mostly be up to Sam. He knew where to pass the ball, he knew where to look, and he could sense what the other team was going to do in advance.

I sat on the bench, tearing a piece of a Pop-Tart Andrew had given me before the game started. The scout was talking to Coach at the side when Sam came over to me after helping lead a drill. "You all right?"

"How come you're not captain?" He looked confused. "You're amazing at soccer-football-whatever. You help and get everyone to improve on their skills. You'd be great."

"You have a certain understanding with them." He nodded at our teammates on the field. "You're perfect as captain for this team. And, by the looks of it, you're full of energy."

I pressed my hand against my bouncing knee. "Is it that obvious?"

"I have an idea I want to share with you and the team. I told Coach but I need to run it by you, Captain." He playfully knocked his shoulder against mine. He grabbed a clipboard and marker to show it to me, his knee pressed against my own.

~

I couldn't get myself to score and Sam must've noticed, because when we were at 1–1 he kept passing the ball to me, and I'd just assist it back to him. Two of those many passes were intercepted by the other team.

We still won 2–1, and now we were in the finals. Against Crenshaw Hills. I'd scanned their practice on one of the indoor fields and they were a fit team now. There'd been a lot of improvement on the team, especially with Michael.

With the final game about to begin and Andrew on the sidelines, I wished Jasmine was here. She would've settled my nerves. Cedric would have too. Or Drake. Or Justin, holding my camera and taking a video of everything. If my dad was here he would've been the loudest person in the crowd.

I wished my mom was here.

"Ready?" Sam asked me and I nodded. He jogged to his spot, which was about six feet away from me.

The referee blew the whistle and the game started.

By halftime, the score was tied at zero apiece.

If we'd gone with our old formation, we would've lost the game, but with extra defense help from Sam's strategy, we were able to keep possession of the ball for longer periods of time. As

I ran off the field I was panting, and Andrew tossed me some water. "You're doing great," he said.

Jon Ming appeared. "They got really good."

"Yeah," Jacob agreed.

Sam ran over and I handed him my water. "We need to try runs instead of short passes. Michael is out to get you every time," he said.

"You don't think I know that?" I snapped.

Sam didn't waver. "Save the attitude for the game." We got into a huddle around Coach and Andrew.

When the whistle blew for us to get back on the field, Coach held me back. "You got this, Mace. Give it everything you've got."

"I will," I said, and took off onto the field. Four corners and one free kick later, time was running out. Brandon dived to grab the ball, shooting it up and curving it into the air. Jon Ming went for the header with another player on the opposing team as I tried to stay in their line of defense. The other player shoved Jon Ming slightly to get the ball and Jon Ming fell, dusting himself off as he got back up.

"Wow," Michael whispered mockingly behind me.

I shot him a look as I ran forward. Jacob had the ball. "Hazel!" a voice called. Sam ran past me. "About fifteen seconds. Run!"

I sprinted once Jacob passed Sam the ball. Sam lay the ball off the side to Jon Ming. Jon Ming moved past a defender, passing it back to Sam—I had to get in line with Michael, the sweeper.

Sam shot the ball into the air, right toward me. I caught it with my feet, but Michael was close by, trying to get the ball away from me. His hands were on my jersey, pulling me back. I reared my leg back to take the shot, but pain shot up my calf and

I fell onto the grass. The goalie dived forward and grabbed the ball. He shot the ball into the air and three long whistles blasted.

Someone lifted me up as I spat out a mouthful of turf. The pain was subsiding from where Michael had dug one of his cleats into my calf, but I knew a bruise was going to form there soon. "You all right? You did good," Sam assured me but my anger toward Michael didn't fade. "Penalty shoot-outs."

Sam and I headed over to the rest of the team. As Coach spoke, my name came up on the roster of players. Everyone headed back onto the field but Andrew held me back. "You got a text."

"You're stopping me from heading over because of a text message?"

Andrew handed me my phone.

> Drake: Jasmine said you guys are in the finals. Do
> good today

She knew. Both Drake and Jasmine knew about the game. Relief overcame me. I took a deep breath, shaking all the nerves out of my body, Drake's voice in my head.

We stood with our teams, me between Sam and Andrew. Crenshaw would take the first shot. Brandon got in the net, hopping back and forth on his feet. One of Crenshaw's players took their shot. Their team yelled. The goal went in—1–0.

Sam walked over, grabbed the ball, and placed it for his kick. He paused, looking up at the sky for a moment. The second Crenshaw's goalie was ready and the referee blew the whistle, Sam didn't even hesitate. He jogged over and kicked the ball swiftly past the goalie's hands and into the net.

Our teammates patted him on the back when he returned. "That looked effortless," I said.

He shrugged. "Depends on how you do it, babe."

"Don't call me that."

"What would you prefer?" He grinned. "*Tomboy?*"

"That's like me calling you *bad boy.*"

"Or Jacob calling you a *pig.*"

"Player," I retorted, any sign of anxiousness within me fading with our banter.

"Bigfoot."

"Cockroach."

"Did you just call me a cockroach?"

"You called me bigfoot!"

"Because I've called you that before. Do I look like a cockroach to you?" We shared a laugh that I immediately cut off as Andrew stared at me.

The score reached 2–2 and my nerves escalated. Austin went for it and was close but the goalie's fingers pushed the ball away from the corner.

We were down to one more penalty each. Brandon rubbed his goalie gloves together. "Come on, Brandon," Sam mumbled.

Michael's attention was on a spot of the net for too long. Brandon must've caught it, too, because once the ref blew the whistle and Michael kicked the ball, Brandon jumped to the right, slapping the ball to the ground. He dived down to hold it steady.

"You'll be fine," Sam said to me as everyone congratulated Brandon on his save. "That scout came all this way for you, you can do it."

I made my way to the box as the ref placed the ball on the ground. I backed a few steps away from the ball when my

Nonna's words rang in my head: *Just do your best. It'll be enough.* With soccer, it was always enough.

The whistle blew, piercing my ears.

I ran toward the ball and kicked it.

The ball flew through the air, barely scraping the goalie's fingertips. When the ball hit the back of the net, my teammates cheered loudly and ran over, clasping me into a huge group hug. Sam's eyes were the first ones I saw—I hugged him tightly to me as he lifted me up. When he moved to put me down, he intertwined our fingers together. The familiar action snapped me out of my happy trance, causing me to release our hands. "Hazel—"

"You said that we would never happen, remember? And I don't want to hurt Cedric any more than I already have."

Then I saw it. The guilt he'd been trying to push away surfaced in his green eyes. Suddenly I was being carried aloft by the others, Sam no longer in my view.

"Good one, Macy," Andrew said before concern crossed his expression. "You okay?"

"Macy." I turned around to face Coach and the scout with his clipboard. He put his hand out for me to shake and I shook it, anticipating the talk about my future.

~

The moment I returned to Port Meadow on Friday night, I went to Jasmine's house. I was used to having her dad greet me at the door while the smell of her mom's cooking would lead me straight to the kitchen. Drake would usually see me before his sister, ruffling my hair before leaving to go hang out with some friends, and I'd walk into Jasmine's room, ready for her to make me watch another *Star Wars* movie or tell me about a new club she joined.

The smile on Jasmine's mom's face when she opened the door was similar to the one she used to wear, even in the absence of Jasmine's dad.

"Macy, come in." She ushered me in and my hands stayed in my pockets. "Why do you look uncomfortable?"

"Jas and I had a little falling out a while ago. Is she here?"

Her mom's expression softened. "She's in her room."

I stood outside Jasmine's door and was about to knock when the door flew open. Jasmine walked to her bed, stopping the music playing from her speakers. I shut the door behind me and took a seat on her desk chair. "Did you just get back?"

"Came straight here," I said.

"Congrats on the win. Drew told me about the scholarship. When do you have to go to your first practice?"

"Late August. Look, can we cut to chase here?" Her silence gave me the answer I needed as I leaned forward, my elbows on my knees. "I should've been more understanding and shouldn't have forced you to tell me what was on your mind. What Beatrice does to me compared to what she says to you—it's not the same thing. I hate that she makes you feel like you don't belong at our school, because you do. You're the most involved person at school. When you're not there, I bug Andrew the whole time about how much I miss you—"

Jasmine let out a soft laugh. "And you tell him, 'Don't tell her I said that.'"

"I'm sorry she and other people do this and that I'm not as aware of it as I should be. She's a racist, plain and simple, and you shouldn't have to put up with that. You have our support—

me, the guys, Stevie, and all your other friends. We're definitely here for you no matter what, and I will be there for you even more in the future. People like Beatrice, they're not even worth it. We can't let what she says get into our heads."

"I know that," she agreed. "You've got to remember that too."

"I know," I said. "I've let her get into my head for a long time. I even had to deal with a mini version of her over the break." Jasmine looked confused. "I'll tell you about it later, but I've learned that I am who I am and you are who you are. If people don't like that, they can fuck off."

Jasmine's eyes went wide and we burst into laughter. "You swore."

"I did."

Jasmine frowned. "I didn't mean to try to change you, especially since you have a boyfriend. Putting you in clothes you don't like wearing? I shouldn't have done that. There isn't anything to change. If you weren't you, you wouldn't be my best friend."

"Can I hug you?"

Jasmine made a weird face at my sudden need for affection but I was already out of my chair and tackling her into a hug that she was quick to reciprocate as we fell onto the bed.

"This is weird," she mumbled.

"I really am sorry," I said. "I shouldn't have exploded on you about opening up."

"I didn't know how to handle my parents separating even after I told you and Drew," she said. "I still don't. And when Dad left, wrecking our family for a completely different life—I didn't know how to feel."

"It's okay to not know."

Jasmine let go and rolled onto her back. "It's one thing for your parents to divorce because they're unhappy; it's another to realize your dad cheated on your mom and knocked someone up. I didn't want to talk about it because, look"—the laugh that left her mouth was pitiful—"I just fit into one of Beatrice's little stereotypes again. My dad left."

Her dejected tone made me frown and I grabbed her hand. "Jasmine, these things happen. Don't see it as fulfilling a stereotype. You don't fit into a box and neither does anyone else in your family. Don't pay any attention to Beatrice. What matters is how you view yourself. You're going to be okay. And your mom? She seems happier."

There was a hint of a smile on my best friend's face at that. "She does, doesn't she?" As I hugged her once again, she cringed. "Yeah, this is going to take some getting used to. I initiate hugs here. Anyway, how was your break?"

I told her everything. When I finished, the look on Jasmine's face mirrored what Andrew's had been, making my stomach queasy. "Have you spoken to Sam?"

"Not since the win."

"I know he, like you, didn't want it to happen like this," she said. "It may seem like he and Cedric have issues but he still cares for his cousin. I'm sure he has as much, if not more, guilt as you do." Jasmine's attention went to her beeping phone and she read the text message. "Brandon and Jacob are throwing a party tomorrow night. When's Cedric coming back? I didn't see him at school."

"Tomorrow evening." My stomach twisted at all the possibilities of how this could go.

"You'll do it then?"

"I have to talk to him face to face. I wouldn't be surprised if he wants to go to the party—I'll have to find a way to speak to him alone."

"It'll be okay," she reassured me, finally initiating a much-needed hug.

~

Saturday night, Stevie drove me to Jacob and Brandon's home. When we entered, red cups littered the ground, music blared in my ears, and the house smelled like alcohol and sweat. Jon Ming flipped through his phone, changing the song that blasted through the speakers in the living room. Austin waved at us from the couch as we passed by, and Andrew and Jasmine approached us.

"You showed up," Andrew said.

I pointed at his foot. "*You* showed up. "

Stevie's hand left mine as she was pulled into conversation with someone else. "Have you seen Cedric?" I asked Jasmine.

"He got here a while ago."

"I need to find him." My phone buzzed in my pocket with a text message from Cedric. "Got to go." Jasmine flashed me her crossed fingers as I headed to the basement where Cedric was.

Cedric stopped midconversation with one of his classmates and walked over to me. "Hey, Mace! Congrats again on the tourney," he exclaimed, pulling me into a hug I immediately reciprocated.

My hand fiddled around with my camera bag. "Thanks, listen, can we talk?"

"I'll get you a drink first, okay?" Cedric was gone, heading up the stairs before I could respond.

A familiar head of curly hair was in the corner of the room—

and he wasn't alone. Sam's green eyes were bright and there was a smirk on his face. The girl in front of him was Beatrice.

Of all people in the school, in all of Port Meadow, it *had* to be Beatrice.

"Here you go." Cedric stood in front of me and handed me a drink, not completely blocking my view of the two.

I took the cup from him. "What's in here?"

Cedric raised his eyebrows. "Do you really think I would spike your drink?"

"I don't know." I flashed him a fake smile. "I barely saw you these past two weeks, maybe you've changed."

He nudged me and over Cedric's shoulder, I could see Sam's focus on me as Beatrice talked to him. My heart dropped as he leaned in to whisper in her ear, his hand curling around her waist as she listened. It was the familiar way he was looking at her, with affection, acting similar to how he had when we were in Redmond. Even worse, he leaned in once again and . . . and then liquid splashed on my flats and I realized I'd dropped my drink.

Almost kicking my cup, I bolted up the stairs, not making it to the front door when a hand pulled me back. "Macy, what's going on?" Cedric looked confused, his eyes wide at the sight of my flushed face.

"I can't do this anymore," I told him, wiping my eyes.

The guilt washed over me in waves at the sight of his confused expression.

"What do you mean?"

My hands went over my face and I sucked in a deep breath. "There's, there's someone else—"

"Someone else? What are you talking about? Who else?"

"I'm sorry, I—I'm breaking up with you." I sprinted out of

the house, passing the people vaping on the front lawn. Passing the people about to enter the party. My heart squeezed in my chest as I ran, my legs taking me in the direction of a nearby park. When I slowed down to a walk as I approached the park, no one was nearby. I sat down on one of the benches, my fingers tapping against my phone screen.

A couple of minutes later, a hand tapped my shoulder. Andrew pulled me off the bench, his blue eyes dim. "Let's go. Jas's waiting in the car," he murmured.

The car ride was silent. When Jasmine parked by the side of my house, I unbuckled my seat belt. "Thanks for the ride home. I'll see you both at school."

I ignored Andrew's protests as I got out of the car. I trudged up the front steps, using my key to enter the house. My dad was the first to see me as I took off my shoes. He walked over to me instantly, wrapping his arms around me. "Honey, you look like your favorite soccer player died."

I sniffed, cracking a smile. "Great analogy."

"I'm cheering you up already."

"I need a moment to myself."

He pressed a kiss to my forehead. "Call me if you need anything."

I went upstairs to my room, furiously changing into comfortable sweats and a sports bra. Then I went down to the kitchen, grabbed a carton of ice cream from the freezer, and made my way to the basement to put on a video game. I was in the middle of a good game when footsteps came from the stairs. Andrew hobbled down the stairs behind Jasmine.

"Macy—"

I interrupted Jasmine by handing her a controller. "Can we just play?"

She grabbed my hand, then took another controller to pass to Andrew, who took a seat next to me. I spent that night with them distracted, neither mentioning Sam.

~

I'd never had a week this awkward in my eighteen years of life.

Before spring break, I had a routine with the two Cahill boys. In the mornings, Cedric would usually meet me at my locker. Or we'd talk before lunch ended about plans to hang out after school or on the weekend. But now he avoided me at all costs, and I didn't blame him.

With Sam, I would usually see him at lunch, at practice, or after school just hanging out. But now I could barely look at him and he knew that, apparently spending his lunch period catching up on work at the library.

Yet I couldn't avoid him when, on Monday at school, I heard him under the railing of the staircase, annoyed. He was talking to Beatrice, whose face mirrored Sam's.

"Why not?" she pestered.

"Because I don't want to. I need to get to class." His tone made it clear he did not want to talk to her again.

"Since when do *you* care about school?" She moved back, crossing her arms.

"Since when do *you* care about my business?" He tried to push past her, but she stopped him with her hand. His glare was strong enough to make me still. "Nothing happened between us on Saturday. I told you before, I wasn't looking for anything you were expecting from me."

Making my way upstairs, I ran over to class. Just my luck,

the first person I had to pass on the way to class was Cedric. He locked eyes with me for a second before acting as if I wasn't in front of him and moved past me wordlessly.

When I got home later that day, I scrolled through my messages, sighing at the memory of Cedric's face. What was I honestly expecting? Of course he was going to look shattered; to him, the breakup came out of nowhere.

As I read over a text message from one of the boys, a hard knock came from the front door. Although I was in a sour mood, Austin looked pretty happy. His tanned skin seemed as if it was glowing. "You look very gloomy. You've been like this all day, especially at practice."

"Thanks for noticing," I muttered as we reached the basement, jumping back on the couch and putting my blanket over me.

He sat down next to me, getting under the blanket with me. "I know what happened at the party. Talk to me."

"I'm upset that Sam was with Beatrice." My throat tightened and I almost cursed myself over the idea of crying over a guy, but it wasn't just him. "I'm upset that I broke up with Cedric."

"You wanted to."

"I did," I admitted. "It's the way I did it that bothers me. I ended it and walked away, giving him no opportunity to discuss it with me or ask questions. I cheated on him with his *cousin*. I'm upset that I did that—I wish I'd done *everything* differently." I remembered Austin's cheery mood when he had entered the house. "Why are you so happy by the way?"

Austin stretched his legs in front of him, his bright-blue socks peeking out. "I had some good pizza and Jon Ming sent me new music he made. More importantly, at that party, I . . . kind of got together with someone."

"I'm assuming romantically."

"You're assuming correctly," he said. "The guy I was texting weeks ago? It was him. Look, I know you don't like romance stuff but Jasmine's with Andrew, Stevie doesn't know I'm gay, and I figured I needed to check in on you. You're the one finding out first."

"That's great, Austin. I'm really happy for you." I wanted him to feel like I had at one point—the good feeling of having someone be on your mind constantly, the awareness you got when they were close. He deserved that. "Are you ever going to tell other people about . . ."

He ran a hand through his hair. "I haven't told my parents, and honestly having you guys know is enough. I don't think I'm ready yet. Besides, we graduate in a couple of months. I think I can wait."

"You're scared."

"I don't know what could happen."

I reached for his hand. "Whatever you decide to do, we have your back. No matter what happens, you're still my friend— even as annoying as you are."

That earned me a light punch on my arm. "I don't doubt that for a second."

28
MEMORY

Boom! Boom!

Justin came out of our front door and spotted me in the drive-way, kicking the ball against the garage door. "Are you okay?"

I stopped the ball with my foot. "I'm great." *No, I'm not.*

This past weekend gave me more time to think. My volun-teering days at the rec center were on hold due to the end of the winter house league season, allowing me to throw myself into school.

I needed to talk to Cedric, to explain things to him, but he was still avoiding me. Seeing Sam didn't help, either, because even while I was avoiding him, he was still part of the team. He dis-tracted me without knowing it during practice. When Coach ran a drill on Monday, I messed up—my attention on Sam, who was working on shots with Brandon—and causing the rest of the team to run laps until everyone's legs burned.

The bristling memory of him with Beatrice the night of the

party flashed through my mind every time I saw him, and I had scornfully pushed it away until today. Today, I allowed myself to be angry, not just at Sam with Beatrice, but at myself for making horrible choices. Kicking the ball felt like the best thing to do.

Justin stood in front of the wall. "Macy."

"Move, Justin."

"Stop being angry, you're acting exactly like—" I kicked the ball toward him, aiming it to hit the wall right beside him. Justin yelped.

"I'm acting like what?"

"Like when Mom died."

My hair had fallen out of my ponytail, the elastic band somewhere in the grass. "You were six when it happened."

"I get it. Sam made you really mad."

"Thank you, Captain Obvious," I snapped, rearing my leg back to kick the ball.

When I did kick it, Justin had his hands out and reached over his head, catching the ball in his hands. "*Holy shit*, that hurt."

"Give me my ball."

"You realize with the way you kick you could break a window, right?"

"Leave me alone," I said, snatching the ball from his grasp.

Dad poked his head through the front door. "What is going on?"

Justin pointed at me. "She's going crazy."

"I'm *not* going crazy."

"You could've killed me with that soccer ball."

"The maximum damage that could've happened was you whining like a baby on the ground for a couple of minutes. It's not that big a deal."

"I don't know what to do with her," Justin said. "Your turn."

Dad walked over to me. "Sit."

As I seated myself on the grass, Justin was quick to grab the ball.

"What happened?" Dad asked.

"Do you really want to hear about my guy problems?"

"You're right," he agreed. "I always thought this would be your mother's department."

"How would she have gone about it, then?" I asked.

Dad crouched in front of me, reaching forward to ruffle my hair. I laughed, pushing his hand away. "She'd do something like that to make you laugh first. She used to tickle you whenever you were upset."

"What would she say?" Justin sat next to me.

"She'd probably ask what was going on in the first place. And you would tell her everything because she'd want you to be able to come to her for anything."

"Like how we do with you," Justin said, and I bit my lip, knowing that I hadn't done that with my dad for a while.

"Something happened during the break between me and Sam." My gaze fell to the ground to avoid my dad's concerned look.

"What had happened with Cedric?"

"I was still with Cedric at the time." My stomach twisted at saying that out loud.

Dad was silent, probably processing the information. "Have you spoken to Cedric recently?"

"He's avoiding me."

"You may not be friends like you were before, but he'll talk to you eventually. He would want an explanation."

"Is that Mom talking or you?" Justin asked.

"That one was me. What did Sam do?"

Before I could explain that the only person I was truly furious with was myself, my phone rang. Pulling it out of my pocket, I answered Caleb's call.

"Can you get over here?"

He sounded off, almost panicked. "Where?"

"The Cahill house."

What? "Why would I do that?"

"Because we can't find Sam and his aunt Liz is getting really worried."

~

"What if he's at a friend's house?" Justin asked in the car minutes later as Dad drove. "He's eighteen."

"Your sister is eighteen and still tells me where she's going at all times." Dad's valid point hung in the air and Justin shut up fast. "His aunt, who's looking after him, is worried about where he is; it's understandable."

"But *this* worried?" Justin mumbled.

"I don't know," I said. "Caleb sounded really stressed when he told me to rush over there."

Dad turned into the Cahills' big driveway. Before I could ring the doorbell, the door whipped open, Cedric on the other side of the threshold. His eyes were slightly red. "Come in."

As I entered the living room, Caleb's frustration was clear. "Seriously? He disappears today of all days? Are you sure he's not hiding out in the pool house?" He directed that last question to Ivan, who said no.

"What's going on?" I asked Caleb.

"No one has seen Sam since last night, and I called everyone to see if they were with him today, but no." Caleb raked a hand through his hair.

"Did anything weird happen last night?" Dad asked.

"Nothing abnormal," Cedric said. "He didn't have any night terrors. I would have heard."

"Night terrors?" Justin whispered to me. I shrugged, as confused as he was.

Ivan tapped Caleb with his phone. "What about the rec center?"

"Austin texted me," Caleb said. "They said he's not there." Phillip pulled his feet up on the couch next to his mom, the cat in his arms. He was worried. His bond with Sam reminded me of my own with Justin. I didn't know what I would do if my brother suddenly disappeared.

Heavy footsteps echoed in the house as Vince Cahill walked in. He was wearing his usual work attire. Silence fell over the room. Mr. Cahill nodded at my dad before turning back to everyone else. "No idea?" The evident stress clouding his expression surprised me a little bit—I wondered what Sam would have said if he was here.

"No, we're still looking," said Cedric.

"He's not at your grandmother's." Vince turned to Liz. "I rang up the house back in England, James checked and no purchases have been made from his credit or debit cards."

"Are Uncle James, Greg, and Aunt Alice flying here?" Phillip asked, biting his nails. Sam's family.

"Not yet." Vince turned to his wife. "If we don't find him in two hours they're coming. He's not at any of the extended family's houses." Vince took a seat on the other side of Phillip. "He doesn't want to be found."

Ivan's eyes shot to me. "Where would he go?"

"Wouldn't you think Caleb would know?"

"No, he's right," Caleb agreed. "You would know."

If he wasn't in the rec center, where we'd spent most of our time playing soccer together, or school or home or at his grandmother's, then he must be at the one place he considered his sanctuary; a place he'd taken me. "The quarry."

"The quarry?" Caleb looked as confused as everyone else in the room.

"It's outside of the city," I explained. "If he's not with his grandmother, then he's at the quarry." Caleb still looked puzzled. "You don't know where it is?"

"I have no idea what you're talking about," Caleb said.

"He said . . ." I trailed off. He hadn't told me that Caleb knew of his thinking place; I had simply assumed it.

"I think I know where you're talking about," Cedric said. "I'll give you a ride."

"Are you certain he's there?" Liz asked.

"It's the only place I can think of." I turned to my dad. "Can I go?"

His face looked serious. "You have your phone on you?"

"Yup."

"If you can't get a ride home when you find him, you call me. You got it?"

"Got it."

Cedric walked out of the living room. I was about to follow him when Caleb held me back by my arm. "Text me when you find him, okay?"

"I will."

~

Cedric's hands gripped the steering wheel so tightly his knuckles were turning white. My anxiousness was growing and overtaking my focus on the obvious awkwardness between the two of us as he drove.

After a long and deafening silence, Cedric parked the car, but didn't move right away.

"I'm sorry," I said. Too quickly. "For not explaining."

"I think we should talk about this when it all blows over," Cedric said, and I agreed, spotting a familiar car in the parking lot. Cedric reached into the back seat and pulled out two water bottles, handing them both to me. "If I know my cousin, you're going to have to make him drink this."

I grabbed them and got out of the car. "Thanks."

"Anytime." He pulled out of the parking lot, waving to me as he drove away.

Walking the familiar route, I zipped up my jacket. There was no one near the water, and I figured Sam would be near the top of the quarry. Trudging up the long path, one hand on my phone and the other on the zipper of my jacket, I reached the top and found him.

Sam was sitting where we had been the first day we had been here. Still behind him, I texted Caleb that I'd found him and put my ringer on silent.

Sam didn't turn around but his shoulders tensed—he knew someone was behind him. Moving closer, I immediately noticed the tall bottle of alcohol.

I sat down next to him and both of us looked at the sun sinking in the distance. "I don't need you here," he muttered.

"I'm not leaving. Also, drinking in public isn't legal."

"You can't tell me what to do." He sounded childish.

"Sam, stop being obnoxious."

"You need to mind your own business and leave me alone." His voice was as cold and hard as steel.

"Is that what you really want?" His eyes were redder than Cedric's—I wasn't sure if that was due to the drinking or the crying. "*Fine*, I'll leave you alone." I started to get up but a hand on my arm stopped me.

"No, don't go." Sam's expression softened. "Stay."

"What is with you?" I sat back down. "Everyone is worried about you."

"Why are *you* here?"

"Because I care about you." *Much more than I want to admit.*

"You shouldn't care about me," Sam said. "I hurt you. It was all over your face the other day."

"I don't care about that right now."

He took another sip of his drink. "Shit, this is going to affect me in the morning."

"Then stop drinking or you'll make it worse."

Sam didn't bother listening, and took a cigarette package from his pocket. He flipped the package over in his hand, and while I was surprised to see it, he didn't take notice of my expression when he handed it to me. "Before I met you, I only had one real friend here."

He paused to shut off the lighter and took a swig of his drink as I still held the water bottles in my hands. "How did you find me?"

"This is your thinking place," I recalled. "You really worried everyone."

"I can imagine," he said dryly.

"That's all you can say?" I stood up. "Sam, you had them worried sick that something happened to you. Even your uncle."

Sam stood up in disbelief, wobbling back and forth. "My *uncle* was worried about me? What did you do? Tie him to a chair?"

"Believe it or not, he cares for you more than you think."

Sam didn't care, ready to take another swallow of his drink. I grabbed the bottle from his hands. "Give it back, Hazel."

"I'm not going to have you in the hospital with alcohol poisoning or liver failure." I held out one of the water bottles. "You can have this instead."

"Give it to me." He managed to take his bottle out of my hand. "I could be doing something much worse, you know."

"Your uncle has your parents on alert and they are probably worried sick about you, and you want to do this? Fine." I threw both of the water bottles onto the ground in case he changed his mind later. "Excuse me for trying to be there for you."

"Wait." He inhaled sharply, his voice cracking. He dropped his head and stood there, defeated. Reaching forward, I took the bottle from his hand and placed it on the ground behind me. Taking a harsh breath, he sniffed, wiping a hand under his eyes.

I hugged him. He reciprocated instantly and I didn't say anything. He didn't need to hear anything or an "It's okay." It wouldn't help him.

After a couple of seconds, he pulled back, taking one of the water bottles from where I had dropped them. He took a seat again, taking a drink of water as I sat down next to him. Dusk had fallen, and his eyes went up to the sky. "Today's the anniversary of Bethany's death."

He wiped his tears away with the backs of his hands furiously. "She didn't even get to fight for her life. It was instantly taken away from her." His voice cracked at the end and I winced at the unexpected sound. "My parents told me at the hospital. I didn't believe them—I half expected Bethany to open the door and laugh loudly that my mum was kidding . . . but she didn't. No one talked about it at all, not until after her funeral.

"That was the worst day. There were so many people at her funeral. We flew Caleb over and I think his face was the worst out of everyone's. He was crazy about her. And now she was . . . she was just lying there, in her favorite white dress and the bracelet Caleb had given her one summer on her wrist. She had a necklace on, same as mine. Hers had an *S* in the middle."

Sam let go of my hands and reached for the necklace, pulling the pendant out from where it was tucked under his shirt. "We got them on our tenth birthday with our given letter, then switched them and never took them off. After the funeral everything went into a downward spiral. She was my twin. My other half."

He was staring at the ground. "About a week later, I got into the biggest argument with my dad. I was upset that he had gone back to work, back to normal, as if her death had never even happened, and I called him out on it. Then I took off and went to Redmond, my grandmother's house, in the middle of the semester. I guess that's when it started."

"What started?"

"Alexis was my first," he mumbled. It took me a moment to register his words, and my expression must have said it all because he was quick to speak up. "It didn't mean anything. I told her that and she said to forget it even happened. We remained friends." So that was why she was so attached to the idea that Sam loved her like she loved him. A pang of sympathy surged in me for her; Sam had used her at a difficult time in his life, and she believed a bond had formed between them.

He took a drink from the water bottle. "After that, Dad dragged me back home. I wanted to forget everything, so I did things I wouldn't even have thought of weeks earlier. That's why everyone says that I changed—I guess I did. I hung out with different people and did things that made my entire family upset at my behavior. I stole things. I would walk into the house absolutely pissed; my mum kind of snapped."

"What did she do?"

"She knew I was acting out, that I was taking Bethany's death very hard. She put me in social groups. I hung out with people who weren't exactly a good influence back home. I got involved in some shit—obviously the arson incident. When my parents heard I was involved, they realized the social groups weren't helping.

"The last thing I ever wanted to do was disappoint my mum and dad. And Greg. I knew I did when they sent me to live here. They also sent me to live here so I could clean up my act. At that time, all I wanted was to forget her. It was hard—*really* hard—and I did bad things."

I handed him the other bottle of water, watching him take a sip out of that one. "Last summer when I was here, I don't know—I kind of gave up. I was very overwhelmed by everything and I didn't think I would ever get used to never seeing her again. Her not being there, not laughing, or singing—her being annoying or sharing birthdays, asking me for advice. I was done with life. I was in the bathroom and . . ." He paused, his eyes on the ground. "And then Caleb appeared, knocking it out of my hands. It shattered on the floor; it looked like a thousand white beads had fallen. We dropped to the ground and I was crying. The most I ever had in my entire life. People have come and gone in my life, but Caleb has never left, even when I've ignored him. He was always there for me, like a brother."

He sighed heavily. "This is the first time I've ever really talked about what happened that night." He whispered the last part of the sentence in pure disbelief and that was when I realized I should start talking.

"You know what I've learned since my mom died?"

"What?" His index finger was tapping at the ground and his tongue prodded the inside of his cheek.

"The worst thing about death—other than dying—is being forgotten. You remember everything about Bethany, and that keeps a part of her alive. Moving on doesn't mean we forget certain things. Instead, we have to understand that what happened happened and continue living."

He drank from the water bottle until it was almost empty. "Isn't that why you take pictures?"

"Each memory is something I *want* to remember. I like remembering my mom. If I forgot who she was, I don't think I would forgive myself. Seeing her in old videos and photos reminds me that she's always with me. That necklace of yours symbolizes that Bethany is with you. Even though you think you don't want to remember her, this shows me that you will. It's okay to mourn, to cry, and to let your feelings out. You don't have to bottle up your emotions, and there are people and resources that can help you, no matter the situation. That's the healthy part of dealing. This whole other outlet of alcohol, drugs, and sex is not going to help you."

Sam's hands were on his necklace. He reached up to wipe the tears away from his eyes but it didn't look like he was going to stop crying. The pads of my thumbs brushed the tears from under his eyes. "It's okay to let it out."

I held him, waiting with a heavy heart as he did as I said. When he pulled away, I wiped the tears off his face once again, pushing his curly hair off his forehead.

"Thanks."

"How about you tell me about her?" I suggested. "It sometimes helps me to talk about my mom."

"She was born before me and never let me forget it. We did everything together and she was always there for me. She forced my cousins to make a sign for me for my first football game. She wasn't just my sister; she was my best friend. Sure, there were times when she was annoying as hell, but that's every sibling. And . . . I'm all over the place here. Um, she had dark-brown hair and green eyes, like you saw in the picture I showed you."

"Like you," I pointed out.

Sam cracked a smile, the first one I'd seen tonight. "Yeah, Hazel. Did I mention we were twins?"

"Don't be a jerk. Not now." Even with the tears staining his face, he chuckled. The picture on Caleb's nightstand came to mind. "Caleb was crazy about her?"

"Caleb met her the same day he met me for the first time. We all became best friends and I know Caleb fell for her not long after that, even when we were kids. When Drake came along? I knew he was hurt by it." Sam sighed. "I shouldn't have fought Drake that day."

"You shouldn't have," I agreed.

"He didn't even date Beth for that long, but he made her happy when we were here that year. And when he broke up with her, seeing him again, it reminded me of how much he hurt her when he ended things, and I got mad."

Sam held his arms around his knees. "You know, since that night I've had night terrors. Same thing every time. I hear everything, I see the lights close in on us—it's fucking scary. They used to happen often but they started going away a while ago."

"How do you feel now?"

He wiped the remaining tears from his face and put his leather jacket back on, zipping it up to his collarbone. "A lot better than I did before you got here."

"If you need anything, I'm here, Sam."

A grateful look crossed his face. "I know. I miss her a lot."

"It's okay to," I reminded him.

"Thank you for being here even after what I did."

"Sam—"

"I was being a horrible person and I know what I did. I'm sorry. I really am."

"I forgive you."

"I don't deserve it," he mumbled.

"I'm giving this one to you," I said. "I know you were being awful and you know it too."

Sam scoffed. "I was so stupid. *We* were so stupid."

"What?"

"I really thought that us being together just for that time was going to make everything I felt for you go away." I reached for the water bottle he was holding, taking a sip for myself because my heart pounded in my ears. "It didn't do shit."

"What are you saying?"

"That all the time we spent together at school, rec center, here, anywhere . . . it all meant something."

"Sam—"

"I'm in love with you, Macy Anderson. That's what I'm saying."

I didn't think I heard him correctly. To have Sam Cahill say those words out loud was something. I wasn't sure what surprised me more: the fact that he had said my real name or that he was in love with me. I didn't think there was a proper response to his words until I settled for, "You're what?"

"I'm in love with you."

"No, you're not." Denial. There was no way he meant that. "You're drunk—"

Sam reached over to grab the bottle of alcohol, wiggling it in one hand. While his plan had been to possibly finish it, enough of the liquor was gone for him to at least be tipsy. "I'm not. I'm not lying."

The seriousness of his tone sent a wave of emotions I couldn't decipher. "Sam."

"You don't have to say it back," he said. "I need you to hear me out."

My heart was pounding loud enough for me to hear it in my ears. "Then talk."

"The first time I saw you was at the rec center a few weeks after I was sent to live here. Ivan said I could play soccer there because of the indoor fields. You were with a few of the guys and I watched your game. You scored." His voice had gotten quieter. His eyes were on the water bottle, too, talking almost as if I wasn't here. "You were always doing your own thing, especially when it came to football. Didn't matter if you were the only girl trying out—it didn't stop you, and I admired that about you. One day in November you were part of hosting the football try-outs at the rec center and it was so obvious you were going to be captain. I overheard Coach say it."

My face flushed.

"Then that day when you clumsily tripped over your soccer ball and fell right into me—"

"I didn't fall—"

"You fell, Hazel, don't lie." A smirk came onto his face. "You didn't know who I was. You didn't flirt with me. I really wanted to get to know you and instead *I* fell. Hard. And I've done stupid things because of my decisions. I'm sorry about what happened with Beatrice. I'm sorry I hurt you. I was jealous—I saw you with Cedric at that party and I acted on impulse, to get a reaction out of you. I didn't do anything with her. I swear it." His head hung low and his hands dug into his hair. "I kept fucking up with you and even with Cedric."

"You're not the only one to blame here," I said. "I should've broken it off with Cedric the second I knew I felt something for you. We shouldn't have thought that what we did over the break was going to settle anything."

"I didn't understand why you would want to be with me. Especially after hearing about the girls I've been with, the rumors. I thought you didn't need to be with someone like that."

"I don't care about all that." I took his hand. "I don't and you can't tell me who I need to be with, Sam. We should have done this right the first time."

"I don't want to hurt you like that again," he said quietly.

"If you're in love with me then you won't." His gaze softened and I leaned forward, pressing my lips against his as our eyes fell shut. My right hand moved down, over his leather jacket, and rested on his heart, which was beating rapidly, like mine. I missed this. Being with him like this.

He pulled back first. "I want to try. This. Us. I don't want to disappoint you."

"You're not going to," I said. "I want to try this, too, but not today. Today is a day about Bethany. A day you can fully remember her, for her. Since we're going to try this, I need you to be fully certain. We can wait until you're ready." I stood, grabbing his cold hands to pull him up with me. "I have an idea."

"What?"

"I'm going to take you somewhere,"

"Where?"

I grabbed the empty water bottles and the bottle he had brought with him.

As we made our way down the path, I threw the bottles and the cigarette pack he had given me into the garbage. Sam grabbed my hand, pulling me to him and we kissed for the second time that night. My hands dug into his hair, bringing him as close as possible.

We didn't say anything after pulling away but there wasn't much more that needed to be said about us as we approached the car. "Give me the keys."

He sighed, reaching into his leather jacket to pull them out. "Can you even drive?"

"I have my license."

"That doesn't really make me feel safe."

I snatched the keys out of his hand. "Get in the car."

Sam climbed into the passenger seat as I started the engine. I drove out of the parking lot. At a red light, Sam murmured, "You didn't take off the necklace." I probably never would.

"Wait," I said, getting closer to our destination. "Is Bethany the reason you had a playlist dedicated to boy bands?"

"She was *obsessed*. I could never delete it."

"Play a song," I urged him, and after multiple refusals, he eventually did. I didn't miss him singing the words under his breath as the music filled our ears.

~

"Where are we?" Sam asked as I got out of the car.

The gates were still open, meaning we had some time before someone would come to scope out the area. Grabbing Sam's hand once he closed the door on his side, I locked the car and led him through the open gates. We walked through the compound I hadn't entered in a while, then I stopped not too far from the entrance. Sam took in our surroundings. "You brought me to a cemetery?"

Sam leaned down to look at the writing on the tombstone in front of us.

HERE LIES

LAUREN "ABRINA" JESSICA ANDERSON

1974-2005

DEARLY LOVED MOTHER, DAUGHTER, LOVER AND FRIEND

"Dad said she used to hate the name 'Abrina' but grew up with it. I wouldn't be surprised if she had rolled her eyes if she saw they engraved that into her tombstone." Visiting the graveyard wasn't uncommon for my family. Every year for the anniversary of her death, Justin, Dad, and I came here. "I miss her every day."

"I miss Bethany every day," he commented.

"Even though they're gone, you know that we'll be okay, right?"

"Yeah."

He wiped another tear away and I pulled him down to sit in front of the grave. "Is there anything else you can tell me about Bethany? Like your motorcycle, BS? It's not really what I thought it was, is it?"

"Bethany and Sam," he recounted. "She went with me to get the license. I've wanted one since I was a kid."

He mentioned how she would force Caleb and him to watch romance movies they'd never have watched otherwise. How they constantly sang around the house. That she had discovered the quarry with a friend's family one summer and brought him to it. How it was their place over the years. How happy she was to hear they were going to have a little brother.

"What about your mum? You have any more stories about her?" His green eyes were curious, and for the first time tonight, I didn't worry about him as we shared stories of our lost ones.

Our conversation moved to the car when the caretaker told us they were closing the gates. Sam continued talking about Bethany, and the more he spoke, the more at ease he seemed. His stories included his family—his brother, cousins, Caleb, even Cedric. I was in the middle of telling him a story about my mom and Justin when my phone buzzed in my pocket.

"Everything okay?" he asked.

"Dad wants me home." I started the car, feeling the slight disappointment of this night being over, but I urged him to keep talking throughout the drive.

When I parked the car in the driveway of my house, I squeezed his hand, saying, "You should call your family in England and talk to your family here."

Sam kept his eyes on the house. A light was on. My suspicions were clarified when my dad walked down the driveway toward the car. "I will."

Opening up the car door, my dad glanced at me before asking Sam, "How're you doing?"

"I've been better," Sam admitted. "But I'm okay."

"I'll give you a ride home in my car," Dad offered. "I'll find a way to send yours over tomorrow." Dad walked over to his own vehicle.

"Are you sure you're going to be okay?" I asked Sam. "You can be honest with me."

Sam cast his eyes down for a moment before pulling me in for a short kiss that left me dazed. "Yeah. Thanks for tonight and everything." He exited the vehicle, entered my dad's car, and the two pulled out of the driveway.

29

WE NEED TO FIND AN OFF BUTTON

Making my way across the threshold of the dining room the next morning, I found food and fruit were on the table where my dad and Justin were eating. "You could've woken me up a little earlier—I just got dressed faster than I ever did."

I took a seat at the table, nudging Justin, who was most likely texting Emma. "Morning."

"Morning," he mumbled, concentrating on his device.

Reaching over the bacon laid out on a plate, I ate as Dad got up and took his plate into the kitchen. "Finish up quick, I'm dropping you off—if we leave now we can make it before the first bell."

I shoved two more pieces of bacon into my mouth and grabbed a banana as Justin ran out the door and toward the car, ready to climb into the passenger seat. I lingered behind with Dad, watching him grab his briefcase. "Did you guys talk much in the car?"

"We did. He was pretty tired, though." I agreed, ready to head out the front door when my dad held me back. "If he doesn't show up at school today, don't be surprised, okay? He needs time to himself and with his family."

Patting me on the back, my father walked ahead and I followed, ready to get Justin to give up the front seat.

~

The lack of sleep caught up with me and I yawned loudly at the end of the school day, making my way down the hallway. Spotting Cedric with a bunch of his friends, I raised a hand in acknowledgment, and he approached me.

"Hey." My attempt to stifle another yawn failed.

"Didn't sleep long enough? Me neither." He did look tired, his normally put-together hair was messy and dark circles had settled under his eyes.

"Are you okay, Cedric?"

"I'm getting by." He shrugged. "Everyone at home is too."

"Look, Ced, can I say something? I'm sorry for how I handled everything at the party. You didn't deserve that." My grip on the straps of my backpack loosened. "I really am sorry, and if you need anything, I'm here."

Suddenly, he furrowed his brow. "You took chemistry last term, right? I'm having trouble with something. Any time we could talk one of these days?"

I nodded, knowing that this definitely wasn't about chemistry as he walked back in the direction of his friends.

Cedric was all I could think of later as I was sitting in Caleb's car behind him and Stevie, heading to Caleb's. Caleb had texted me earlier to see if I wanted to hang out after school. Now a small part of me was regretting my answer as he sang along horribly to the *High School Musical* soundtrack.

His falsetto voice was cut off by Stevie slapping him on the shoulder. "I should stop asking you for rides home."

"Princess, tell her," he urged me. "The movie is a *classic*."

I shrugged, not wanting to have any input into their argument when Stevie said, "I haven't even watched the movies."

The car slammed to a sudden stop that nearly caused whiplash for all of us. My head hit the back of the driver's seat and I rubbed it in pain, hearing the honks from other vehicles around us. "*Caleb!*" I warned him, but he didn't move the car. In fact, he was in the middle of the road, not moving at all.

"None of them?" he asked in shock.

Stevie let out a harsh breath. "I haven't watched any one of them. Now please drive, you're causing a scene." He completely ignored her comment, still stunned at what he had learned. "Caleb, drive!"

"I'm in shock." Someone swerved around the car, giving him the middle finger. "How is that possible? It's childhood."

"Then clearly we had *different* childhoods, Caleb."

I kicked the back of his seat. "Caleb, *drive!*"

"Shit." He pressed his foot on the gas. "Tomorrow, you, me—a marathon. I don't care how long it takes. We're even going to watch the bonus scenes."

Caleb and Stevie's arguing continued as we got onto the elevator, and his horrible singing didn't stop until we reached Stevie's floor first. "Caleb?" The doors opened. "We need to find an Off button for you."

"I'm bringing the popcorn and the movies, expect me at your door—*tomorrow*."

"Bye, Macy." Stevie exited the elevator.

When we reached Caleb's place his aunt came over to us as we took off our shoes—Caleb wiggling his pink socks at me—and reminded him, "Romero, you're doing dishes tonight."

"Got it!" he yelled, urging me to head down the hall. She said something back to him in Spanish. "I was responding, not yelling!"

He made his way over to his aunt and I went to his room, where a stack of notebooks and his open laptop lay on his bed. I picked up the picture on his desk as he entered the room. Caleb reached under his bed and pulled out two notebooks similar to the ones he carried around.

I sat on the bed while he settled for the floor in front of me, crossing his legs. He handed me one notebook. Most of the book was filled with words covering almost every inch of white space, except for some of the last pages. I skimmed through it, moving by sentences of Caleb talking about her, how she was that day, how she acted, his thoughts of her.

"I knew I loved her when I met her. Even when we became best friends," Caleb said. "She had hobbies, something new almost every week. She went through this phase of making bracelets and she forced me and Sam to make them with her, and I made one for her.

"That day was the first time we really talked. About my parents' death, moving countries with my sister, and how we ended up here with our aunt. How weird it was coming to Port Meadow and being the new kid with a strange accent. I loved talking to her, I loved it when she talked back to me. I told Sam I had feelings for her. Surprisingly, he was fine with it; in fact, he encouraged me to tell her."

He flipped through the other journal until he found a picture. In the photo she was wearing a white dress and was hugging a younger version of Caleb, who was in a tux and had neatly combed hair. They were both smiling in a snow-covered garden. She looked like Liz, with her straight brown hair, and had green eyes like Sam.

"That was on their fifteenth birthday when they came over during winter break. It was a big party; but then again, everything with the Cahills is extravagant." Caleb's fingers moved through the journal before fetching another picture.

He handed me a strip of photos from a photo booth. They were of him and Bethany making funny faces at the camera. The last picture was Sam pushing Caleb out of the photo booth as he and his sister looked happy, not paying attention to the camera taking the picture.

Caleb sat next to me on the bed. "She had a good voice too. Really talented. She practiced like crazy for tryouts at the art school she ended up going to." Caleb reached down to his ankle. He pulled his pant leg up and his sock down to show the small lily on his ankle. "I wanted a tattoo one day and she suggested this. It was her favorite flower—it reminds me of her."

He cleared his throat. "When she met Drake, I wrote a lot more." He handed me the second notebook. The amount of writing within this book was far more than I had ever seen in his other notebooks. "I wrote about a love triangle."

Realization made me take a deep breath. "About the three of you."

"She introduced us to him and everything. She was happy with him." Caleb may have sounded sad but his eyes sparkled at her memory. "And he was good for her. I was honest about that in the story."

"Did you finish the story?" I asked.

"I did. I showed it to her and watched her read the entire thing. She realized who each of the characters was. I didn't expect a response right away, but was hoping to get a sense of what she was thinking. Sam inadvertently interrupted the conversation. It was fine. She looked happy and that's all that mattered to me in the moment. A week later, we got into an argument."

"Over what?"

"It was the first time I asked her how she and Drake were doing. He was her first boyfriend and I was her friend, so I thought I was just looking out for her. She tried to change the subject and we ended up fighting when she said this."

Caleb turned around, taking off his shirt to expose his shoulder blade and the quote I had spotted once before. *Curiosity can be a risk you sometimes don't want to take. —B. C.*

"Why did she say that?"

"She didn't want to hurt me by telling me anything about their relationship. She knew that I had feelings for her but she was in love with Drake, and then that relationship ended and she went back home." Caleb put his shirt back on. "Then I never saw her face to face again. It was hard to accept that she was gone but eventually I found my way through it. Sam didn't. He went through a lot of bad moments. He kind of lost himself, and there were times when I thought I was going to lose him."

A sigh left my lips at the knowledge of what he was referring to. "He told me."

Caleb released a harsh breath. "I had already lost one of my best friends; I wasn't going to lose another."

At the sight of his rapid blinking, I was quick to give him a hug, tightening my arms around him. Tears sprung to my eyes for what felt like the hundredth time these past two weeks. But I was tearing up for the loss of someone he had a great bond with; of someone he loved.

"You give good hugs," he mumbled while hugging me back, and for some reason that made me laugh. That was Caleb, managing to find humor in any situation. Pulling back, he wiped under his eyes. "I'm glad we became friends with you and everyone else."

"I'm glad I'm friends with you guys too. Even with your weird antics, theories, and love of Disney movies," I admitted with a teary smile. "Wait, how did the book—*your* book—end? Who did she end up with?"

"It's unknown," Caleb said. "I wrote that she went on to focus on her career. It made sense at the time when I wrote it, and it would still make sense if she were still here. Bethany wasn't made to stay in this town." He stood up and placed the notebook on his desk. "Wherever she is, I like to imagine that she achieved her dreams and is happy. That's all that really matters, no?"

~

Cedric and I were in the dining room of my house two days after I had spoken to Caleb. We'd been focused on chemistry for the past hour, with me answering anything he needed to know for his upcoming test. I must've made a face at the mess of our schoolwork on the table because he pointed at the disaster. "Most of this is your stuff. You're messy."

"*I'm* messy? Have you *seen* your room?"

"You're the one who had a pizza box under your bed and didn't even know."

"*Andrew* left the pizza box there!"

I pulled out another chair, laying my legs on it to get more comfortable.

"Have you spoken to him?" he asked, surprising me.

"No," I said cautiously. "He hasn't come to school."

"Yeah, I've been getting his schoolwork. He's taking time off. He's been talking with his family back home a lot. Mum's also been with him, and Phillip and our cousins keep him company."

My fingers tapped against the table as we fell into silence. Then Cedric abruptly said, "It was Sam."

My heart pounded irregularly in my chest. It was clear he wanted the truth. "Yes."

"He told me last night. Apologized and everything."

My fingers stopped tapping against the table, curiosity urging me to ask, "What did you do?"

"I told him to fuck off and get out of my room." Cedric's tone was scornful. "I should've known something was going on anyway. It's the little things. You guys become friends when he refuses to give anyone else the time of day. And he was in Redmond when you were in Redmond—I realized it must've happened during the break."

"I'm sorry. I really am."

Finally looking up at me, he shrugged. "It's fine." *What?*

"You seem to be taking this very well."

"You're my friend, Mace. It'll be okay."

No. There was more to it judging by his nonchalant expression. "You just . . . seem very calm. You're not telling me something."

"Mace," he sighed. "Sam and I aren't exactly the type of relatives to argue and forget about it by making jokes the next day or week. We hold on to grudges for a long time. And this one has gone on for years." I said nothing, waiting for him to keep going.

"Mum had put me in a little soccer league back in Bath and I loved it. I remember being the little captain and I was the best of the team. Sam was in the same league but in a different group until he got switched to mine." Cedric paused, looking to find the right words to use. "He upstaged me because he wanted to show everyone he was the best, and it's been like this since then. Grades? He was better. Always better even when he didn't try. Girls? That was the worst. I remember one summer we went to this overnight camp up north. I liked this girl and was going to ask her out only for her to say that she wanted my cousin. And it was the same every time. Listen, I did like you a lot at one point, and when Austin said you had a thing for me, I thought here's my chance to finally have the kind of girl who . . . who—"

"Who Sam would never go for." I felt myself go cold, and then suddenly heat up with anger at the realization of what he was saying. "That he wouldn't go for a girl who didn't wear makeup? Who dressed like me, whose majority of friends were guys and loved soccer?

"You thought that Sam wouldn't go for a *tomboy*. You thought that Sam wouldn't fall in love with me because I was completely different from what he would usually go after. You were wrong." Cedric's eyes widened. "He said he loved me."

Cedric sat right up now. "He what?"

"It's still hard to believe. Not impossible." Cedric looked away, but I wasn't finished. "And Sam trying to upstage you? It's not his fault that you took everything that way and ended up turning everything into an argument. Thinking that Sam trying to one-up you made you turn to rugby, and you love playing rugby, Cedric. You're one of the best flankers I know."

I punched him softly in the shoulder and he smirked. "I'm pretty sure I'm the *only* flanker you know."

"You've got to stop thinking that everything between the two of you is a competition. Sam has no idea why you two have such a strained relationship but he cares about you. He loves his family and I know he wouldn't trade any of you—even you—for the world."

"I shouldn't have done that," Cedric mumbled. "Used you, I mean."

"I'm sorry," I said. "I tried to block out my feelings for Sam by being with you. I'm sorry for pulling you into a relationship that never would have worked out in the first place."

"I'm sorry too." There was sincerity in his voice.

"Maybe you and Sam could talk too? I know he has a lot to be sorry for, and maybe you could set right all those stupid arguments you two have had for years. He feels guilty for what he did, Cedric."

"I know he does." He looked hesitant before saying his next words to me. "Are we okay?"

"We're okay."

"Are you sure?"

I fished a Pop-Tart out of my backpack and handed it to him as a symbol of peace.

That night, I spent most of my time scrolling through my phone at my desk. Jasmine's contact name would occasionally pop up as she procrastinated by sending me the latest posts she had found. Ignoring the yelling down the hallway from Justin's room as he was probably engaged in a video game with one of his friends, I received a text message.

Drake: I heard you won. Congrats, captain

I was ready to type back to him when he sent another.

Drake: Sam apologized by the way. Had a feeling you had something to do with it. Thanks, Mace

30

CHANGE

It was a normal day at Wellington and my friends looked content. The chatter at our table during lunch only got louder when Austin said something funny, everyone around me bursting into laughter. Stevie took a seat between Jon Ming and Brandon, and Caleb's relaxed expression faltered at Stevie's frown at him. "What?"

Her index finger was pointed in his direction. "This *weirdo*—"

Caleb looked offended. "Rude."

"—decided to come to my apartment to watch *High School Musical*."

"Because it's a classic."

"Caleb, you're seventeen! And then thought he should make me watch what felt like every other movie in one evening." Stevie huffed before turning to me, lowering her voice. "Anyway, I was just in the bathroom and people were talking about you and Cedric."

It was bound to come up anyway. "It's whatever." Clearly it wasn't, because someone approached me from behind and Jasmine stiffened next to me, giving me the impression that we knew who it was.

"Caleb, Sam's not here today?"

Caleb mumbled no as I turned around to meet Beatrice's condescending stare. It didn't help that her group of followers stood behind her. "Macy, I heard that Cedric dumped you."

"How does that concern you?"

"It doesn't," she claimed. "I knew he would anyway. Probably came to his senses."

"Okay," Jasmine spoke up. "You've said enough."

"Beatrice," I said, exasperated, "Sam's not even here. Go. Away."

"Tell us the truth, Macy: he just didn't want to date a freak."

"You realize what a horrible thing that is to say, right?"

"Beatrice." Caleb looked as tired of her as we were. "I'm sure the rest of your friends are waiting for you somewhere. We're trying to eat before lunch ends and we can't do it if you're attempting to fight Macy here. Do you mind?"

A snort came from Austin and Jon Ming. Beatrice glared at the three of them.

"I wasn't talking to you," she sneered and by this point, *like always*, our voices carried throughout the cafeteria because *like always* people in this school found the need to stop talking among themselves and listen to others' conversations.

"What do you want to talk about?" I dropped my fork and turned to face her from my seat. "Me with Cedric? Or do you want to talk about Sam? Because I really don't care."

"Just admit that you only came here to stir up trouble, Beatrice," Austin mumbled.

Beatrice gave him a pointed stare and didn't think twice when she said, "At least Macy can admit that Cedric dumped her." *I never said that.* "You can't even admit that you're gay."

Everything shifted. My heart dropped as Austin stiffened and the color drained from his face. Caleb's lips parted in surprise, the twins froze, and Andrew looked at Beatrice in disbelief. The worst part was that Austin wasn't ready.

And even if he was, it hadn't come from his mouth.

People heard, judging by the quietness of the cafeteria. Stevie, who was the only one in our friend group who didn't know, shot up the second Beatrice had spoken. She was already rounding the table in her direction when Brandon reached out to hold her back. "Are you serious?"

Jasmine stood up in equal disbelief. "What the hell, Beatrice?!"

Andrew held her arm as Jon Ming disdainfully said, "That was a shit thing to do."

"Guys," Austin started but my own anger got the best of me and I stood.

"You don't fucking do that." Beatrice flinched, not expecting that word to come out of my mouth. "You had no right to do that."

She'd tried to spite me and Jasmine for as long as we'd been in this school, trying to put us both in categories we didn't need to be put into. We didn't deserve that, and Austin didn't deserve this. No one did.

Whispers scattered around the cafeteria and all eyes were on our table, but Beatrice didn't care. "Maybe next time don't kiss guys at parties if you don't want to be—"

"*No,*" Jasmine hissed, getting in Beatrice's face and trying to keep her voice low. "You *don't out someone.*"

Beatrice looked ready to argue with Jasmine and I was ready to speak up when Austin rounded the table, getting in Beatrice's face. "You really don't see a problem with what you did? I'm gay!" he declared. His eyes flickered around the cafeteria before he turned back to Beatrice again. "I wanted to be able to tell people when I wanted to. It's the twenty-first century and it may not seem like a big deal to you, but it is to me. And you clearly knew that. So fuck you."

He walked out of the cafeteria. Jon Ming grabbed Austin's things and followed him, as did the rest of the guys and Stevie.

"Why?" Jasmine surprised me, her question directed toward Beatrice. "You don't have to act like this. Earning the reputation as the mean girl isn't a great accomplishment, and you don't have to live up to it. You could do better." Beatrice didn't say anything—it looked like she couldn't even think of a response.

Jasmine's words inspired my own and I said, "I never thought I would say this but I forgive you." Jasmine tensed. "*I* do. Only for what you've said to me—*not* for all the insensitive and frankly *racist* things you've said to Jasmine. If she wants to forgive you in the long run, that's her choice. Austin too. It's not on them to forgive as much as it's up to you to apologize."

Jasmine linked her arm with mine and we exited the cafeteria to find our friends while the rest of the school stared at us in silence. Jasmine didn't say anything but the smile she gave me as we pushed through the doors made me grin back. When we found our friends at one of the staircases, I said to Austin, "I'm so sorry."

"It's not your fault." He sighed. "She's—"

"We know," Jasmine said, sitting down on the stairs next to him. "Don't worry about her or what anyone else says. We're here for you." Jasmine's promise to Austin made me beam, and a part of me knew that she knew we would always be here for her as well.

"She's right." Jacob extended his hand for a low five that Austin hit with his own.

"Only two more months in this place," Stevie pointed out.

Austin dramatically sighed. "Can't fucking wait."

~

If you'd asked me a few months earlier about anything involving change, I would've focused on *changing* the topic.

On a very bright spring day after school, on a day when I didn't have practice, as we strolled through the park I listened to Jasmine and Andrew on the other side of me discuss the latest show she had forced him to watch. The rest of the guys were attempting to show Stevie how to properly kick a ball while Caleb, with my camera in his hands, tried to capture everything.

My friends were constantly changing, especially with the school year coming to a close. For the first time, I wasn't scared about it. I wasn't scared when I pulled out the official letters I had received the day before on my phone. One letter presented the details of my enrollment at the university I would be attending in the fall. Andrew patted me on the back with a grin as I showed them the other letter, from the scout who'd come to the tournament, informing me of my place on their soccer team and the scholarship I'd earned. "Have you told everyone?" Andrew asked.

Jasmine stopped Stevie's training session, grabbing the attention of our friends with my news. She took my phone, showing my friends the documents with excitement in her voice as she explained. Everyone came over to congratulate me, and Andrew said, "Your first goal in first year is to become a starter."

I hit my best friend lightly on the chest. "Let's not get our hopes up."

"You never know, Mace," he teased.

Minutes later, the boys and Jasmine were playing around with the soccer ball when Austin took a seat on the bench near the maple tree. *The* maple tree. The memory of almost falling right in front of here, and what happened after made me shake my head. "You doing okay?" I sat down next to him.

"I'm good, Mace. What about you?"

"I'm doing okay too." He looked at ease despite what happened today. "How did it feel? When you told off Beatrice?"

"Besides *amazing*, the 'fuck you' part felt especially good." A pleased look crossed his face. "Someone needed to say it to her, to be honest."

"She shouldn't have done that." My fists clenched at how Beatrice hadn't thought twice about it. "Taken this away from you."

"I know that. You know that. But there are probably a million people like Beatrice out there. I'm happy I got to say something like that to one of them." Austin was beaming, knocking his knee against my own playfully before saying, "She's wrong, by the way. About you and Jasmine, she always was wrong about how she saw you two."

"I know."

The familiar click from my camera cut through the air. Caleb moved it away from his eyes. "I should be a photographer."

Stevie looked at the picture as Austin got up to join her. "Stick to writing."

I cracked a smile, my eyes falling back to the tree as Caleb sat down next to me. "What are you thinking about?"

He followed my gaze, taking a picture of the tree.

"That's where Sam and I met."

"Really?" Caleb wasn't looking at the tree anymore; instead he pointed ahead at the figure walking toward us in his leather jacket. "Speak of the devil."

Andrew attempted to kick the ball over to Sam with his good foot and Sam was quick to set it down with his feet, raising a hand in acknowledgment. Our friends greeted him with a pat on the back, a handshake, or, in Jasmine's case, an overeager hug.

"Look who's back," Caleb said, getting up from the bench as Sam approached us. "You got my text."

Sam reached forward, giving Caleb a hug his best friend easily reciprocated.

"Better?"

Sam nodded. When they let go, his eyes fell on me.

Even if Caleb hadn't asked him the question, it was obvious that Sam did look better. His eyes were brighter—his usual confidence was present, including his ability to look at me once and make me forget everything around us.

Sam picked up the ball, his smirk making me want to roll my eyes at whatever he had to say—but this time I was too happy to see him.

"Rec center?" Brandon suggested and they all headed in that direction. The two of us hung back.

"Hazel." Sam tilted his head. "I've rendered you speechless."

"Shut up."

"There she is." I didn't know if that smile on his face would ever come off—I hoped I'd be seeing it more often.

"You mean what you said to Caleb?" I asked him.

"I mean it." I linked my arms around him in a hug he was quick to reciprocate. "I had a lot of time to think. I talked to Drake and Cedric."

"I talked to Cedric too." With the mention of his cousin's name Sam released a long exhale. "He'll speak to you eventually," I said.

"How do you know?"

"Because even through everything he's your cousin. He will." Sam looked down. "What's on your mind?"

"My mum, dad, and Greg," he said. "We all talked a lot over the past few days. I told them I didn't want to disappoint them. That I wasn't going to act out like I did. I mentioned what we talked about that night. They'd like to meet you." He grew amused at my surprised expression. "They'll be here for graduation."

"That's really good, Sam."

"Also, I couldn't stop thinking about what you said about my uncle. That he was worried about me that night."

"I think that despite your rocky relationship, he cares. It might take some time for him to properly show it, but maybe one day you guys can be in the same room without fighting."

Sam linked our hands together. "Caleb texted me about your university choice. How do you feel about the change?"

"I'm not scared of it anymore." My confession filled me with relief.

"I also made a choice a few days ago." He pulled out his phone, showing me the screen.

The institution's name was familiar, and my jaw dropped in surprise. "You're going to *this* university? It's not that far from me."

"About an hour's drive. Might be less on the motorcycle."

I was in a daze, maybe because of the way his eyes were on me or at the information on the screen. *He's not going back to England in the fall.* "You're serious?"

"The game plan is to try out for their team."

"You're planning on playing soccer too?" I shook his hands eagerly and Sam grew amused at my excitement. "You're definitely going to get on the team."

"Hazel—"

"No, you *are*," I assured him. "You're good, and I know you have ways to find training of all sorts during the summer and now. Trust me, you'll get on."

Sam's expression softened. "I missed you."

"I missed you too." When he kissed me, I threaded my fingers in his hair as his grip on my waist tightened. I pulled back first, ready to speak, when out of nowhere, grass was flung in our direction. I was quick to brush it out of my hair, annoyed at the culprit. "*Caleb.*"

Caleb stood with my camera in one hand and a handful of grass in another, which he also threw at us. "What the hell are you doing?" Sam said, taking more grass out of my hair.

"I don't have any flowers so grass was the next best thing. Did you ask her yet?"

"Ask her what?"

"To be your girlfriend." Caleb turned to Jasmine, who held the ball in her hands. "He's a lost cause sometimes."

"It was implied," Sam said.

"Don't make it implied," urged Caleb. "Make it *happen.*"

Jasmine tapped Sam, growing annoyed. "Would you just ask her?"

Sam rolled his eyes at his best friend's antics, turning to me. "Hazel, would you—"

"Would you what?" Caleb interrupted. "Do me the honor of being my wife? Dude, are you asking for her hand in marriage or starting off your relationship?"

Sam turned back to me with an exasperated sigh. "Would you be my girlfriend?"

We were doing this right and I wasn't planning on making a wrong choice this time. I nodded and Caleb let out a sound of happiness. "C'mon, Caleb." Jasmine tossed me the soccer ball.

As they walked to the rec center, Sam said, "Took us long enough."

My hand was linked with his. "How long?"

"Seconds, minutes, hours?"

"Days."

"Seventy-two," he answered, pointing toward the tree. "Right over there. Feels like forever ago."

He squeezed my hand. "Football?" Sam started to follow Jasmine and Caleb but I pulled him back to me, one hand on his face. "Wha—"

"I'm in love with you." The surprise was clear in his eyes. And I kissed him once more, moving my hand over his racing heart. He felt the same. There was no doubt. "I just wanted you to know that."

The smile on his face didn't waver as he took the ball from my hands and we followed our friends to the rec center to play the game we both loved.

ACKNOWLEDGMENTS

I don't know how I can express my gratitude to all who have contributed to making this possible but I'm going to try.

To my childhood and high school best friends (you know who you are): Our funny moments and our emotional conversations over the years found their way into this novel. Thank you for impacting me and this story in ways you may not even know.

Thank you to my mom, who has endlessly supported me and encouraged my love of reading. Thank you for fueling my passion for words by constantly buying me books over the years.

To my grade twelve AP English teacher, Mrs. DiCostanzo, the advice you have given me over the years will always stay with me, and influenced the development of this story. Thanks for being one of the best teachers I've ever had.

A thank you to the numerous people I've met through Wattpad, whether briefly or for the long run—you are a supportive community on a platform filled with amazing interactions, each of which makes me happy to be a member of the ever-changing platform. To Danielle, whom I met all those years ago at summer camp, thank you for introducing me to Wattpad at a time when I had yet to know of the many opportunities to come.

A big thank you to those at Wattpad—every editor, illustrator, marketing and promotions team member, and everyone involved in making this, one of my biggest dreams, come true.

To I-Yana Tucker, my talent manager, thank you for never giving up on me, for answering my questions, for the check-in phone calls. I appreciate you more than you'll ever know. A big thank you to all the editors involved: Whitney French, Deanna McFadden, Jen Hale, and Rebecca Mills, who've worked on this story to make it the best it could be and one that I love.

Lastly, to the fans who loved Macy, Sam, and the characters in this universe—the gratitude I have for you all is bottomless. From every kind word and piece of fan art to making me laugh over your comments at two o'clock in the morning and motivating messages that led to this point: thank you so much. Without you guys, this would not have been possible.

ABOUT THE AUTHOR

Nicole Nwosu grew up in Toronto, Canada, and first started posting her stories on Wattpad in 2014. Her most popular story *The Bad Boy and the Tomboy* has accumulated over a hundred million reads on the platform and won a 2015 *"Cover-to-Cover"* Watty Award. When she's not writing, Nicole spends her time catching up on binge-worthy TV shows while balancing her studies at Western University.

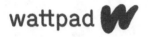

Where stories live.

Discover millions of stories created by diverse writers from around the globe.

Download the app or visit www.wattpad.com today.

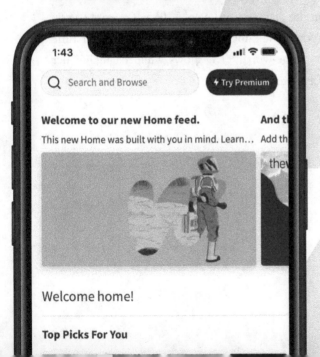

 premium

Supercharge your Wattpad experience.

Go Premium and get more from the platform you already love. Enjoy uninterrupted ad-free reading, access to bonus Coins, and exclusive, customizable colors to personalize Wattpad your way.

Try Premium free today.

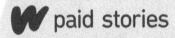

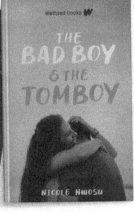